NOT FOR GLORY

A HISTORICAL NOVEL OF SCOTLAND

J R TOMLIN

ALBANNACH PUBLISHING

For as long as but a hundred of us remain alive, never will we on any conditions be brought under English rule. **It is not for glory**, nor riches, nor honours that we are fighting, but for freedom — for that alone, which no honest man gives up but with life itself.

The Declaration of Arbroath, 1320

MAP OF SCOTLAND AND NORTHERN ENGLAND

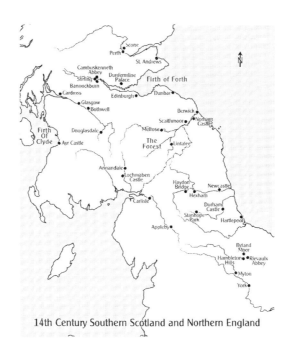

14th Century Southern Scotland and Northern England

CHAPTER 1

JUNE 24, 1314

Bannockburn, Scotland

The English host was trapped against the waters of the Bannockburn. The bristling hedge of Scottish steel shoved once more into the desperate knights, and Sir James de Douglas eyed the banners flying above the writhing mass. Those included the massive scarlet banner with the Planta-genet leopards that proclaimed that King Edward of Caernarfon was somewhere in the chaos. James bellowed, "A Douglas! A Douglas! " Battle fury swept through him—rage and hatred unleashed for the losses and the pain. He thrust his sword into an English neck. For his father... For Isabella… For Thomas... For Alycie... For all of the dead…

With every opening in their schiltron, it was the same. Slam with his shield, slash with his sword, and when his man went down, a stab to the throat. And then on to the next as blood ran down his sword to dye his gauntlets scarlet.

Around him, his men screamed, " Scotland! Scotland! On them! " Hungry for revenge, they had spent their lives fighting the invader and had become savagely good at war. Their feet slipped in the blood slicked grass. They stepped over bodies as their schiltron pressed forward.

An arrow sliced in from the right, striking James's shield. He lifted it but no more arrows came. Archers would have been the last chance for the English, but King Robert de Bruce had planned well for them, holding back his five hundred Scottish chivalry to sweep behind the line and attack the archers.

James's men bellowed as they hacked their pikes into the bellies and faces of English horses, into the gaps in gleaming armor, and chopped with their weapons. The English fell back, horses screaming as they went down the steep edge of a gully.

The enemy had nowhere to go. Under the hooves of English knights, men lay dead, wounded, shrieking in pain. Their commanders yelled orders to retire while James slashed each man who came before him. The English shouted curses, thrust with lances, and swung swords as they were forced back. Ribbons of scarlet rippled through the Bannockburn's waters. They fought with the desperation of trapped men.

Next to James, one of his men shouted as he chopped his pike. Another horse went down. Blood and mud splattered. The rider threw himself free, landing flat on his back. James slammed a foot on the knight's chest and thrust his sword through the man's throat.

"Forward!" he roared. "They fail!"

"Sir James!"

James spun at a hand on his shoulder and jerked his sword arm into position.

A wide-eyed squire dodged backward, stumbling on the broken earth. "The king sent me. He wants you."

An unhorsed Englishman screamed as a slashing hoof

crushed his head. He fell atop a knight already dead. James's own men wore helms and studded leather marked with the blue and white Saltire of Scotland, now streaked with mud and blood and gore. The steel tide surged against the crumbling mass of a panicked foe. Another step forward.

For six hours, they'd fought since the cool of dawn, hacking at an army that seemed without number. His arm suddenly was heavy with the fatigue from a day of slash and thrust.

The English trumpets shrilled thinly. *Harooo Harooo... Retire... Retire...*

He blinked the sting of sweat from his eyes. *Where was Walter Stewart?* In the chaos, James spotted Walter's blue and white checky pennant. He grabbed Iain's arm and pulled him out of the line of pikemen. "Find Sir Walter. Tell him that he has sole command of our men." He shoved his sword into his black leather sheath and jerked a nod to the squire. "Lead on."

The lad led James across the broken sod, past a sprawled knight, his armor still agleam as his blood soaked into the dry earth. They passed thousands of shrieking men screaming "Scotland!" as they hacked at the English. For a moment, a wind from the east gusted the smell of the salt sea and cut through the fug of blood and shit. *Who would have imagined such a battle?* A body clad in a studded brigandine marked with a Saltire lay pierced by the shattered remains of a pike next to a gutted stallion. A crow, its black feathers gleaming in the sun, took flight from the guts spilled onto the ground with an angry *kraaa*. They trudged past it all, and the uproar faded behind them into a rumble.

Beyond a stand of alder, leaves drooping in summer's heat, the king's scarlet lion banner hung limp in the still air. The lad pointed. James slapped his shoulder and strode through the welcome shade of the trees while reaching up to wrench off his helm.

Robert de Bruce's hand rested on the hilt of his sword, his head tilted as he listened to what the Keith was saying. At the Bruce's feet sat a helm topped by a gold crown. Enemy blood streaked his armor and cloth-of-gold tabard. He ran a hand through fair hair dripping with sweat. "Jamie," the king exclaimed.

James worked spit into his parched mouth. "Your Grace."

"Bring him water," the Bruce said and the squire scurried away.

The Keith said, "King Edward fled the field."

James felt his eyes widen as he looked from his good-father to the king.

"Come." The Bruce strode through the alders so they could watch the battle. On a distant hill, Stirling Castle loomed gray against a cloudless noon sky. The king shook his head. "If someone took command they might still win the day."

"They're in full flight." The Keith pointed toward the battle and past to the deep gully cut by the Bannockburn. "They're forcing their horses down the slope into the burn. Already it's mired with bodies. Some are fleeing for the River Forth."

"Our men are so weary they can barely lift a pike," the king said, squinting at the roiling mass of the battle. "How many hours can a man fight? If the battle turned now, we'd be in a desperate case."

The squire ran up with a cup and flagon and thrust the cup of water into James's hand. He gulped the drink, and it ran down his throat like rain after a drought. He held the cup out and let the squire refill it. "But without their king?" His voice was clearer now.

"I want to pursue Edward," the Keith said. He slid a glance toward the king. "No one is left to rally them. Aymer du

Valence fled with Edward. They say young Gloucester died in the first charge."

"We don't know where Robert de Clifford is or Humphrey de Bohun or Ralph de Monthermer. And Gloucester… I pray God you're wrong for the sake of his family. But even broken, such a vast army is dangerous. Like a wounded boar." His gaze was fixed on the chaos of the battle. The sound was a roar of a distant sea. Remorseless. "I won't chance it."

"Did King Edward make for Stirling Castle?" James asked.

The Keith jerked a nod. "I pursued him so far. Mowbray must have refused him entrance. They turned south."

"No, Lord Marischal. I'll have sixty of your chivalry. That will leave you a full four hundred if we have need of them." The Bruce skewered James with a look. "You'll lead the sixty to follow the curst English king."

James blew out a long breath. His whole body was a mass of weary aches. He looked at the cup in his hand, lifted it, and dumped the water over his head. It ran through his hair and down his cheeks to drip from his close-cropped beard, mixing with sweat, until he shook his head hard like a wet hound.

The king and his good-father were watching him.

"We'll skirt the battle and take the North Park road." James scraped his wet hair back with a hand as he pictured the way. "We can ford the Bannockburn to the east where its banks are lower."

"Sir Robert's horse and one for Sir James," the Bruce said, with a thrust of his chin at the waiting squire. The lad gave a quick bow and ran.

"How many ride with him?" James asked.

"Five hundred…" His good-father narrowed his eyes. "Mayhap more."

"I can't take them with sixty knights."

"I know that," the king said. "Harry them. Capture any who fall behind. See them out of Scotland."

"It's too bad to let him escape," the Keith said.

"Do you think I don't know that, man?" The king glared at the Keith. "Even now with your men, could you defeat them if I dared give leave? They number more than our chivalry, are better mounted. Experienced knights all. And I dare not lose my only mounted men."

"I could defeat them!"

The Bruce put a hand on the Keith's shoulder. "You saved our lives for us, breaking the English archers with your charge. If you hadn't, it is we who would have died this day. But this you cannot do." The Keith bowed his defeat, though his tight face showed how reluctant he was.

James turned at the rattle of harness and took the reins of a horse from the lad. He blinked trying to remember which squire this was and shrugged the thought away.

The king laid a heavy hand on his shoulder. "Whatever you do, do not try to fight them, Jamie."

He bowed and swung into the saddle. "Let's find me my men, my lord." He twitched a smile that felt more like a grimace.

His good-father mounted, his face knotted in a frown. James shook his head at him. He couldn't argue with the king's stand. Even fleeing, the guards around King Edward and Aymer du Valence would fight to the last man. Outnumbered, upon lesser mounts, he doubted the Keith's knights could defeat the English king's guard, however determined the Keith might be.

Behind them, the king was shouting commands. Hours of fighting remained, albeit that wasn't James's problem now. Sir Robert de Keith set his horse to a canter, and James followed. To the left flank of the battle, Scottish knights stood beside their mounts, tending their light coursers, pissing, scratching, talking, and laughing, though the laughter had a weary sound to it.

James grunted. "My banner is still with my men. I'd not care to be taken for a Sassenach on the road."

"Best have one of the men retrieve it." He pulled up and gave his troop a frowning survey before he called out to young Loccart, knighted only the day before, "Sir Symon, you and your men are to follow Sir James."

The knight, his sweaty red hair still smashed to his head from a helm that rested at his feet, blinked up at James. Sir Symon picked up the helm, donned it, and swung into his saddle. "Mount up."

Loccart sent one of his men to retrieve James's battle banner. The talk died as they mounted, muttering and giving James long looks. These weren't his own men, and they knew him only by reputation.

James stood in his stirrups and shouted, "The English king ran like the craven dog that he is. We're to see he keeps running." He paused before he went on. "We'll not stop even to take a piss. Not until the damned English thieves are out of our lands."

He wheeled his horse and gave the command to move out. He sent a dozen men to spread out ahead and scout as they headed toward Stirling Castle to find the English king's fleeing party. The victory should have had the men in good spirits, but a day of bloody battle and a ride with too few in their party should they face a real fight had their faces somber. James felt their unease at his back.

As he rode, James peeled off his gloves to flex his hands and worked his shoulders. If he let himself stiffen, it would go ill in a fight. A man could never relax.

James led them wide around the battle, but the sound of screams and the blare of horns followed them. Sir Symon spurred his horse to catch up as they wended their way past a thick stand of oaks and down the low slope to the River Forth, a gleaming gray ribbon. The fresh sea air of the firth blew in his face as he turned toward the ford.

"Will we find them, you think?" Sir Symon asked.

"Aye, we will."

They rode in silence except for the clatter of harness and armor until Sir Symon said, "When we do—"

James shrugged. How could he know what would happen? He would follow the Bruce's command, albeit the chase still might come to a fight. Before he voiced the thought, one of the scouts galloped down the far slope and into the river, water spraying. "Riders ahead, my lord, coming this way," the man shouted.

James pulled up his mount with a jerk and the animal danced under him. "How many? What banner?"

"Four score. Fresh. They've seen no fighting. Under a pennant with a red lion. They rode out of the Torwood."

Wheeling in a tight turn, James yelled, "Close order." Many pennants had a lion device. A pennant meant it wasn't one of the great lords though, especially not with such a small number in his tail. He tightened his hand on the hilt of his sword as he kicked his horse to a canter, splashed through the low water of the ford, and gave the horse a smack on the flank. Its haunches bunched as it labored to keep a fast pace up the slope. This would be a ruinous spot to be caught. He spurred it, and it heaved to the top of the rise.

He pulled up and narrowed his eyes in the glare of a bright summer sun: a band of armored riders, eighty strong. The yellow pennant wasn't one he knew, but from the shout and the sudden halt of the armed party, he suspected they knew his. He snorted and glanced up at his banner. The night before, Robert de Bruce had cut the tails from his pennant and raised him to a knight banneret. His heart had pounded at the honor, but the stars on a blue chief had not changed. He smiled as he pulled his sword from its sheath.

"Will they fight?" his young companion asked.

"We'll soon know." James nudged his horse a couple of paces ahead to yell, "Who goes there?"

"Who asks?" came the answer from a knight in unsoiled armor, yellow tabard bright in the afternoon sun.

James raised his blade. "Swords to the ready." Sir Symon shifted his shield onto his arm as he urged his horse a pace forward and to James's right. He heard the sound of hooves and clatter of weapons as his men formed up on him to attack.

"Wait!" The knight rode half-dozen paces toward them. "The Black Douglas?"

"Your name and your title."

"Sir Laurence Abernathy of Saltoun." The man kneed his dun another step forward. "You've fought the English? There's been a battle?"

"You want to join them? They are dying on the banks of the Bannockburn. It runs red with their blood. And I pursue their king."

"They're defeated?" The man gaped, open-mouthed. "Truly?"

"Do I look like I jape?" James knew how he looked, blood and dirt streaked as he was.

Abernathy was shaking his head. He slowly raised his sword arm, hand empty. "No. King Robert— He'll take me into his peace. I've heard he does those who return and swear to him. I'll aid you in pursuing King Edward."

James snorted. Of course, the Bruce would take the man's oath. Another traitor taken into the king's peace, but hell mend him if he liked having Abernathy at his back. That Randolph had proved true, and his good-father as well, didn't mean he would trust the rest of the pack of traitorous dogs. Yet the English king had almost ten times his number, and he needed these men.

James leaned to hawk and spit. He'd take the devil as an ally against the invader and swallow the foul taste of it. Straightening, he eyed the man and gave a silent sigh. "Your word then. You'll swear to King Robert when we return to his camp. Until then, you aid me."

"My word as a knight. I swear it."

James laid his sword across his saddlebow. The thought of turning his back on traitors always made the skin between his shoulder blades itch. "Then welcome home, Sir Laurence." James's mouth twisted in a grim smile. Behind him, the men were muttering, and he heard a curse.

"What happened?" Sir Laurence asked as James and Symon nudged their horses to a canter. He motioned his men to join theirs.

"We won. And the damned English lost." He had no reason not to tell the man more, however much he loathed returning traitors. "We trapped them in a bend of the Bannockburn and our pikes tore them to bloody shreds."

The ash and oak giants of the Torwood spread before them, the old Roman Road wending its way through. James led them into its shadows. The shade of the green canopy cooled them from the heat of summer sun and battle, and James pushed them to keep a fast pace. At a shallow burn where sunlight broke through the leaves to dapple silver, splashing waves, James stopped to water the horses. They had no time for rest.

The scouts returned with no news. He sent them again to search the road near Linlithgow.

"Won't they make for Berwick?" Symon asked as they rode beneath the towering trees.

In the dappled shade, James scanned the dusty road. "Castle Dunbar is nearer. The towers there have passage down the cliff to the sea where galleys are kept." James nudged his horse ahead, too weary for idle chatter. They rode in silence, the thud of hooves accompanied by a whisper of the breeze through the leaves.

The sun was half dropped behind rolling hills when they emerged from the forest, a mosaic of purple and green and the yellow of gorse flowers stretching before them. James spotted three of their scouts atop the nearest low swell, waving their arms over their heads. He spurred his horse to meet them.

"We found them! They halted to rest!" A bald scout, thin as a pike, beamed as he pointed to the south. "Just past the next hill." Overhead, a hawk flew in slow circles.

"Swords to the ready!" James shouted. They had no time to waste. His sword sang as he took a practice swing. He wheeled his horse and spurred it to a gallop. It stretched its legs into a ground-eating stride, hoof beats rattling like hail. They topped the low hill.

A bowshot away, knights held the reins of their horses, squatting and talking, and a few were mounting to ride—hundreds of knights in battered armor and tabards still bright beneath streaks of dried blood. A tall man with a crown atop his gilded helm sat a dappled gray charger. Next to him, a standard-bearer mounted a dun. Above them streamed the scarlet Plantagenet leopard banner.

"Wedge!" James shouted. They formed the flying arrowhead with him at its point. Sir Symon took the place on his right; on his left rode Sir Laurence, sword in hand. He heard horses thudding behind him. "A Douglas! A Douglas!" he shouted.

English knights scrambled onto their lathered mounts. Voices bellowed, "To horse! To the king!" Horses reared and plunged as riders jumped into the saddle. One jerked its reins free. Its knight ran after it a few steps, threw down his shield, and dropped to his knees as it departed in an unfeeling gallop. The fleeing men streamed around the kneeling knight like a gleaming river surging past a rock. They flogged their horses as they coursed after the king.

James cursed and jerked on the reins, pulling his mount to a rearing halt. Symon was off his horse, sword at the throat of the kneeling Englishman. The man dropped his sword, shoulders sagging. "I yield."

James gritted his teeth. He couldn't disobey the Bruce's command further than he had, but letting them escape made his face hot with fury. "Symon, chase down yon mount and bring your prisoner. You'll have to catch up to us." At least, he would make the English flight to Dunbar a dangerous and miserable one.

They rode through the warm summer twilight that never fully darkened. Once when the English stopped to water their horses, James swooped in on them, screaming his battle cry, but let them gallop away. One of the Lacys who'd stood facing a tree taking a long piss moved too slowly and yielded to James's sword at his back. Hands bound, he joined Symon's prisoner, horses led by one of their men. The rutted road turned and twisted through the hills in the purple night.

During the long ride, every muscle clenched and cramped from James's neck to his toes. He wanted to rub his thighs where the muscled burned, but they were encased in mail. Summer nights were short, but this one seemed never to end. They'd fallen behind, so he kneed his horse to a lope. Shortly, he heard ahead the thud of hooves and clatter of armor and weapons.

A breeze sighed, carrying a scent of the sea. James breathed it in deep. At last pewter fingers stretched above the eastern horizon to outline Dunbar Castle high atop a cliff. Gulls squalled as they plunged to the water. Shouts too far to make out came from the walls and the sound of horns in challenge. A drawbridge crashed down.

"Merciful St. Bride, we've done what we were sent for." He slid from the horse and grabbed his saddlebow when his legs wobbled, needles of pain flashing through cramped muscles. He listened to shouts of welcome as the English king went beyond his reach within high, thick stone walls. Metal squealed on metal as chains lowered the portcullis of Dunbar Castle.

"They might yet ride for Berwick," Symon said. "Mayhap we could take more prisoners."

James stretched his back and a joint popped. He grimly contemplated climbing into the saddle and decided to walk for a few minutes. He turned to go the way they had come. "They will escape by sea. At least Edward of Caernarfon will. I must return to the king."

* * *

James spied Cambuskenneth Abbey, a mass of gray granite topped by an enormous square bell tower, where the bells tolled, sweetly and unceasing. Bells clanged from every steeple in Stirling Town in the distance. On and on they cried out… A carillon for Scotland's great victory. He let out a gust of a sigh as he reined up at the carved wooden doors twelve feet high and climbed from the saddle.

They'd snatched two hour's rest near Dunbar before riding for Stirling. Between the battle and the pursuit, James had lost count of the hours since any of them had slept or eaten a meal. Symon had swayed in the saddle for the last hour, and the men slumped like sacks of grain.

He lifted his helm to tuck under his arm. "Symon, see to the men. Find where the prisoners are held and where we are to lodge. Rest and eat. I'll see to Sir Laurence." He nodded toward the spread of gray stone buildings. "If you need aught, find me." He waited as the prisoners were pulled from the saddle and turned to a guard, shifting his feet as he leaned on a pike. "The king?" James asked.

"In the refractory, my lord. It's been a fair to do since the battle," the man said as he opened the door.

James strode into the cool dimness of an arched entry toward voices in a far room. The warm air, heavy with the scent of incense, pressed like a blanket. Holy St. Bride but he was weary.

Through the doorway was a vaulted refectory, walls whitewashed and lined with polished oaken tables stacked with gold and silver plate, gleaming jewelry piled high, weapons, helmets and painted shields, stacks of bright tapestries, fine worked harness, and two tables heaped with golden spurs by the hundred. The room hummed with the scratch of quills upon parchment and the voices of clerics murmuring as they counted the English treasure.

Robert de Bruce sat in the carved abbot's chair. James's breath went out of him at the sight of the king. They had won. The king lived. Until this moment, he hadn't believed the truth of it. James had thought they would lose. That at the end of the day, they would die.

The shadows under the king's eyes looked bruised, and his face was drawn with fatigue, but his armor was polished and his cloth-of-gold tabard clean of the blood and filth of battle.

"Your Grace!" James strode past Abbot Bernard bent over a parchment to oversee the clerics counting the captured loot. A squire scurried in with a silver flagon. "I couldn't take him. The English king reached Dunbar and took refuge there, sire." He dropped to a knee in front of the king, and a laugh welled up in his chests. "But we won!"

The king dropped a hand on his shoulder and squeezed

hard. "Aye, Jamie. We won." They shared a long smiling look. "Now tell me how you did with the pursuit."

James rose to his feet. "We harried them and took Sir Anthony de Lacy a prisoner. We accomplished little else, I fear. Aymer du Valence was not with them. I saw no sign of him or his banner. On the way…" He muffled a snort. "I was aided by Sir Laurence Abernathy. He'd approach you if he might."

The Bruce narrowed his eyes at James's companion, hanging a few steps back. "Sir Laurence. You aided my good Sir James. Yet you've been in England with my enemies."

"Your Grace." Sir Laurence dropped to a knee. "I was with the English, but…" The man quailed under the Bruce's frown. "I beg you accept me into your peace, sire. I'll serve you well. I swear it."

Bruce turned his head at a footstep from a side door. A tall man, threads of gray in his dark hair and dressed in a tunic blue and gold samite, stepped through the doorway and bowed to the king. The Bruce gazed down at the suppli- cant. "So be it. I accept your oath." The king gave Sir Laurence his hand to kiss. "And I take you into my peace." Sir Laurence rose as the Bruce waved him away. Sir Laurence looked happy to make for the door.

James placed his helm on the table beside a bowl of summer berries and rubbed the back of his neck. "How many did we lose?"

"Few knights. One of the Ross lads, young William. Of wounded, we have many, mostly from pikes that shattered under the weight of warhorses. Gilbert de la Haye will bring a report, and we'll know more when my brother and Thomas return."

The stranger said in a choked voice, "Nothing compared to our losses."

"James, here is an old friend. Sir Ralph de Monthermer."

The king's mouth thinned as he shook his head. "His step-son, the earl of Gloucester lies in the chapel."

Gilbert de Clair killed? James realized his mouth was open and snapped it closed. One of the greatest names in England, the nephew of King Edward of Caernarfon, a good-brother to King Robert through the king's wife— "How?" James asked.

Monthermer's face clinched in pain. "In the first charge, Gilbert plunged into the pikes. The king had called him a coward, and he was in a rage. God forgive me that I didn't teach the boy better. He had courage more than enough but in a temper, no judgment." His mouth worked for a moment. "What am I to tell his mother?"

The Bruce stood and grasped Monthermer's arm. "Now England shares the pain that we Scots have had these many years. But I'd not have wished it on you and your lady wife or my wife's sister, his wife." The king turned his gaze back to meet James's eyes. "There is a body in the chapel that will cause us little grief though, Jamie. Lord Robert de Clifford lies there."

"Clifford…" James felt his face heat and his heart thudded. The grasping man who had claimed so much of Scotland–including his own lands and those of the king. He would have killed the man a dozen times over. "At last!"

"And John Comyn. William le Marshal. Sir Edmund de Mauley. Sir Giles d'Argentin… The chapel is filled with bodies—more than thirty of their lords. The bodies of knights and commons are being taken to churches in Stirling Town." He shook his head. "God have mercy on them because we could not."

"Why should we?" James clenched his hands against his thighs and forced his voice to softness. "Any more than they did to my father–starved in the Tower. To your brothers. All three of them hanged, drawn and quartered. Isabella caged like an animal."

"We did what was needful. Now there will be no more slaughter. We'll have prisoners for their ransom."

James raised an eyebrow and slid his eyes toward Ralph de Monthermer.

"No. Not Sir Ralph. I owe him too great a debt and a friendship. He is my guest here, but I've sent Robert de Boyd out with a good troop of men-at-arms to see the killing stops and prisoners brought who will pay well for their freedom. I'll trust you to see Sir Ralph safely over the border along with the body of his step-son."

James's anger ran out of him like water from a cracked flagon. He was too weary to contain it. "If that is your pleasure, sire." James gave the baron, once styled as earl whilst his stepson was a minor, a half-bow.

"Give him a day's rest and…" The king broke off at loud voices in the hallway. He turned toward the door at the sound of his brother's bellowing voice mingled with the clank of steel.

"By the Holy Rood, I want a day out of the saddle," Sir Edward de Bruce said as the door was thrown open. "Albeit this day's ride was worth the trouble. I bring you gifts, Robert." Blond hair windblown and tabard dirt splattered, Sir Edward stood aside to make a sweeping motion to the man behind him. "Your Grace, may I present Sir Humphrey de Bohun, Earl of Hereford and Constable of England, who is now our—guest."

A man, much of the Bruce's age, his brown hair lightly touched with gray at the temples, strode proudly past Sir Edward. His head was bared, and he wore gold-inlaid mail under a filthy silk tabard embroidered with small golden lions. The man's face was a proud, frozen mask.

Men, armored nearly as finely and all mud and blood

besmirched from the battle and their flight, crowded in after Bohun. Their eyes darted from the king to Monthermer to James.

Sir Edward made a wide, bowing gesture to the other prisoners. "I present you Robert de Umfraville, Earl of Angus; Hugh, Lord Despenser; John, Lord Ferrers; Edmund, Lord Abergavenny; John, Lord Seagrave; and Maurice, Lord Berkeley. Lesser knights I sent ahead to Stirling Castle to be held, but I knew these you would want to greet." Edward grinned.

"Indeed, all lords I knew in years past. I am most glad to offer them our welcome." The Bruce sat and stretched his long legs out, his eyes gleaming. "My lord of Carrick, where did you find these noble guests for me?"

"At Bothwell Castle where they had taken refuge. Gilbertson there suddenly found his loyalty to you and gave them up to me and the castle with them."

"Well done." A soft and dangerous smile curved the king's mouth. "Indeed, these are guests with whom I would have speech." For the first time, he turned his gaze to the troop of noblemen who stared at him, faces frozen with hostility. He motioned to a squire and waited until the lad filled his goblet and placed it in his hand. He took a drink and gazed at the vaulted ceiling for a minute before he chose a berry from a bowl at his elbow to toss in his mouth.

"Damn you, you traitor." Bohun's face knotted like a fist. "You have us, but don't play the king at his pleasure with me. I know what you are."

The Bruce raised an eyebrow. "You'd curse me, sir earl? Call me a traitor? Instead, you should give thanks to the Blessed Virgin. My pleasure…" The Bruce's teeth gleamed as his wolfish smile broadened. "…would be to see you on a scaffold—with your belly ripped open as your king had done to my brothers. My *pleasure* would be your head over the gate of Stirling Castle."

Bohun sneered. "And give up our ransom? I think not."

Robert de Bruce nodded slowly, smiling still. "You speak truly, my lord. I am a Christian king, and I do not heedlessly murder my prisoners—unlike a king who had become no more than a ravening dog."

"King Edward was no... no dog!" Bohun sputtered in rage. "You— King *Hob*. You're not fit to speak his name. Brigand that you are! Thieving, *treacherous*—!"

"I suspect I can find somewhere to cool that temper for you, but first we'll speak of other matters." The Bruce fastened his still smiling gaze on the earl of Angus. "Aye, there will be no executions. Not even of a traitor who has given me good cause."

"Traitor? To you? Who murdered my good-brother." Robert de Umfraville, earl of Angus, flushed red, and he thrust his face toward the Bruce. "I have never sworn fealty to you. Never!"

"More fool you. If you had, you'd not be a prisoner in my hands," the king snarled. For a moment, his smiling mask had slipped. He took a drink from his goblet and paused before he continued in a low, mild tone. "As the earl of Hereford so sagely observed, I shall expect ransom for your release. And the first payment will be the return of what is mine." The king rose to his feet and paced slowly toward Bohun. "Those of mine you and your king have foully imprisoned... My wife... My daughter... My two sisters... My dear friend, Bishop Wishert... Young Andrew de Moray... Donald of Mar... They shall be returned forthwith. Then we will talk about the gold it will take for you to see your own lands again. Gold to rebuild the Scotland *you* savaged."

He turned his back on the prisoners and looked to his brother. "There are dungeons beneath Stirling Castle where you may lodge these guests. Make sure they are the deepest and darkest. There these lords of England will cool their tempers. And there they shall stay until I have returned to me what is mine. The lesser men you may ledge more pleasantly until they are ransomed."

CHAPTER 2

JULY 1314

Stirling, Scotland

James led his score of men, horse's hooves clattering, up the road towards Stirling Town, its red-roofed buildings clustering around the foot of the gray cliff, toward where the Bruce stood with Abbot Bernard of Arbroath. Abbot Bernard, the king's chancellor, wore a gray robe of the Order of Tiron. Dark hair fringed the blunt, snub-nosed face of the king's chancellor.

Abbot Bernard was shaking his head as James pulled up and jumped from his horse. "Slighting Stirling Castle? I know it's a danger to have it taken again by the English... But Stirling?"

"Jamie," the king said as Abbot Bernard frowned.

This discussion had gone on since their victory, and his news wouldn't wait. "A party approaches, sire. Andrew de Moray and an escort of English."

"Only him and no others?"

"Not yet. I have a watch on the road and orders for news to be brought as soon as they cross the border."

The king nodded. "If they want the Earl of Hereford and the others back with their heads attached, they'd do well to heed my warning. I give you my word on it. They shall not see the light of day until our own are returned to us."

James flashed him a look. How many captured Scots had the English put to cruel execution? William Wallace... The Bruce's own three brothers... The gallant Sir Christopher Seton... Sir Alexander Scrymgeour... The Earl of Atholl... Sir Simon Fraser... More loyal Scots and dear friends than he could count... So many who would not return... Yet, the king wouldn't serve those he'd captured after the battle thus as they deserved. Revenge was past seeking. England did not hold enough blood to repay what this war had cost. Better to rescue the victims than seek vengeance. No, James couldn't argue, and yet...

"There." James pointed.

Around a bend in the road, horsemen came into view, a score in all, led by two men brightly clad. Their armor and weapons clattered as they came.

As they neared, a rider at its head left the group and came at a gallop, gold hair and dark cloak flying in the wind. The lad reined up sharply a few yards away and leapt down so that he was standing, wide-legged, tense-faced, panting. For long moments, he gazed speechless, with an intensity that was painful to see.

Robert de Bruce took a step towards him. "Welcome home, Andrew."

Andrew's mouth moved though at first words did not come. "Sire... Your Grace..." He looked around as though drinking in the sight of the tall oaks, the heather, Stirling Town in the distance. "They told me—of the prisoners you took at Bannockburn. They said that you demanded my release; I could not believe it. That I would be free."

The English party came jingling up and halted just short of young Andrew de Moray. He glanced over his shoulder at the gray-haired knight who led them. "Here is Sir Roger who was my..." His mouth twisted. "...my host these past years."

James bit back angry words. What was the point? The man had no doubt followed the commands of his own king. Young Andrew was not the only child they'd imprisoned these many years. It was over and past mending, except to bring them home.

The man frowned and shook his head. "I dealt with him as kindly as I was allowed, my lord. I've no taste for ill-treating children."

James Douglas dropped his reins and gripped the hilt of the sword at his hip. Through gritted teeth, he rasped, "You will give the king his title. Or you will see a dungeon, *Sir*."

The man's face drained of color. "I beg his grace's pardon. No offense..."

"You may go." The Bruce gave an abrupt gesture of dismissal. "Mark you, though. The other prisoners had best be returned to us promptly. You have a month or Bohun and the others will meet my brothers' fates. My patience grows thin." As the men turned their horses to leave, he said, "Come here, lad."

He gripped Andrew, wide-eyed and a little white around the lips, by the shoulders. "Never doubt that had it been in my power, I would have brought you home sooner. Now I'll return you to your mother and your uncle, the bishop."

Andrew's color was coming back, but he swallowed hard. "They're here?"

"They will be. You've arrived before them." The Bruce smiled and gave Andrew a gentle shake. "How does it feel to be home?"

"It's a wonder. It *smells* like home. Isn't that strange, Your Grace? The scent of heather and salt sea. It's what I remembered most."

James smiled. "Not so strange to me. I remember that from when I returned home from exile as well."

"They thought I'd forget." Andrew's eyes were solemn. "But I didn't. I could never forget my own country or my own people."

"I never thought it," the Bruce said gently.

"You'll take my oath? I shall be your man. I swear it."

"Gladly, lad." Robert de Bruce, king of the Scots, held out his hands. "Your father's lands and his titles are yours. Lord of Avoch and Petty and Bothwell, as they should be."

Andrew dropped to his knees and reached up for the king's hands. The solemn look on the lad's face made James's chest ache. Had he ever been so young? He remembered the day he had knelt before Robert de Bruce, not yet a king, on a spring day with the scent of the heather all around them. Yes, mayhap he too had been young and unstained all those years ago.

In a clear, ringing voice, the lad made his oath, "I, Andrew de Moray, become your man in life and in death..."

* * *

Outwith the stable, James strode to join the Bruce to give him news of the approaching party. "They will be here in an hour or two," he said as they walked toward the door of the manor house.

"You're sure the queen is with them?"

"My scouts said two women are in the party under Gilbert de la Haye's banner." Two men with pikes guarded the door. James greeted them and followed the king up the steps, wondering at the king's frown. This was good news surely, but the Bruce's hands clenched as he walked through the high arched Great Hall to his bedchamber. Within, a squire was polishing the king's helm and another brushing a velvet cloak.

"Lay out my best garb," the Bruce said, "and bring hot water." He paced around the chamber, rubbing his lips with his fingers, his forehead creased whilst the lads scurried to do his bidding. James propped up the wall with his back and crossed his arms.

One of the squires laid out a blue tunic of silk with a lion worked on the breast, black hose, a belt of gold links, and a crimson cloak. The other hurried in with a basin of steaming water scented with lavender. "Very good. Sir James will play the squire for me," he said and waved them away. As they bowed their way out, the king stripped his sweat-soiled tunic over his head and tossed it down. He twitched a crooked smile. "You wonder that I am vexed?"

"Surprised, sire. I thought…"

"We were happy? Aye, we were. But whilst I've been free, she's spent all her youth locked in a nunnery. Allowed nothing fine—no pleasures. She'll come home to find my bastards whilst she was denied…" The Bruce made a choking noise and turned away. He ran a damp cloth over his furred chest and threw it hard into the basin, sloshing water over the rim from the force. "She loved music. Laughter. Gay company. And they locked her in a room with two grim old women, year after year. Eight years of it."

"You think she'll blame you?"

"How not? You know what she said the day I was crowned? That we were but king and queen of the May. That it would not last. She was afraid of exactly what happened. And after, I must face my sisters and tell them through my fault three of our brothers were tortuously murdered. Holy Jesu God! I'd rather face the worst battle of my life than this."

The Bruce raked a broad hand through his hair; his chest heaved as he sucked in a great breath.

"It was the damned Sassenach who did it. Not you. They'll know that." James dropped the tunic over the Bruce's head, fastened his belt, and draped his cloak around his shoulders.

"I should have protected them. Had I sent them to Norway straight away after my coronation, to my sister there, they would have been safe."

As he fastened the golden lion rampant pin to hold the king's cloak, James frowned and shook his head. "You can't know. They might have died in a storm on the way. Sickened in the winter." James tried to think of something that could comfort the king for all he had lost. There was nothing, any more than it comforted James. He met the king's eyes. "You have the courage to face it as you always have."

Robert de Bruce took a deep breath and squared his shoulders. "I'll meet them in the Great Hall."

James opened the door for him and followed. The vaulted chamber was immense but in the summer's heat only a small fire burnt in the great hearth. Walter Stewart and Robert de Boyd were seated at a bench, talking as they shared a flagon of wine. Walter, in a blue embroidered surcoat of the Steward colors, leapt to his feet, and Robbie, a hint of laughter in his eyes, rose more slowly.

Walter exclaimed, "Your Grace, we heard. The queen will be here?"

"Pour me some of that wine," the Bruce said.

"You must keep a proper court now, Your Grace." Robbie grinned. "My lady says these years in the heather have made us fit for nothing but heathens, so it won't be easy."

The Bruce took a long drink of the wine that Walter handed him. "Aye, I've been thinking on that. How is the lad settling, your stepson? After being locked up in England so long?"

"Andrew is as wild as a falcon cut loose from a cage. There's no mischief he won't get up to celebrating his freedom." Robbie shook his head at the king. "As should you be. Why a solemn face? Is that any way for the queen to see you?"

"It has just been so long a time." He smiled but it was little more than a grimace. "Has the lad an eye for the ladies?"

"He's seventeen—still young for that."

James laughed. "Not too young at all. At that age, I was after anything in a kirtle. Surely you were as well, sire."

"At seventeen, I was already wed. That was the year Marjorie was born, and her mother died birthing her."

Robbie was right that the king had to show a cheerful face to the returning prisoners. James leaned close to the king and said in an undertone, "What will they think to see you with this sour mien? They'll think you didn't want them to return."

The Bruce nodded and upended the wine goblet. James saw the effort it took for him to smile. "So I shall keep a court. That means I expect the rest of my nobles to wed. Including you, Walter."

"Me?"

Robbie snorted. "What lass will you curse with him?"

James kept a grin back as his young cousin glared at Robbie. The door banged open. Gilbert de la Haye beamed in the doorway, though travel soiled and his dark hair stringy with sweat, and said, "Your Grace…"

A woman brushed past him, as plainly dressed as a nun in a gray robe, but her blond hair was uncovered. She stopped and stared at the king, flushed with excitement and eyes wide.

The king took one step toward her. "Elizabeth," he said in a choked voice.

She ran to him then and threw herself against his chest,

wrapping her arms around his waist. "Robert."

"God be thanked." He pressed a kiss to the top of her head and rested his cheek against it. "Holy Jesu God be thanked."

James looked past the two to a figure silhouetted against the sunlight in the doorway. He squinted, for surely she was too slender to be one of the king's sisters. He strode to the door. She was smiling, as drably dressed as the queen but as unlike a nun as could be imagined in spite of her eight long years locked in a nunnery. Her eyes were wide blue like her father's and her hair a reddish-brown, wind-tossed mane. He hardly recognized her as the hoyden she'd been when they'd fled the English. "Lady Marjorie!" He reached for her hand and bent to kiss her fingers.

Behind James, the Bruce gasped. "Marjorie! Lass!"

"Father!" Marjorie pulled free from James to run to her father's arms, laughing. The queen pushed back from the Bruce's chest and made room for the princess. The Bruce held her against him whilst the queen wrapped her arms around them both, murmuring something incoherent. The king's face clenched, and he squeezed his eyes closed. Tears ran down his face.

"Father," Marjorie clutched him. "I thought I would never see you again."

James swallowed a rock that seemed lodged in his chest. Lady Elizabeth met his gaze. She was still beautiful even as she wept. James smiled at her and went to drop to a knee at her feet. "Your Grace," he said and took her hand to kiss. "Welcome home."

Lady Marjorie sniffled and stepped back from her father. She took a handkerchief from her belt and mopped at her face. "My lord father," she said in a choked voice, "you must think me a goose."

"I'd have to think the same of myself, lass." The Bruce shook his head as he took the cloth from her hand and wiped his own cheeks. "I'm unmanned but—God in heaven, how I missed you. Both of you."

James rose to his feet, grinning at Walter. "Cousin, didn't I teach you better than to stand gaping? Come make your courtesies to the queen and Princess Marjorie. My ladies, this is Sir Walter, the High Steward. He's not much to look at but did proudly at Bannockburn, so we decided to keep him." James twitched a grin at Walter's scowl. "You'll frighten them back to England with that look."

"I blame Jamie for Walter's manners. I've heard he was never properly buffeted about the head as a lad." Robbie gave a sorrowful shake of his head.

Marjorie hid a giggle behind her hand. Walter blushed red. He opened his mouth but couldn't seem to find a reply to suit the japes.

"Oh, I think it is safe that nothing would frighten us that much. It has been long and long since I've heard laughter." Lady Marjorie shook her head at James. "And your smile I remember well from days as we fled through the heather. You outdid all the men in hunting, and I thought you quite wonderful."

"Don't think I'm a still green lad, my lady. You can't make me blush like another I won't name." He winked at her and she giggled again. James prodded Walter's shoulder, and the young knight dropped to a knee. He took Lady Marjorie's hand to kiss her fingers.

"Leave Walter be, both of you. He's not here for your japery." The Bruce was silent for a moment. "None of us have had a surfeit gaiety these last years. But I swear it will be put to right." He looked from his daughter to his wife. "We'll find musicians. And somewhere in Scotland must still be acrobats. We'll make up that—" The king's throat work as he swallowed. "We'll make up that we couldn't bring you home sooner. You have my solemn word on it."

The queen took the Bruce's hand in hers, but her smile was a little twisted. "Not solemn, Your Grace. I had enough of solemnity locked in a room of that nunnery. Truly, it was grim and solemn indeed. Now we'll have gaiety, I pray you."

* * *

James settled back in his place at the head of the table and drank. The fruity taste of the claret in his mouth made him smile with satisfaction. The Great Hall of his manor in Perth was heavy with the smell of roast venison and berries fresh picked. Under it was a hint of the rose scent Elayne wore. The manor's stone walls were draped with his banner and tapestries embroidered in gold, crimson, and blue, gifted from the king and seized from the great stores of treasure the fleeing English had left behind. A minstrel in the gallery played a harp and sang a song of a knight helplessly in love. James drank deep from his cup.

Love… He mustn't think of Alycie. The memory cut like a sword. He drained his cup. *Holy St. Bride, keep me from thinking of her.*

It was his duty to think of his lady wife. She smelled sweetly of roses. Her tight-bodice gown was of yellow samite; the long sleeves draped when she folded her hands modestly in her lap. Her silvery-blonde hair fell in waves to her waist beneath a gauzy veil.

It was the third hour of the feast laid to welcome him home. A hundred guests crowded the benches, his retainers and allies who had ridden back with him from Stirling and some who had already returned home, raucous with drink and laughter, sharing stories of the battle. Symon de Loccart smiled when James met his gaze with a nod. James's good-father frowned, and his good-mother kept glancing at him from the corner of her eye.

His wife picked at her food. She thanked him prettily when he offered her the queen's piece of the haunch from the point of his knife. But she kept her eyes fixed on her hands, and what he could see of her cheek was pale.

He said, "The court abides at, for a time, to Cambuskenneth Abbey. And Lady Marjorie is with the queen. She is not so much older than you." He frowned, counting the years. "She must be eighteen years old now."

"Is she, my lord?" Elayne murmured.

"Lady Christina and Lady Mary had also arrived the day before I left." He took a gulp of wine and pulled a deep breath, feigning a smile. "Lady Mathilda and Sir Aodh are to join the court, as well. The queen is in need of a lady-in-waiting."

She finally raised her gaze to his and her cheeks flushed. "Do you mean you'd want me to serve the queen?"

"The king has summoned the parliament, and I must return. I thought to take you with me. The court will go north, I think, to Dunfermline after a time. Further from the border. The king means to slight Stirling Castle."

Her back was stiff as she slid her eyes toward him. "Will you stay with the court? After the parliament?"

"My duties lie elsewhere."

He was sure her sigh was one of relief. He stood and pulled her firmly to her feet. "Come, it's time to retire." He nodded to the company as he rose and walked quickly from the hall, her hand held in place on the crook of his arm. James shoved the door to the bedchamber closed behind them. He'd commanded a flagon of malmsey for the bedchamber. It was sweet but would be better for her tastes. This would be easier if they both were drunk, he supposed, and better this was done and done now.

He poured them both a goblet of wine.

She sat on the edge of the curtained bed and took a long swallow. "Should I call my maid to undress me, my lord?"

"Drink your wine and then I'll help you." He propped himself on the edge of the table and sipped the cloying wine. "You might enjoy being the queen's lady-in-waiting. I won't command you, but the princess is near your age. There will be dancing, and it will be gay, I think. Mayhap you'd be happy."

She drained her cup, and he held out the flagon to refill it. She seemed less timid, he thought, but she continued to stare down at her cup. "Your father was angry, you know. You needn't have told that I hadn't..." He took another drink of his wine. He needed it, as well.

"My lady mother asked questions I couldn't answer," she said.

"We both have a duty." James knew he sounded angry and softened his voice. He pushed himself to his feet and sat down his cup. "I promise it won't be so ill."

She nodded and drained her cup in two gulps. He took it and pulled her to her feet with a hand on her elbow. She trembled as he unfastened her laces and buttons. He let her gown fall in a puddle around her feet. She was passive as a doll under his hands. His breathing was fast, and he wasn't sure if it was anger or lust. But he knew he must try to handle her gently. Her skin was milky white and soft when he stroked her shoulder. Her breasts still buds that wouldn't even fill his hands. She kept her eyes straight ahead as he pushed her silken smallclothes from her body. When he was done, she raised her wide eyes to stare into his.

"You are fair," he said.

"I—" Her throat worked as she swallowed. Her whole body was shaking. "I shall do my duty."

"Whatever they told you when you were in England, I am not a cruel man. I won't hurt you." He thought of telling her that he wanted a wife who did more than her duty. Loyalty. Kindness. Even desire would be welcome. But mayhap those would come. "Climb into bed, Elayne."

He pulled the coverlet back and let her climb in. She stretched out. Her eyes were closed, her head turned away. He pulled off his clothes, knelt on the bed beside her and stroked her breast. She shuddered. He wanted to command her to open her eyes, to look at him, but the words stuck in his chest. He gently used a hand to part her legs.

* * *

The drizzle came and went, and there was more slate than blue in the sky. The river was running high as they crossed it below the cliff where Stirling Castle loomed above them. A rumble like thunder shuddered, and a puff of smoke rose from its walls. The king was destroying the castle. Never again would it be held by their enemies. He turned his horse's head west and signaled the party to follow. Every field they had passed was drowning in the late summer rains.

Wet and hungry, James tugged his cloak close as they slogged the last mile of the road and cantered toward the towering gray bell tower. He stepped off his horse into a puddle and pulled a face. He wanted a hot meal in front of a crackling fire to warm his feet. He looked about, wondering where their rooms would be in the vast outlying buildings of the abbey, when a guard ran toward him across the yard. The Privy Council was already gathering, and Sir James was wanted.

"Where is the chamberlain?" he asked and thrust his reins into the man's hands. "I can't meet with the council, wet and travel soiled."

A sturdy man of middle years scurried out the main doors. "My lord, you have chambers in the east wing. With so many here, even the abbey is crowded, but a fire is lit in your chambers, and I'll see you to it."

"I thank you, sir." The rest of his party was clattering and splashing into the yard behind him, surrounding Elayne's canopied litter, led by Will Dickson, whom James had named his steward. James motioned him over. "Find me something dry in the wagons and bring it. And then see they're unloaded, and my lady wife is settled in the rooms they've given us. I'm called to the council."

A half-hour later, James strode into the council chamber, still chilled and hungry, where rushes scented with lavender covered the floor. A tapestry of the Scots defeating the Norse at the Battle of Largs covered a wall and in the center of a long polished table. The chamber was full of men awaiting the king's pleasure, all in finery fit for the royal court instead of their usual armor: Maol, Earl of Lennox; Niall Campbell; Uilleam, earl of Ross; Angus Og, lord of the Isles; Gilbert de la Haye, Lord High Constable of Scotland. The short man speaking in a low voice to his own good-father had to be William de Soules, Lord of Liddesdale and hereditary Seneschal of Scotland, newly returned to the king's peace a week before. Robbie Boyd stood propping up a wall, his arms crossed over his chest.

Soules nodded to James with an arrogant smile. "I've heard much of your exploits, Lord Douglas."

"My lord," James returned the smile with a twitch of his eyebrow. "Welcome home. It may be chill for you after so long in England."

Robbie gave James a wry smile that twisted his scarred cheek.

Edward de Bruce, earl of Carrick, looked up from the chair where he sprawled and drawled, "Ah, Lord Warden of the Marches, we thank you that you deign to grace us with your presence."

"The trip took longer than I expected, Sir Edward. I crave the pardon of the council." James bowed to the king's brother, who had always disliked him. In looks, he was much like the king, blond and broad shouldered, and brave as any man alive, but be arrogant, haughty, and with more bravado than brains. "A household makes slow travel."

Thomas Randolph, standing next to a window, turned, so his back was to Sir Edward and winked at James. Laughing, he said, "S'truth. Allow twice as long as traveling alone, so I've found since the king married me off."

James grinned. "Aye, my lord, and through your wife we're by way of being cousins now." Thomas Randolph, earl of Moray, had wed one of his Stewart cousins on his mother's side. "Is your lady wife here at the Abbey?"

"I bade her stay in Moray for the sake of the bairn." He laughed and his face colored. "She scolded so that I let her come. It was a long weary trip with her litter."

James moved to the table and said, "Abbot Bernard, I trust you're well and recovered from watching over all that English treasure. Is it locked safely away?"

The chancellor looked up and smiled from his chair at the foot of the table. "I've had worse jobs, Sir James. You know much of that treasure the king will gift to those who fought for him there." His brown hair fringed a sturdy, plain face. "Bishop Lamberton arrived late last night from London."

James took a seat near the Abbot Bernard. "So soon?"

"I fear so," Robert de Bruce said from the doorway, and behind him stood William de Lamberton, Bishop of St. Andrews, his hair gone quite gray and stoop shouldered during his years in an English dungeon although only in his fortieth year. They all jumped to their feet except Sir Edward who slowly uncoiled his body to rise. The king took his seat at the head of the table and waved them to their seats. "Tell them your news, William."

Bishop Lamberton remained standing, his face grim. "They refused our terms for peace."

Sir Edward pounded a fist on the table whilst Niall Campbell slumped, his forehead in his hand. Thomas Randolph silently shook his head and looked toward James, but the others were on their feet shouting curses. James gripped his hand into a fist and slammed it on his thigh—so much for any hope for peace.

"Silence," the Bruce said. He glared at them until the room was quiet except for the sound of rain on the stone walls. "So, was it the terms? We could hardly ask for less—that they recognize Scotland's independence and our sovereignty."

"No. It was not the terms. They will not consider any terms. They still name you a traitor and all of us rebels."

"Are they fools?" Maol of Lennox demanded. "They cannot mount another invasion. Not possibly after their losses and a hundred of their lords still in our hands."

"They appeal to the Pope to renew the excommunication and interdict against you, Your Grace."

"Again?" James shouted, amid laughter.

Lamberton sank into a chair at the left of the king. "They won't invade, not soon. Eventually? Yes. If we can't force them to treat with us, we can expect to have to face another army even larger than the last. They are—" He frowned as he pondered his words. "They are convinced that our kingdom is theirs. That they cannot defeat us for the nonce does not mean they might not with another army in another year. They'll cling to their false claims and hope for victory over us in the future—whatever the cost to them now."

James leaned forward on his elbows and stared at his clasped hands against the polished wood of the table. The few losses of the English had been nothing. He looked up. "How can they know the cost? Their cost has been that!" He snapped his fingers. "Compared to what it has cost us. So we must let them know what war truly costs. Let them see if they want to pay."

"Aye," Angus Og growled.

"Can we afford to do that?" asked Niall Campbell. James looked at the man in surprise. He was the last James would expect to cry against war, but his face was drawn and pale. Niall was no older than the king, but to James he looked ill. "We need to give thought to raising our sons and reaping our harvests. Not to the English."

"Will they leave us in peace to do that?" Thomas snorted. "I think not."

"No," the Bruce said. "Bishop Lamberton is right. If we don't force them, they will be back. So James will take the war to them. Yet again." He nodded to James. "Albeit burning York didn't force them to terms before, it will not now."

"Then somehow we much reach further south," James said, but he chewed his lip. Going further south than York was a risk they'd not dared take. They'd be cut off by the strong forces in the southern reaches of England. That Scotland could not afford. "Mayhap as far as Richmond and the River Wear with a strong enough force, but I think no further."

"My galleys could reach further than Sir James. Let me attack their ports. Harry their merchant ships." Angus Og beamed as he stroked his long moustaches that drooped below his chin. "No one can catch my berlinns at sea."

Uilleam of Ross glared at his life-long enemy. "Mine can."

"Good," the king said. "Then whilst Uilleam and his galleys harry the eastern coast, Angus Og will do the same on the west. And we must push a force into England—my good Sir James and my brother together. If the English won't make peace, then they must make war. James, you and Edward will thrust into the Midlands. Burn what you cannot seize, as far as Richmond if you can."

Bishop Lamberton cleared his throat. "It isn't enough, Your Grace. I'm sorry. It won't be enough."

"You are right. So are you fit for a trip to France, my friend?" the king asked.

Lamberton raised his eyebrows. "To King Philip?"

"Exactly. Discuss renewing our treaty with the French king. I have little reason to think Philip loves his good-son. Mayhap it will accomplish little but to fash our enemies to the south, but that alone is worth doing. I do not believe that the French are ready for a treaty. So I'll also send Thomas to Norway to renew our treaties there."

"Aye, Your Grace. I am fit for a trip to the French court."

"About Ireland," Sir Edward said, and it was not a question. "I tell you if the Irish rise against them, the curst English will be in grave case. Two wars will be more than they can fight whilst they snarl at each other at home."

The king spread both his broad hands on the table and stared past the wall. James wondered how far his gaze went beyond these walls and across Scotland. Finally, the Bruce nodded. "Send a letter to the king of Tyrone. If he will support you, I'll give you my support as well and give you an army to take with you to Ireland."

Edward de Bruce's face went blank with surprise. James bit down on a smile.

"I shall," Edward said. "He will give me the support I need."

"Mind you. I'll not support you unless they agree to crown you high king. And I am none too sure you can win. If they do then I'll do what I can, and every day the English fight there means they're not fighting in Scotland. If we can draw their fangs, so they can't attack us on our western coast that will be a happy day." He nodded to Abbot Bernard. "Now to the matter of tomorrow's parliament."

The abbot stood with a rolled parchment in his hand. "I'll bring before the parliament a most urgent matter. Those who owe fealty to Lord Robert who serve the English to the harm of us all must be dealt with: Henry de Beaumont who claims, *jure uxoris*, the earldom of Buchan for his wife, Alice de Comyn; Robert de Umbraville, earl of Angus; Sir Ingram de Umbraville, late Guardian of this realm. Others of their ilk serve our enemies. We will give them notice that this must end. They give themselves into the king's peace within the twelve-month or their lands and titles shall be forfeit."

James watched the faces of the men around him. The earl of Ross had made peace with the king, albeit few in the room had forgiven his treachery in turning the queen over to English imprisonment those years ago. But he didn't seem to give a tinker's curse if others paid when he hadn't. Niall Campbell had lifted an eyebrow. James suspected the coming was no news to the Bruce's good-brother.

The chancellor continued, "I will propose to this the parliament for a vote." Several of the lords leaned their heads together to whisper comments as muttering spread through the chamber. "If they do not return to the king's peace and offer their fealty, all their claims will be forfeit to the king to be disposed of to those who have served him and the kingdom better than the traitors."

Now James raised his own eyebrows as he leaned back. Those were vast estates to be parceled out if they were forfeit. Niall Campbell twitched James a smile. Yes, Campbell had earned a share of any forfeiture, mayhap even an earldom. So had James, though he didn't look so high. He was sure that some of those men named would cut off both hands rather than put them in the king's to give him their oath.

"Good." Robert de Bruce slapped his hand down on the table. "Then it is settled. I shall call another parliament for the spring to discuss other matters, but until then you have your duties set out for you. For tonight, Lady Elizabeth expects you in your finery, as do I."

CHAPTER 3

ONE WEEK LATER

Young Gylmyne knelt to fasten the fine worked leather belt around James's waist over his crimson velvet tunic with sleeves fashionably puffed. James smiled as he tugged the tunic straight. The lad had yet to find the knack of hanging his clothes straight. James hoped that soon he would. He was a Loccart, a cousin to Sir Symon, and only in his thirteenth year. Surely he would learn to be less hack-handed soon.

"Are you ready," he asked Elayne. She was lovely in a blue gown with long dagged sleeves touching the floor, her skirt embroidered with white roses. The maid the queen had sent to her draped Elayne's mantle around her shoulders.

Her mouth was drawn into a thin, bitter line, but she nodded. "Yes, my lord." She dutifully took his arm. He felt her stiffness as he escorted her down the stairs, and she never looked up at him. They descended in silence.

At the foot of the tower, they joined the hurrying guests in the bailey yard. It was a peacock's show of silks and velvets in every color as they filed in through the doors. The evening was gray, and everyone was eager to enter and escape the drizzle. Inside, the high vaulted hall was ablaze with torches in polished sconces. Guests milled about the tables as heralds announced the names and titles of the lords and ladies. Music of harps and pipes and drums at the foot of the hall mixed with the laughter and chatter of the guests.

A little page in red led them toward down the center aisle. James paused to make their courtesies to Robbie Boyd and Lady Caitrina. Elayne embraced her when Robbie told her that Caitrina's son had been returned to her, complimented her own mother on her new velvet gown, and asked Abbot Bernard where the court would proceed upon leaving the abbey. *She may indeed be happy at court,* James thought. *She had not a happy day in his company, he was sure, nor he in hers.* Aodh of Ross was limping from the wound he took at the battle trying to save his brother and his wife, Lady Mathilda, on his arm took part of his weight. When Elayne said she had heard of his brother's bravery and his own in trying to save him, Aodh blushed.

James patted her hand on his arm and said, "They're taken with you." She didn't reply as they went to their places next to Lady Marjorie and her uncle Sir Edward.

Robert de Bruce and Elizabeth de Burgh strolled into the Great Hall. The king wore black tights and a red tunic embroidered with lions, but Lady Elizabeth outshone him in green velvet, with a tight-laced bodice that showed her full bosom and her hair was in a silver net, winking with sapphires. On her brow was a slender gold crown. She smiled like a girl at her first ceilidh as the king led her past the bowing throng to seats of honor at the high table before a banner of the Scottish lion as large as a ship's sail. A dozen others were sat closer to the king, the earl of Lennox, the earl of Ross, Bishop Lamberton, Bishop David of Moray and the frail, blind Bishop Wishert, last of the Scots to be freed from an English dungeon. Lady Elizabeth paused to kiss Wishert's hand and say a quiet word to him before she took her place standing beside the king. James and Elayne were well to the king's right with Edward de Bruce and Lady Marjorie between them and the king.

Elayne curtsied prettily to the princess, and Lady Marjorie pressed a kiss to her cheek. "My lady-in-waiting, Marioun of Ramsey." Marjorie tugged the hand of a wisp of a lass, no more than twelve, with bright eyes and blonde curls tumbling down her back. "I have so looked forward to our all being friends."

They bowed their heads whilst Bishop David made neat, quick work of a blessing.

Robert de Bruce looked around the hall, his expression so happy it made James's chest ache. "Our people are freed once more. Tonight, we'll have naught but joy. To the queen's safe return." The king took a filled goblet from a squire and lifted it. "To the queen!"

"Lady Elizabeth!" James shouted, joining a hundred other voices. "To the queen! To the queen!" James drained his cup and motioned for a page to refill it when he and Elayne were seated.

For once Sir Edward nodded amiably enough at James before he said "Robert should have seated you with young Walter." Sir Walter, now the High Steward of Scotland since his father's death was on the other side of the king and queen past two score nobles.

Lady Marjorie made a face at Sir Edward. "Cannot we talk of something pleasant?"

Her uncle raised a sun-bleached eyebrow. "You dislike him? Why?"

She rolled her eyes and leaned forward to speak past James to Elayne. "I am returned a week, and all they will speak of is finding me a husband. I'd rather make merry at least for a time."

James grinned. "Sir Edward is not the one to press you to wed, my lady."

Marjorie gave him a curious look and a wicked smile. "Is there a story about my uncle that would entertain us?" He would never have thought she had spent eight years locked up in a nunnery for she was sparkling with gaiety. She wore a deep blue samite gown that shimmered in the torchlight, setting off her eyes. Her hair, held back by a slender gold coronet, hung in waves like silk down her back almost to her waist.

"No, there is not," Sir Edward said.

"Not at all." James took a drink of the rich red wine in his cup to wash down a laugh. "Your uncle is a braw knight and beloved of so many, he is hard pressed to choose."

In fact, Sir Edward bedded more women than James could count, and his bastard with Ross's sister was the talk of the realm, but that was a story Sir Edward would not be pleased to have told.

Marjorie laughed and asked Elayne if she was joining the court. The moment passed when Elayne said she was. The pages kept the cups filled all night as James helped Elayne to dishes that came and went, of swan, of rabbit in wine-current sauce, of compost of carrots and pears, of sturgeon in a golden saffron sauce, and spiced honey biscuits. She nibbled as she chattered to Lady Marjorie. They both clapped when a troop of acrobats swarmed it tumbling and jumping on each other's shoulders to form a tower. When her mouth wasn't in a bitter line, Elayne had a delicate beauty, but Marjorie's laugh made him smile. She'd been a child when they'd fled with the king through the highlands, full of laughter and a child's tricks. Odd that such a terrible time also had pleasant memories. She'd missed so much locked up by her English captors.

He watched a stilt walker juggling colored balls as a

tumbler leapt through a burning hoop and an old man who got a bear to dance clumsily to the tune of a pipe.

"Sir James, do you ignore me?" Marjorie smiled and her eyes sparkled.

"Of course not, my lady. I was remembering those days when we fled through the Highlands. You know I have no sisters. I grew up in a Bishop's household. You were the nearest I had to a sister, I think." He smiled at her fondly. St. Bride but he hoped she would find happiness now. "You've been missed."

It was foolish that seeing Marjorie grown to a woman made him sad, so he looked at Thomas Randolph and his Isabella near the king. She was heavy with child and her round face was plain to his eye though she glowed with happiness. James watched as Randolph cut her a morsel of a sturgeon and fed it to her. He leaned close to whisper something in her ear, his hand resting upon her swollen belly. Randolph had found joy with his sweet, plain-faced bride. But that was fair. Someone in the midst of this benighted war should find joy.

James might have given Elayne a child the nights he had lain with her. He prayed so for both their sakes. He wondered what she would do if he put a hand her belly if she were with child. Shudder, he supposed as she had in their bed. Albeit, she would suffer his touch as her duty, and he'd touch her for his.

"Do you ride, Lady Elayne?" Marjorie asked. When Elayne murmured that she preferred her litter, Marjorie nodded. "Some ladies do. But I'd smell the sweet, free air and feel the wind. Would your lord husband and his men escort me on the morrow, do you think?"

"I must attend the parliament, but in the afternoon if your lord father permits. In the company of your lady-in-waiting, of course." He nodded to Sir Edward and put a hand on

Elayne's arm. "You look weary after our long journey. We should retire."

He'd been too long between women, was all. It was making him mawkish. His night with Elayne had been more punishment than pleasure, as much for him as for her. James shouted for a maid when he led Elayne up the stairs to their chamber. He kissed her hand as the maid peered around the door. "Shall I help my lady?" the woman asked.

"We don't need you." James touched Elayne's shoulder with his fingertips, soft like velvet.

She jerked away and lifted her chin. "Mayhap I'm with child."

"It's soon—too soon to know."

"If I am, you needn't touch me." Strangely calm, she looked into his eyes. "I don't want you to touch me."

"I'm your husband," James was so angry he forgot to keep his voice down. "You have no right to tell me nae."

"You can force me." Elayne tilted her chin to an imperious angle. "You can find a woman anywhere. If I'm not with child... Then I'll let you do that to me. I know I must give you an heir." Her eyes narrowed. "I hate when you touch me. The Black Douglas." She spat the words. "They say you're the devil's spawn. My father married me to you, but he can't make me not hate you."

Mayhap I should force her. It is my right. His hands were shaking. With anger? He was not sure. He had the right, but... Holy St. Bride, he could not. *What kind of man can kill in battle, but cannot take his own wife?* Silent, he turned his back. "I'm of a mind to check on my men and make plans for the foray the king commanded." He took his sword belt from the peg where it hung and buckled it around his waist.

"As it please you."

"Sleep well." Without looking, he closed the door behind

him and made his way down the narrow stairway. Outside, he nodded to Richert. "Are the men settled for the night?"

"Aye." Richert gave him a cocky grin. "Will you want an escort?"

Half an hour later, James took the road toward the town with a score of his men in his tail. Stirling Castle was outlined against the moon, misshapen as a rotting tooth, half its walls demolished. The king was wasting no time in slighting it to the ground, but such a strong castle was no small task to destroy. "Richert," James called, "on the day after tomorrow, we'll ride for Douglasdale. See that the men are ready to leave at daybreak. Choose a score of men to remain with my lady wife when we leave."

"I'll see to it, my lord."

"Good." James put his heels to his horse and cantered away, leaving his men to follow as best they could. He had told Elayne that he intended to make plans for the foray, and that was not entirely a lie. The command from his liege could not be delayed, and it was long since he'd forayed with Edward de Bruce. He'd need a strong force and trusted lieutenants. The king's brother would not make it an easy raid. Edward de Bruce had a liking for open battle that would not do them well deep within England.

After dark, the streets of Stirling Town were quiet. The city gates were open and a pair of guards stood on each side leaning on their pikes. They sprang erect and bowed as James passed. James followed the winding street up the hill past a lone farmer standing beside his wagon shouting, "Neeps for sale. Neeps and onions for sale cheap." This year's crops had been poor even before the English invaded, and he'd burned everything before them. He wondered how soon there would be no food in the market or in people's bellies.

"We'll need sumpter horses for returning what we find in

the south," he said. "Choose men to send to the Lanarkshire market. It's a good place to buy them."

"How many horses?" Richert asked.

"As many as they find."

A pack of dogs raced past them into an alley, growling and barking after some prey. A blacksmith working at an open forge stopped to watch them pass, and an ironmonger shouted that he had a fine razor that would please my lord. But the shadows had grown deep, and the streets of Stirling Town were grown quiet. James pulled up beneath a sign painted with a mug of ale, weathered and peeling that creaked in the sea wind. A torch flickered beside the doorway. James swung from the saddle. He handed his reins to Richert. "Return with my horse at daybreak. I'll spend the night here."

Richert gave him a questioning look. "Without a guard?"

James grinned. "I have enough guard on my hip." He shoved the door open and sucked in the rich smell of ale. Next to the fire three men-at-arms croaked out a bawdy song whilst a giggling woman put a pitcher of ale on the table in front of them. A few torches on the walls smoked as much as they threw out light. The room was crowded, men-at-arms and townsfolk squeezed together on benches.

A bony woman with a thin, crooked nose bustled toward him, a rag in her hand. "Welcome, my lord." She shooed away a scarred faced man from a table near the kitchen and pulled out a rickety chair before she swiped it with her rag. "I'll send a lass with a flagon of ale, my lord." She smirked. "She's as tasty as the wine, but the cost for her would be extra."

James snorted. He knew better than to trust the horse piss an inn would pass as wine. "Have her bring me ale instead." He tossed a handful of pence onto the table. "I'll judge for myself on the lass."

The woman scooped up the coins and hurried away, yelling, "Megy, move your arse."

A lass, probably no more than sixteen, scooted out of the kitchen door, a pitcher of ale and a battered pewter cup in her hands. James looked her over as she poured for him. She looked to be clean, her hair was combed until it shined, and her breasts were of a size that would fill a man's hands. When she looked up from pouring to smile at him, she was no beauty, but that would be much to expect in a whore. She had a round face and a pug nose, but her eyes were a pretty blue. They flashed with a look that stirred him.

He took a deep drink of the ale and nodded. "Aye, that's good." He patted his thigh for her to sit. "Your name is Megy?"

She curled gracefully onto his lap. "It is." She gave him a cheeky smile. "And your name is my lord."

"Some call me that. But you may call me Jamie." James picked up the cup and drained it. In the time since Alycie had died, he'd not lain with a woman except the once with his wife—a cold memory. Megy's full breasts pressed against his arm as he reached around her to put down the cup, and he was already hard. He stroked her dark, soft hair and knew needed this. "Show me your room, if you please. We'll take the ale with us." He grasped her waist and lifted her to her feet.

She picked up the pitcher with one hand and clasped his with the other to lead him up the stairs. She smiled over her shoulder as she opened her door. "Your bed at the court must be a cold one to come into town."

"Cold enough." He kicked the door closed.

Megy took the hem of her kirtle and pulled it over her head to toss it aside. She wore no shift beneath it. "You'll find my bed warm, my lord." She smiled up at him, curved and soft and pink, her blue eyes gleaming.

"Show me." He pulled against him to stroke her flank, and her deft fingers moved to the lacings of his breeches.

* * *

James blinked when he stepped into the bright afternoon sun. He stretched his back and groaned. There was nothing more miserable than sitting on a hard bench and listening to men quibble and argue. But at last, it was over. If Lady Marjorie still wanted to breathe the sweet, free air, he would not argue, albeit were he wise, he would ride for Douglasdale.

"Sir James," a high, young voice called to him.

He turned to see Marioun of Ramsey waving to him. She smiled at him, and he smiled, too.

"Why are you alone, lass?" he asked.

"Lady Marjorie sent me to fetch you." She took his hand boldly as a child and pulled him around a corner and toward the stables. "Our horses are saddled."

"We cannot ride without a guard." James pulled his hand loose and turned on his heel to scan for his own men. When he spotted Iain, he shouted for him to gather a score of men and have them mounted. He tucked Marioun's hand into the crook of his elbow. She was a small, willowy mite, and her giggle as they walked made him smile.

"There she is." She pulled her hand free and darted ahead, lifting the hem of her gown. "Lady Marjorie, I found him."

Marjorie stood stroking the neck of a braw palfrey, a gray with a mane that shimmered like sliver. She beamed at him. "A gift from my lord father." And Marioun led her little bay mare beside the princess's mount.

Iain headed the troop of men riding into the yard, leading a black courser that James favored. He knelt and cupped his hands for Marjorie to step into the saddle, but Marioun he grasped by the waist as she giggled. The sound warmed like the sun as he tossed her upon the mount.

Marjorie was off like a falcon freed from its jesses, her happy shout floating behind her. James curst and set his heels to his horse's flanks. If she were thrown... But she bent over the gray's neck and flew toward the cliffs, steady in the saddle. The sea wind whipped her hair as she galloped up the heathery slope. Behind them, Marioun yelled, "Wait for me!"

James pulled beside Marjorie. If he grabbed her reins, she might fall. That she would be furious was no matter. But her horse was blowing from the gallop and slowed to a canter.

She straightened, still laughing. "Blessed mother of God, I needed that." She threw her head back so the sun shone on her face. "They'll never cage me again." A sea tern coasted on the wind, high overhead.

The creak of saddles, clank of bits and the thud of hooves came up behind them. "You rode so fast," Marioun said, her palfrey prancing as she trotted beside them.

"Let's rest a while by the sea before we start back," James said. The green and purple of heather was dotted with patches of yellow-bloomed gorse, but gray outcroppings lined the edge of the cliff. Marjorie nodded amiably, so he led them to a spot with a large flat rock where they could sit.

"I love the sea wind in my face," Marjorie said as James held her bridle, and she let him help her dismount. James breathed deep the moist air, scented with heather and the salt scent of the sea. Sitting on the gray boulder, they looked down the high, stony cliff. It was peaceful with the occasional of a sea gull cry and the faint rustling of tall gorse around. The gray-green sea dashed itself against the bottom of the gray cliff, beating uselessly against an immovable surface. It minded him of his pain over Alycie's death. Like him, it was forever always reaching for safe harbor, but the cliff loomed before him, and no matter how many times he crashed himself against it, he was forced back into deep water, back into the cold hollow his life had become.

When he looked at Marjorie, escaping his own thoughts, her face had tightened into desperation. She tilted her chin to look up at James and said, "They'll never cage me again. I'm free now, and I'll never give that up." For the first time in the square set of her chin, he saw in her face the look of her father.

James pressed his lips together to keep back the words that life caged them all. Tonight he would try to be gentle with the wife he hadn't wanted, who hated his touch. One day soon Marjorie would wed a man her father chose for her. Mayhap all life was a cage, and none of them escaped. *If life was a cage, why had he fought all his years for freedom? For what?*

Marioun strolled gathering an armful of heather blossoms to pile in her lap. James sat on the cold stone watching Marjorie and tried to think of some words of comfort. None came until she stood and brushed off her skirt. "You don't believe me, but I swear it."

CHAPTER 4

AUGUST 1314

Durham, England

It was full daylight when James crested a low ridge, and the English city of Durham spread before him. Behind them smoke furled into the sky in long streamers from fields and orchards they'd put to the torch. Ahead, from beyond the horizon and past the River Wear, a pillar of smoke twisted and writhed into monstrous shapes as Edward de Bruce burned his way to Richmond. But below, the streets of Durham were silent and empty.

Robbie Boyd pointed toward columns of smoke rising beyond the river where Sir Edward was burning as he advanced on Richmond. "You should have been the one to advance to Richmond," Robbie Boyd said. "As the king commanded."

"No. I only told him that I could, Robbie. He didn't say that it couldn't be Edward." James shrugged. "I'm not going to quarrel with the king's brother in the field with the king not here to back me. You know what Edward is. What matters is that one of us raid as far south as we may."

Robbie grumbled under his breath before he said, "Ofttimes, he acts as though he is the king."

James shrugged and held up a hand to halt the columns behind him that stretched for a mile in good order. There were shouts as the halt was conveyed back and his two thousand men climbed down from their saddles, stretching weary muscles, checking their girths, scratching and talking. Beside James, Robbie Boyd wiped the sweat from his face and cursed the late summer heat. James grunted in agreement and said the fires made it even worse when they breathed in smoke and ashes.

From the red stone castle, a horn sounded a wavering note.

"They might decide to fight," Robbie said.

James snorted. "Unfurl my banner," he said over his shoulder to Gylmyne who carried it furled. Every castle in the north of England had pulled up its drawbridge and prayed they would pass. They had indeed passed the castles. The towns and the farms—those were a different matter. They'd cut a swath through England with hardly a sword drawn.

James wheeled his horse and motioned for Loccart to join him. "Symon," he called, "Ride back and take a column of men to watch the castle. Stay out of bow range but I want to know if they find the stomach for a sally against us. And I want a pair of men on watch at every street corner."

"Aye, Sir James." Symon turned his horse and rode back along the lines of men the way they had come.

"The whole town looks abandoned," Robbie said as he rubbed the long scar on his cheek. "Mayhap they've all fled."

It wouldn't be the first they had reached where all the people had fled, but Durham had many people and rich merchants and clerics. "Or they're in the cathedral. I'd wager that's where the gentry are." James eyed the square towers of Durham Cathedral, magnificent in the shimmering sunshine. "The bishop won't have abandoned the cathedral or want it burned. But let us ask him and see."

James gave the command to move so the men climbed back in the saddle and the talk died away. They moved as long columns with no wagons, but Johne Duncansone followed in command of two long strings of sumpter horses.

Thousands of hooves clattered on cobblestones like a hailstorm as they passed houses with doors swinging in the summer breeze. The houses were silent. He called an order, and a couple of men jumped from their horses to kick in the doors as they passed. Crouched in an open doorway, a dog snarled at them. A thrust of a sword silenced it. A piece of torn cloth pinwheeled in the wind. Except for the stamp of hoof beats and calls of "Nothing here," the city was silent.

"Company," Robbie said as a of score men seated on horses under a white flag rounded a corner.

Magistrates in fashionable tunics in wine and green and blue and brown along with six black cassocked priests on palfreys surrounded a compact man, spare with gray in his brown hair and eyes like onyx, magnificent in robes of shimmering purple and a heavy gold crucifix hanging onto his chest. "The bishop," James said. Richard Kellaw, the prince-bishop of Durhum. The bishopric of Durham was one of the most ancient and powerful in all of England. From the scowl on the bishop's face, he was mightily unhappy at greeting a Scottish army on his doorstep.

James held up his hand and shouted for a stop. As the command echoed back through his columns, he nudged his horse forward. He motioned Gylmyne, carrying his immense starred banner, and Robbie Boyd to ride beside him. They pulled up to wait, a few steps in front of the columns of men.

There was an uneasy silence broken only by a horse stamping and the creak as men shifted in their saddles.

"Your excellency." James nodded and gave a mild smile. "How kind of you to save me the ride to your cathedral, though I mean to admire it before we leave Durham."

"You serve an excommunicant, a false king. Would you dare to set foot in—" His voice faded in the face of James's raised eyebrow.

"Did you ride out from your cathedral to me of remind of that?" He let his smile broaden. "I hope not, for I have ample torches, and my men and I have acquired a taste for burning."

"You—" The man sputtered for a moment, his hands twitching as he clutched his reins. "You must not, my lord. You would not! On pain of damnation. The cathedral is sacred to St Cuthbert and the Holy Virgin!"

"I am persuadable, your excellency." James looked around. "A magnificent city and a resplendent cathedral. How much will you pay to save them?"

The bishop jerked his head to look first to one side and then the other, eyes darting. "I must save the cathedral, but... Our treasure is very little. I can pay you a thousand gold marks. It will empty our treasuries but to save the cathedral..."

James laughed. "Have you heard that I am a fool? Is that the name the English call me?"

"No." The bishop licked his thin lips. "No."

"You wear gems and gold worth as much as that. Do you want to save your city or no?"

A heavy-jowled magistrate, a thick gold chain of office about his neck, shouted at the bishop, "It's the Black Douglas, man. Give him whatever he wants. We have no choice."

The bishop's Adam's apple bobbed as he nodded. "Two thousand marks, my lord? Surely that will satisfy you."

"Aye. Along with your cattle and grain, that will satisfy me."

The bishop's mouth worked. "The food stores, too?"

James jabbed a finger at the heavy-jowled magistrate. "You. Have you a son?"

The man blinked rapidly. "Yes, my lord."

"Then he'll do for a hostage until payment is received. For that, you will have a truce and my word you are free of further tribute for a year. I shall accept the hospitality of the cathedral whilst my men gather grain stores. Is it agreed?"

"Yes," several of the magistrates shouted. They seemed to think they were escaping easily, and James wondered if he should have held out for more gold. The head magistrate trembled so hard his jowls shook as he nodded and looked at the bishop.

The bishop's lips were pressed to a slit, his face whey-white, but he bowed his head. "It is agreed, my lord."

"Good. Robbie, take half the men. Grain, any food stores, cattle in the fields— Gather all of them outwith the city. Have the sumpter horses loaded and start them for home under a strong guard. I want to be ready to turn north when Sir Edward returns." James flicked his hand at the churchmen and magistrates. "To the cathedral then. And Durham is safe—for the nonce."

The question was if the English king would give a damn if the north of England burned and starved. He feared that Lamberton would prove to be right.

* * *

"Are you certain you agree to such a thing?" James said. "God help Scotland if your uncle ever becomes king."

"The decision is made. Anyway, my uncle won't." Marjorie quickly glanced around the Great Hall of Ayr Castle.

Servants were busy preparing for the parliament, arranging benches before the dais and strewing fresh lavender into the rushes that covered the floor, but no one was near, so she put a hand on his arm and leaned close, "The news is not about yet, but Lady Elizabeth is with child."

James leaned back against the wall as he raised his eyebrows. "By holy St. Bride, that is good news."

"Aye. And you can't tell me, Jamie, that anyone wants a woman as heir to the throne. Not in the midst of a never-ending war. The last thing in heaven or earth that I want is to be tasked with that." She shrugged and looked quickly around to be sure no one would hear. "A crown would be little more than a cage. I won't have it."

He put a hand on hers and squeezed. "When you're married…"

She pulled her hand free and turned away, smoothing her gown. "When I am married to your cousin, I'll give them an heir to be sure of succession. Then no one will demand more of me. You know my feelings." She gave him a knowing look. "How is your lady wife?"

His face scalded with heat. "The midwives and Lady Elizabeth are with her. They say it the bairn will not be born today. Though she is…" He cleared his throat. "She is having birth pains, but the first is always slow coming the midwife said."

She turned back to him and gave him a sympathetic smile. "I hope she has a son, Jamie. I do. That would be best for both of you."

Abbot Bernard walked through the door beyond the dais, parchments in his hands and three monks in black robes at his heels. He nodded absently to James and then unrolled one of the scrolls as he began speaking to the clerics with him. James straightened. "She seems happy—with the court, I mean. Don't you think?"

"So I think."

They watched Abbot Bernard for a moment. Her wedding to young Walter would be well timed with so much of the nobility gathered for parliament. It would be a feast such as Scotland had not seen in many a year. Walter would be a good husband for Marjorie. He was a good man, and if she was no more than passing fond of him...

"I don't mind, Jamie. I know my duty and Walter—he suits me well enough. He knows I won't sit in a solar, embroidering all the day."

He frowned at her. "Of course, you will not."

She gave a fierce little nod and motioned to the narrow wooden stairs to the minstrel's gallery. "Escort me up? I'll wait above. I'm sure Lady Boyd and my aunts will want to watch."

"I suppose your wedding feast will be very grand."

She rolled her eyes. "My dress is the finest I've ever seen. It has enough cloth of gold and velvet to satisfy the most elegant. Lady Elizabeth has seen to that. I think she has made up for several years of her confinement with the planning. It will be a grand feast indeed."

"Wait." He spotted Walter standing in the doorway of the Great Hall and motioned to him. As Walter strode toward them, James took Lady Marjorie's hand. The bones were as fine as a bird's wing and as fragile. But there was nothing weak in her spirit. She was her father's child. "God keep you, my lady. I'll be at your wedding feast."

"I'll thank you not to court my betrothed, cousin," Walter said, but he smiled and Marjorie offered him her hand.

"Merely showing you how it's done, Walter." He grinned at Walter as bumped him in passing.

Walter snorted and tucked Marjorie's hand into his arm as they started up the narrow wooden stairs to the minstrel's gallery. James rubbed his forehead. It was aching a bit. He hated when he was helpless, and childbed had no place for a man. All he could do was wait for news of his wife, whilst he dressed in his finery like a damned peacock. Sometimes he did long for the days when the only demand was for his sword. He flicked his hands down his fine wool tunic. He refused to wear a color other than his own blue or the black that the English had named him with. He snorted. The toes on his shoes were fashionably curled and his hose tight as they should be. He brushed a piece of lint from one of his full sleeves. In a few days, he'd be back in his armor and thanks be to the merciful God for it.

One of the pages bowed to him. "Sir James, the Privy Council has a place next to the king."

James nodded and followed the lad through the stream of courtiers who had begun filing in to their places. James sank onto the middle of a bench to the right of the throne.

Robbie Boyd, Lord of Noddesdale, joined him and gave him an unusually serious look, the deep scar on his cheek deepening with his frown. "You think the king will agree to it?"

"To what?"

"Letting Edward take an army to Ireland."

James looked over his shoulder. Men were moving about, talking in low voices, but none other of the Privy Council had come in yet. "I think two Bruces in Scotland is one too many as far as Edward is concerned. And the king knows it."

Boyd opened his mouth to answer, but Thomas Randolph strutted through the crush and dropped onto the bench beside Robbie. He said, "My lady wife promises that later in the year she'll present me with an heir to join our daughter."

Robbie grinned. "Not bad, my lord. Keep trying and one day you'll be man enough to catch up with me."

"This whole birthing thing—" James wiped the sweat

from his forehead. The idea made him sweat. "God in heaven, let's keep out talk about war."

Both men just laughed at him. The vast room was rapidly filling as noblemen were shown to their place according to their rank. His good-father Robert de Keith, Marischal of Scotland sat beside him and nodded. "My lady wife and Lady Elizabeth are with her. They'll send any news." James nodded.

Maol, Earl of Lennox, Niall Campbell, Uilleam, earl of Ross, Angus Og, lord of the Isles, Gilbert de la Haye, Lord High Constable of Scotland, wended their way through the crowd and took their Council. The room was like a field of bees, buzzing with murmurs behind them when Sir Edward strutted in, resplendent in green velvet embroidered with gold thread, and took his place nearest the king.

Bishop Wishert leaned heavily on a page who helped him to the bishops' benches on the other side of the throne, followed closely by Bishop Lamberton, frowning with worry as he watched the man so frail since his return from English imprisonment. Master David, Bishop of Moray had already taken his place, and he gave James a friendly nod as Bishop Dalbyle of Dunblane joined them.

Abbot Bernard laid a parchment with a pile of others on a table as he stood behind the throne. There was a flurry of movement in the doorway, trumpeters blew a flurry and a herald shouted, "Be upstanding for Lord Robert, King of the Scots."

Robert de Bruce, splendid in a crimson tunic with a lion rampant picked out in jewels, strode to the throne, nodding to their bows, and waved them to sit as he took his place. He motioned to Abbot Bernard.

The abbot bowed. "I hereby declare The Act of Succession to the Throne to be open to discussion by the parliament. Should such an unhappy event as Lord Robert's death take place before he has a trueborn heir, it is his wish that the parliament make provisions for the governance of the realm." He paused.

There was a murmur of whispers, but no one stood until James rose and said, "Lady Marjorie surely is the king's true-born heir until there is, with God's blessing, a son." He sat down, his face burning. Sir Edward darted a glare his way.

The king leaned forward, his elbows on the arms of his throne. "I will not put such a burden on my daughter. I cannot bequeath what would be an affliction to a female and one who has already paid so much for our struggle—to lead battles and rule a contentious realm. I won't place my enemies on her shoulders." He looked at Walter. "If she were queen, she would still have a regent, and that would perforce be my brother. I'd name him heir in such a case and be done with it." He motioned to Abbot Bernard.

"It is proposed that in the event of the death of Lord Robert, king of the Scots, without a son of his body in wedlock, that his heir be his noble and beloved brother, Lord Edward, earl of Carrick, but should Lord Edward die without a son born in wedlock…" there were a few whispers since the earl's child by the sister of the earl of Ross was still the talk of the court, but Bernard raised his voice and the muttering died away."…born in wedlock, the succession shall revert to his grace's daughter, Lady Marjorie or heirs of her body, and he proposes that the parliament name Lord Thomas, earl of Moray as Guardian of the Realm in case of a minority. Does the parliament agree?"

James grunted his "Aye" along with the rest of the assembly. They had little choice and a few voices were raised to happy shouts. Edward was a bold knight after all, but James thought of Marjorie's news that Lady Elizabeth was expecting and prayed for it would be a son.

Once the clamor of assent had died down, the chancellor continued, "On the matter of recent raids into England and the English military dispositions, Sir James, Lord of Douglas will be heard."

James rose with an unaccustomed flutter in his stomach. He was well used to battles, but speaking before hundreds, he had never done this before in his life. His throat felt tight, and he cleared it. "My lord Chancellor." He realized his hands were shaking, so he clenched them into fists against his thighs. "At the king's command, I raided into England as far as Dunbar, burning as we went and seizing cattle and stores to return to Scotland. At Dunbar, we spared the city when they paid two thousand marks in tribute for a year's peace. Sir Edward reached as far as Richmond, and then at the king's command we returned by Swaledale and Stainmoor where we carried off a large number of cattle." He worked spit into his ashen mouth and wet his lips. "However, we see no sign that it has persuaded the English to come to the bargaining table. My friends in England..." He paused at a ripple of chuckles that went through the room. He smiled at his feet for a moment before he went on. Everyone knew he paid well for "friends" who brought him news. "Friends in England tell me that Aymer du Valence, earl of Pembroke, has been named to govern the north of England and drive off incursions." This time the laughter was louder. "So far the men of the North of England are more eager to fight each other than to fight us."

James sat down and wiped his sweaty palms on his thighs.

Bishop Lamberton stood. "We feared as much. Every approach for negotiating peace on my part has been spurned."

"The English stubbornness in admitting our independence and my sovereignty does not surprise us." The king looked at his brother. "Edward, I want the parliament to hear the contents of your letters from the Irish."

James sent Robbie a wry look. It wouldn't be a terrible

thing to send the hot-headed man out of Scotland and at the same time divert the attention of the English. Edward de Bruce was a good man in battle, but one day his hot temper and stubborn pride would cost them. And James wondered what that cost would be as he watched Sir Edward stand.

"The kings of Ireland are ready to rise and push the English into the sea. Donald O'Neill of Tyrone has pledged to support me. The O'Connor and Brian Ban O'Brien are ready to rise with their clans, as well. They and their allies can bring twenty thousand men to our banner. With the earl of Ulster still in England, it leaves the English ripe for defeat."

"Is O'Neill committed then?" The king frowned. "Fully? And agreed to swear fealty to you as high king?"

"He is." The king's brother hesitated. "He has sworn he can bring others to it. But not all have yet agreed."

"And you have comitted to go." The king was still frowning, tapping a hand on the arm of his throne.

"I have. O'Neill expects me to join him in May with all the men I can raise from Galloway and Carrick. We'll be two thousand. And those you promised me." He gave his brother an uneasy look and sat down.

After a pause Robert de Bruce nodded. "I said if they agreed to crown you that I'd give you an army. This falls short of that. Well short of it. But I will send an army—four thousand chivalry, under the command of Thomas Randolph."

Edward jumped up. "Under my command! You promised the army to me. Not to send your—your lapdog nephew to command it."

"How dare you!" Thomas leapt to his feet, and slapped his hand to his hip, but like the rest of them, he carried no sword. "You'll not speak so, uncle or no."

James was on his feet and shoving his chest against

Thomas, grabbing his arms. Thomas tried to jerk free, but James held on.

"Try! Just try," Edward yelled. He spun back to face his brother. "An army. You gave me your word."

The king uncoiled from his throne. "Silence. Both of you. Lord Edward, I shall remind you the lapdog, as you name him, is our nephew. Yours as well as mine. And if you want an army from me, you'll take one under his command."

Thomas shook with fury, and James tightened his hands on Thomas's arms.

The king scowled at the two men. "Another word or a blow between you and you'll both have time in a dungeon to consider the meaning of *lèse majesté*. I expect your excuses for this behavior. And you shall give each other the kiss of peace." After a short, silent pause, the king shouted, "Now!"

James leaned close to Thomas and whispered, "You heard him. Do it." He eased his hands away from Thomas's arms.

Thomas lifted his chin and said clearly, "I should not have cursed you, uncle. I beg your pardon. And yours, Your Grace. It was badly done."

The king's brother muttered a grudging apology and the two men pressed their cheeks together in what might pass for a kiss of peace. But James saw Thomas's fists working. In a ringing silence, they both resumed their places.

"We'll need ships to take the army to Ireland," Edward said.

"That we will discuss later." He gave his brother a pointed glare. "My lord chancellor, does that conclude the business of the parliament?"

"There are certain forfeitures and appointments to be approved, Your Grace."

At the king's nod, the chancellor hurried through the rest of the day's business. James kept looking at Thomas out of the corner of his eye. Robbie was squirming in his place. The sooner this was over, and they could discuss what Edward leaving for Ireland would mean the better.

After the king's retiral, everyone hurried out, exchanging wary glances. This was a matter of fierce factions.

"I need a drink," Robbie Boyd said as they stood watching the crush at the doorway.

Sir Edward shot Thomas a murderous glance before he bulled his way through the crowd, the lords dodging aside. No one looked eager to argue his right to knock them aside.

"We all do," James replied darting a glance at his good-father, being carried along by the crowd. "You know more about this kind of thing. Should I send my page for news? Or…"

Robbie shook his head. "It's best to leave them alone. They'll send word when they want you."

"I suppose."

Thomas offered his hand. "I owe you thanks. I almost struck him, and that would have been…"

James clasped his hand. "Disaster." Thomas was generally not a hothead, but he didn't take his dignity lightly. "I need no thanks, and I don't envy you leading an army with him when he's angry."

Since most of the lords had filed out except for a couple of knots of men with their heads together whispering in the corners, the three started for the door. "My uncle usually cools his temper after a while though, by the Rood, he is hot tempered enough. I'd best see to it. I have uncles to make peace with." Thomas twitched a wry smile and followed after Sir Edward.

"I have a good flagon of uisge beatha in my chambers that is in need of drinking." Robbie gave his shoulder a hard buffet. "Tell your squire where to find you, Jamie. We'll empty it whilst you wait for news."

"Sir James," a voice called, and he turned to see * running

toward him, beaming. "My lord, you must come. They said it's a son!"

"So soon?" James took off at a run past the lad, through the passage and up the winding stairs, two steps at a time. "Are they all right?"

He ran at James's heels, panting. "Lady Elizabeth said to fetch you. And that it is a lad. They must be well. Mustn't they?"

James reached the landing on the parapet level. There was the sound of a bairn crying, and he threw open the door. Lady Barbara bent over the bed, and beyond her he could see spread Elayne's honey-colored hair. For a moment, his breath caught, but Lady Barbara smiled. "She did well. It's a braw lad." The hawk-faced midwife held a bundle of bloody cloths in her arms.

The queen sat in a chair next to a cradle he'd had made where there was a fussing sound. James strode to it. He knelt and looked at the red, wrinkled mite, its head covered with a tuft of black hair. With a single finger, James brushed the dark fuzz. He stroked the palm of a hand, no larger than a sparrow's claw that waved in the air. The tiny hand closed around his finger. "William," he said keeping his gaze on the bairn. If he looked up, someone might see tears that were burning his eyes. "He is William. For my father."

"A good name," the queen said softly.

After he blinked his eyes clear, he stood and went to look down at Elayne as her mother brushed her sweat-damp hair back from her brow. Elayne watched him warily, so he just stroked his fingers over her hand where it was clenched on the coverlet. "You are well?"

She nodded.

"Thank God. And I thank you – for my son." He frowned down at her. "Elayne, I've hired a master mason. He's to begin a manor house on a hill in Lintalee overlooking the Jed Water. It is a beautiful spot."

"I..." She licked her chapped and dried lips. "I don't want to go there."

"Jamie," Lady Elizabeth said. "There will be children with the court now. Your son would be most welcome if you'd let your lady wife remain with me."

Elayne sent the queen a look of wide-eyed gratitude. He bent and kissed her forehead. "Of course, I'll allow her stay, Your Grace." To see his son, he would be nearly as often at court as at his new home at Lintalee—or at war.

CHAPTER 5

JULY 1314

Carlisle, England

James kneed his horse to dodge a stone the size of a man's head thrown from the top of the tall barbican. He hated the city of Carlisle. Where in Hell did they find so many stones? Was the town made of them?

His men slammed their ram into the gate, wide enough for two wagons to pass, and boards groaned. Shouts of defiance came from above. A line of his men hacked at the boards four hands thick with their axes. Archers on the walls loosed their bows, arrows glittering as the arrows rained down. James lifted his shield as they thudded around him. His horse snorted and danced, but one of the men at the ram shrieked as he fell. A moment later more rocks came like a hailstorm. His own bowmen were shooting at the English, but they were well hidden behind the battlement of the walls. His men's arrows bounced off or sped harmlessly past.

King Robert was at one of the other gates. They'd hoped that a simultaneous attack would spread the defenders too thin. A futile hope. It was now clear that Carlisle had too many for such a trick to work, and the governor of Carlisle, one Sir Andreas de Harcla, obviously knew his business. James wheeled his horse, his jaw clenched in frustration. He couldn't order a retiral until he had a sign from the king. An arrow hit James's shoulder, caught in the mail, and he grunted at the blow. He jerked the arrow free from where it had hung in the mesh of his armor.

Sir David de Brechin trotted up. Tall and thin with silver-gray hair, his long, elegant face was twisted in a frown. "We're losing men too fast. We won't breech the gate."

If James retired before the king's signal, the defenders might rush the king, so he must keep some of them busy here. Even if it cost him men. "I know. But we must hold the attack longer."

The ram hit the gate again. But his men were faltering under the onslaught. James saw Iain at the head of the ram catch an arrow in his shoulder and go to his knees. Some of his men's shields bristled with arrows like hedgehogs.

On the wall, Englishmen jeered, and one shoved his bare arse through a crenel and wriggled. Another flight of arrows slashed into his men.

The sound of the king's trumpeters, two long low blasts that rolled across the hill, gave the order for retreat. "Back to camp," James shouted. "Blow the retiral." His trumpeter blew the command. They'd been at this for nine days, nine miserable days. He hated Carlisle. Damn the English to hell, but as much as he hated them, the English, he hated sieges more.

"Keep order. Don't give them a chance to rush us." Another arrow stuck in his raised shield. He yelled for his chivalry to move up to cover the retiring men who were backing away, shields raised to protect themselves from the constant rain of arrows. The men on the walls were hooting and shouting taunts. But once his men were out of bow range, he commanded them to move faster for camp. This night was over, and they couldn't have much longer to take the city.

Past the long lines of campfires and rough tents, on a hill overlooking Carlisle and the River Dee, the king's tent and his own had been erected. By the time James threw himself from his saddle and tossed his reins to a groom, it was midafternoon, and the sun blazed down. Sweat dripped from his face and down the back of his neck. Storming into his pavilion, he wrenched off his helm and threw it across the tent. He strode fast back and forth across the small space and kicked the sole camp chair, so it thudded into the side of his narrow cot. Gylmyne peered doubtfully into the pavilion. "Sir James…"

"What?"

Outside there was the tread of horses, the rattle of swords and armor, and the king's voice calling for his squire.

"The outriders brought in two youths. The lads claim they're your brothers."

James strode to push past Gylmyne and stared at the lad standing there, his wide shoulders heavy with muscle as he shifted nervously. Thick hair, black as ink like James's own. The shadow of a new beard darkened his jaw. Not tall though. *Dear God*, James thought, *he is so like our lord father*. "Is it Hugh?" James said.

The lad took a step toward him. "No, I'm Archibald." He jerked his head toward the fat lad standing behind him. "That is Hugh."

Dark eyes darted nervously in Hugh's moon face, and sausage-like fingers wiped themselves on the closed woolen cloak of a cleric though surely he was too young to have taken orders. "We… we wanted to come—to join you, but they wouldn't let us. Our mother… Her husband…"

James snorted a little laugh. "Well, I doubt King Edward

would be well pleased if they sent you to join me." He caught Archibald by the shoulder and jerked him into a hard hug, pounding him on the back. "But I am pleased. I am well pleased." He released Archibald and looked Hugh over. Not what he'd expect of a Douglas, but his brother, so he thumped Hugh on the shoulder.

Hugh winced at the blow, but a smile warmed his eyes, and they weren't darting with fear any more. "They watched us close and talked about putting us in a dungeon. They never did. But they wouldn't let Archie serve as a squire. Well, he wasn't an heir." He shrugged. "I didn't matter so much since all I'm fit for is a cleric."

James shook his head. He'd not thought there was a chance of finding his brothers, not since his English step-mother had taken them deep within England after his father had died in the Tower. "You'll have to tell me how you got here. And we'll make plans." He threw an arm around Archibald's shoulder. "I can always use a squire."

Hugh stared at James and gave a feeble smile.

"We'll find a place for a cleric, too, Hugh. I will see you right."

"So they found you instead of you finding them, Jamie." The king emerged from the doorway to his tent, his immense crimson and gold Lion Rampant banner waving high over-head from a lofty pike.

"Aye, Your Grace." He rubbed his chin. There was no time for sentiment with a town to take. Archibald and Hugh were making awkward bows to the king and shuffling their feet. "Gylmyne, find a place for my brothers in the camp and food."

He started to follow the Bruce into his pavilion but stopped and turned back. "You're both welcome with me. I'll—" He swallowed something that had closed up his throat. "I'll do for you as our lord father would have wanted."

Hugh was blinking at him, but Archibald grinned and nodded, so James ducked into the king's large tent. The Bruce dropped heavily into a camp chair and waved a hand toward a silver flagon and goblets. "I'm glad for you, Jamie."

"Archibald. I hadn't seen him since he was—" James poured the wine and tried to remember. "I think he was two when I went with our father as a page to Berwick. Two." James breathed out a laugh. "He followed me like a puppy. I was ten and I rolled him in the mud once. Hugh hadn't been born."

The king nodded thoughtfully and took a drink of his wine.

"Half-brothers, really. And I don't know them." James went to gaze out the entrance into the golden afternoon sun and the high walls of Carlisle Town. "I knew your brother Thomas better than I'll ever know them." He turned back to the king. "They put his head over the gate here after they killed him. Is that what this is? That it was at Carlisle that they butchered your brothers?"

Robert de Bruce face knotted, and he tossed back the rest of his wine. "You know not."

"Do I, Your Grace?"

"You think I'd waste our men on revenge? And what revenge would it earn me? I can't kill Edward Longshanks who ordered the foul deed. He's dead and beyond me." He held out his goblet for James to refill. "No, I wouldn't mind punishing Carlisle, but you should know that's not the reason. If we can take Carlisle, it will threaten them. Force them to treat with me. But we don't have long."

"A week. No more. The forces rallying at Brough Castle can be ready by then. It would have been sooner if Clifford were still alive." He looked at this liege lord. He shouldn't have challenged him albeit there was more revenge in this than the king wanted to admit, but as far as James was concerned, he had a right to it. Still… James took a drink of the wine. It was sour for his taste. Still, it was better than the water they usually drank on a raid. But this was not merely a raid, though he'd looted and burned Hartlepool two days before.

The Bruce shrugged. "Harcla. He's doing well. Better than I expected. So…"

"So we need another tactic. One we haven't used against him yet." James swirled the dregs in his cup. "When Thomas Randolph took Edinburgh, he attacked a gate with a strong force, strong enough to draw all their defenses, and took a small group to climb a weak spot on the wall."

"So he did." The king raised an eyebrow with a wry twitch. "And you hate being bested by my nephew."

* * *

Even before dawn, the next day promised to be hot and muggy as James dodged in a crouched-jog from tree to tree. The leaves were full of whispers. Already sweat beaded in the mud that daubed his face and bare chest. Behind a hoary oak next to the deep ditch that surrounded the city wall, he dropped to his knees and motioned over his score of men.

"Richert, Iain, close behind me with your pikes," he whispered. "And by all the saints, not a sound. Anyone falls going down the edge of the ditch, don't open your mouth." He patted the rope and board ladder he carried himself tied on his back. "Pray that the sentries don't spot us before we reach the wall. And pray they're pulled off by the king's attack."

The wall here was high compared to most of the city, so the English would think it was too high to be attacked. He'd spotted it days ago, and had pikes made even longer than usual. Going in with a score of men to try to open a gate was a deadly risk, one the king had been more than reluctant to take. In the pre-dawn, the wall was a black hulk

James dropped to his belly and wriggled his way to the edge of the ditch, swung his legs around and dropped over, hanging on. When he let go, he slid a span down the rest of the way, clamping his teeth when the hard ground ripped his skin. Once the metal hook of the rope ladder clanked on a stone. Going up the other side would be harder, but it wasn't straight up so they could work their way. The hard part was making sure they made no noise. "Quietly," he whispered and strode four paces and crawled on hands and knees. At every movement, James expected a shout from the guards, but it was silent. Only a thin sliver of silver growing in the east changed as they went. It took a few moments, although once there was an alarming clatter of falling pebbles. They all froze into place, but there was no sound from the wall.

His men knew their parts, so James didn't need to give orders. He pressed his back against the wall, sweat from exertion and nerves dripping down his face and his ribs. His men spread out, each squeezing as close to the wall as he could. The mud that daubed their bodies would make them hard to spot, but with no armor, any fight would be as dangerous as any could be. James grasped the hilt of his sword. He'd have to kill any guard before he could call for help. It didn't matter how many times they did this, his heart still hammered like a galloping horse. If they could open the west gate, he had a hundred mounted men out of sight of the walls, ready to answer his call. But they had to wait for the king's attack on the east gate to draw the sentries away.

In the dawn light, James began to make out the shape of the trees and when he looked up he could see the top of the wall. A morning wind rustled the grass and a branch creaked. A crow called a harsh warble. In the quiet, James heard the far off shout of thousands of voices and the long *Harooo* of the king's trumpets calling the attack.

Within the city, the trumpets of the English blew defense. James heard men shouting closer and a curse, the rattle of swords and the pounding of running feet. Iain moved but James held up a hand. It was too soon. He must give them time to run to the defense of the eastern gate. The king had brought what should look like their whole army. Almost, it was.

The sounds of running faded into the distance. "Now," James said softly. Hurriedly, he loosed the rope and board ladder from where it was wrapped around his shoulder. Iain poked the point of his pike through a hole in the hook whilst Richert did the other. James craned his neck to look upward as they lifted the hooks. It was simple, yet not an easy task to hoist the ladder on the fifteen-foot weapons high enough to hook over the edge of the crenel. Then they'd drop the pikes and the ladder would be in place. They'd done this a number of times, but they could never be sure that a sentry wasn't waiting at the top to unhook the ladder and send them crashing down. The hooks caught with a clank.

James pulled his dirk and put it between his teeth to have both hands free to climb. He thrust down with a foot on the first board to be sure the hooks were firmly caught and then climbed–fast. At the top, he vaulted over, scanning the walk for a guard. Already, Iain was clambering over the edge. James crouched as Richert followed and another head appeared behind him. James plunged down the steps, leaping three at a time to the cobbled street. "To the gate!"

Two guards stood, leaning on halberds. The towering wooden gate banded with iron was triple barred with beams. One guard shouted in surprise as James barreled into him and kicked the tall weapon aside. Kneeling, James plunged his dirk into the guard's neck. His men were already swarming the other. And in an instant, the street was filled with soldiers. James spied leather brigandines studded with steel and Harcla's cross and starling on their chests. There was a line of them on foot, no time to count but twenty at least. Richert caught a blade and ducked under to gut his attacker. "To the stairs," James shouted. He grabbed Richert's arm and shoved him behind.

"What are you waiting for?" a dark-faced man shouted. "On them." They closed in. Wielding his sword in one hand, his dirk in the other, James cut one down. A second man reeled away gushing from a slashed neck. Richert hacked, a red spray flying from his sword as they backed, step by step.

"Up the stairs," James shouted. "Up!" Two halberds flashed in the sun toward Richert's head. James leapt to meet one with his blade. His side exploded in a moment of blinding pain. He heard a scream. Iain cut the legs out from under his attacker. Another sword slashed. Someone was lifting him, but he couldn't see. It was a blur of agony, and he was in a gray mist. For a moment, he opened his eyes and groaned as he was pulled over the wall. The ground far below was spinning.

* * *

James was wrapped in wool blankets but he shivered. A face bent over him. Through a fog, he recognized Master Ingram. James winced when fingers poked and prodded at his wound. He clenched his teeth, but a cup was put to his mouth. His head was tipped back, and he gulped down a mouthful of a bitter wine. He gagged, but they forced down another swallow.

His head felt heavy and numb. "My cautery iron is heated. I need four men to hold him," a man said from a long way away. Voices buzzed in his ears. He felt a heavy weight hold down his arms and his legs. When he saw the iron glowing red hot, he jerked his head to look up at Richert who knelt, leaning hard on him. Richert look frightened, James thought for a moment, and then pain burned through his side. He threw back his head, gulping in air, but it had the stench of burning flesh. He screamed. After that for a while, he knew nothing.

When his eyes opened a slit, he was wrapped in furs, but his body floated within them. He tried to lift his hand. It didn't move. He must be dead he knew when Alycie brushed his hair back from his forehead and wiped his face with cool water. Her lips pressed softly to his. He smiled when he closed his eyes to sleep.

His next awakening was throbbing with pain. The wagon he was lying in bounced, and he gritted his teeth. Pushing the furs back, he tried to sit up, and a fiery stab of pain went through his belly. He fell back, gasping. Rain pounded onto the canvas above him.

"My lord." Richert's face was looking down at him, freckles and all. "They said you mustn't move."

James grabbed Richert's arm. *Yes, he was real.* "What's happening?"

"The king commanded a retiral. We're on our way home."

"The men?" He fought the pain to prop himself onto his elbows. "How many got away?" Sweat dripped down his face.

"Iain, Johne, and I got you over the wall. The rest—" Richert pushed him back down into the furs. "Rest, my lord. You bled like a pig at the slaughter, but the king's physician cauterized the wound. You'll recover. He swore to the king."

He closed his eyes and drifted away.

He dreamt fire was blazing around him, houses and fields aflame. He hurled the torch in his hands. Sweat ran down his face as he ran. A hot wind blew on his neck. Where were his men? "Wat?" he called. "Wat? Richert? " No one answered. In the distance, he heard trumpets. *There is a battle. Why am I not there?* A burning beam crashed before him and flames roared in his face. He whirled, looking for a path, a way out of this hell. But he was trapped within the flames he had set. They roared...

The room was dimly lit, the bed soft beneath him, the air sweetened with thyme. His own chamber, he remembered as his head cleared. You would think it would have brought him better dreams. His body was sticky with sweat, and he threw the counterpane back.

Archibald looked up from a stool, a dirk and whetstone in his hand. "You were tossing and mumbling, but I didn't dare wake you. The physician gave orders you should sleep."

James looked down at the red, angry slash, scabbed over now and healing, across his belly. "I've rested. Is there water for washing?" He rolled to his side. The pain made him hiss in a breath, but it was nothing he couldn't stand. He wanted the feel and smell of sweat and sickness off his body.

Archibald thrust his chin toward a ewer on the table. "Aye, though it won't be very warm."

James's mouth twitched. He should tell Archibald to heat it since he was a squire now. "Where is Hugh?"

"The king sent him to Glasgow Cathedral– gave him a post there. He was happy about that. I think he was still afraid you'd try to make him fight."

James eased up from the bed, hobbled to the table, and picked up the ewer. "He didn't look as if he'd make much of a fighter. He can give prayers for our souls instead. "James shook the memory of his dream from his head as he poured water into the bowl. "We'll most like need them."

Archibald was right. The water was not very warm, but it felt good as he sluiced his face and his chest.

"There is talk of attacking Berwick." Archibald drew the

blade across the whetstone. "The king has been meeting with Sir Robert Boyd."

"Berwick? Attacking it soon?"

Archibald shrugged. "They've not told me their plans, but I suppose soon. I heard one of Boyd's squires say they'd leave tomorrow to raise their levies."

"Find me my clothes, Archie." James scowled. Why would they plan an attack without him? For Berwick—from which his father had been dragged in chains. If there were any attack upon it, he must be there. "Up. Let me sit there." His muscles trembled with weakness, but giving in to it would do him no good.

Archibald jumped to his feet, and James sank onto the stool with a sigh. "The physician won't be happy," Archibald said. He dropped the dirk on the table and hurried to a chest at the foot of the bed to pull out a blue tunic.

The brush of heavy linen over his wound made his belly burn like fire, but James tugged his hose into place. Archie slipped the tunic over his head. He stamped into his boots and Archibald knelt to fasten his belt. He picked up his dirk that Archibald had been honing to thrust into the sheath at his side. By the time they were done, he felt like crawling into a corner like a beaten dog. Instead, he downed a cup of wine. There. He felt more like a man, but Archibald was giving him a doubtful look.

"You're not supposed to be up. I hope the king doesn't blame me."

"The king knows me." He patted his brother's shoulder and hobbled through the door, moving gently so as not to awaken the pain. It was the quiet of a dusty summer mid-afternoon. James could hear friars chanting in the chapel. A lay brother knelt scrubbing the floor. He could smell bread baking in the abbey kitchen. As best he could, James ignored the wobble of his legs as he walked, albeit he had to keep a hand on the wall to stay erect.

When he opened the door to the Privy, Robert the Bruce looked at him with a scowl. "What are you doing here?"

"I'm well enough, sire." James straightened and tried to stride to a chair without hunching over. "And if I am still Lord Warden of the Marches then my place is here."

The king sighed. "Sometimes you're a damn fool, Jamie. You're weak as a bairn yet. It wouldn't do harm for you to miss one battle."

"If the battle is for Berwick...?"

With a frown that turned the scar up his cheek into a crevasse, Robbie was examining James. "I've seen more color in a snowfall than you have in your face." He got up and went to the sideboard to pour a goblet of wine and plunked it down in front of James. "You've had naught but pap and broth since they brought you back from Carlisle. At least, that should keep you on your feet until you're in your bed."

James took a drink of it because the truth was—Robbie was right. "What about Berwick? Are we going to lay siege? My men still have a blockade on the roads, do they not?"

For a moment, the Bruce clasped his hands and pressed them to his forehead as though dealing with James was more than he could stand. But then he leaned back and said, "Aye, your men have kept a blockade on food and supplies reaching the city, and our galleys have cut off supplies from the sea, but enough has slipped past that they hold out. But a siege? No."

"I heard how well a siege went at Carlisle," Robbie said.

"We lack engineers trained well enough to build siege engines and men trained to use them. And a relief army is too likely to come to their aid. No, we'll go back to what has worked in the past. Another of your secret attacks, James."

"Then I must be part of it. Besides, Berwick..." The king

knew he'd sworn holy oaths to take the town where his father had been shamed and dishonored. That was an oath that he meant to keep.

"I know your feeling about Berwick, but you cannot think you are strong enough to lead an attack. After being forced to raise the siege at Carlisle, we can't let the English believe we've lost our ability to win. I'll lead the attack on Berwick myself."

James shook his head. "It will take time to prepare for an attack. Robbie will need to go to Kilmarnock to raise his spears. That will be more than enough time for me to recover from this scratch. I can send Richert to Douglasdale to gather my forces." The king was glowering at him but hadn't said nae, so James plunged on. "What is your plan?"

"I'll lead a raiding party from the sea and open the gates. A small boat can slip in without being seen."

"You can't," James said. "The risk is too great. Give me a week to regain my strength, sire. That's all I need. I'll be ready."

"It's only by God's grace you weren't gutted on that wall at Carlisle," the Bruce said.

He couldn't argue because that was true, but he'd always known he would die in battle one day. He'd choose it over being starved to death in the Tower of London or hanged and drawn on a scaffold.

"Aye, but I wasn't. And if it happens, better the Douglas die so than the king. You can't take such a risk." He twisted in his seat to try to work out the stiff, aching discomfort in his belly, a mistake that sent a shaft of pain through him like a spear. He gripped the edge of the table, grimacing.

"I've taken greater risks than that," the king said.

Once such risks had been needful. James raised his eyebrows and gave the king a stern look through odd flecks of light dancing before his eyes, and his stomach roiled.

The Bruce sighed. "Very well, my lord warden. You have a week, but if you can't move then without going pale as whey, I shall lead the attack. Now hie you to your bed." And James was glad enough to obey. He would be ready. They would make another try for the city that had been so stubbornly held in enemy hands.

CHAPTER 6

MARCH 1316

Annandale, Scotland

James kept his face bland as much as he wanted to grind his teeth with frustration. Since his humiliating flight from Berwick by boat when their secret attack failed, the king had stubbornly refused to allow another attack. The king would not be pleased when he asked again, James knew. He stood to the side as Robert de Bruce's strode into the Privy Chamber. Robert de Keith, Niall Campbell, Gilbert de la Haye, and Walter Stewart gathered around him. He greeted each in turn, spoke a word to Abbot Bernard, kissed Bishop Lamberton's ring, and squeezed James's shoulder.

The king seated himself at the head of the long table, and Walter took a place at his left. James took his preferred chair in a chair at the foot of the table as the others scrambled for seats near the king. He could tell a great deal by watching the other's faces.

"Is there word from Ireland?" the abbot asked.

"Not since they defeated Butler at Skerries." Gilbert de

Haye steepled his hands. "The last word was that they were retracing their steps to take Cerrickfergus Castle so that it was no threat to their backs. That was two months ago."

"It weather is too severe to attempt a crossing. This is the worst winter I've ever seen. And after the rains and poor harvest last autumn, Ireland must be the worry of my brother and my nephew. We have enough to deal with here," the king said.

It had been a quiet winter with icy roads too bad for travel or fighting and with snow blowing into your eyes every time you set foot outdoors. The last two days the weather had broken, and everyone prayed the respite would last. Forced into each other's company with the court, even his wife had been courteous enough as he'd recovered from his wound. She'd even gone so far as to kiss his cheek whilst he sat at the fire by William's cradle. She'd said, "I prayed every day that you'd heal. Everyone says you are the greatest knight in the kingdom." But she had escaped him at every chance with the excuse that the queen and the infant princess needed her in attendance, and she slept in the queen's chamber.

Bishop Lamberton on the king's right smiled. "I have news from Berwick-upon-Tweed. Friars have brought news that their food has almost run out. Even the English soldiery is on short rations and no ships have been able to reach them from England. Nor have the soldiers been paid. It's said some are near rebellion."

"It's too bad we can't take advantage of their weakness," Gilbert said.

"Perhaps we can." The king rubbed the bridge of his nose and frowned thoughtfully, and James sucked in a breath. At last... "We must eventually make another try. They would not expect a winter attack, and our men are capable of surviving a little cold."

"Not so little, Your Grace," Niall Campbell put in.

The king raised an eyebrow at his good-brother. James brushed a spot on his tunic. He smiled at coming to the council with a lump of William's porridge on his chest. The lad's method of feeding himself included attempting to feed his father as well, but none too accurately. James worked the spot off with a fingernail as he listened.

"As you said yourself, never have we seen such a winter and there is no sign of it breaking for spring. Even with the warmest woolens, could an army make a march in this weather?"

The king looked at James. "What do you think, Jamie?"

"If you allow, we will do it, sire."

A heavy hand hammered at the door before it was flung open. A guard gaped at Sir William de Keith of Galworthy, who stood panting, red-faced. "Your Grace. Forgive me, but it's the queen's command. Lady Marjorie—" He paused. "She's been thrown from her horse."

The Bruce's chair crashed over as he leapt to his feet. "By the Holy Rood, who let her ride? In this weather? In her condition?" He glared at his son-in-law.

Walter was shaking his head, hands raised. "I did not. How badly is she hurt? Where is she?"

The flush drained from Sir William's face to leave him pale. *He's afraid to say how bad it is. Holy St. Bride...*

"The guards carried her up to her bower."

The young knight stumbled back when the king shoved him out of the way and ran for the stairs. "I told her." Walter Stewart faltered, his chest heaving. "I said not to venture out. But she hates to be..."

"Caged," James whispered. "Go on, Walter. What are you waiting for?"

Walter nodded and strode for the open doorway, and then he broke into a run. James pushed himself slowly to his feet. The room was silent except for the heavy breathing of men as they stared at the table. Marjorie was young. But young women died if a pregnancy went awry. And this might be as badly awry as was possible.

"I'll see to the king," James said. He turned and followed through the corridor and up the winding stairs, his feet ringing on the stone as he broke into a run. On the landing, the king and Walter Stewart stood outwith the closed door, whispering servants keeping well back from the two grim-faced men.

The Bruce's face was pale as whey. "Elizabeth called—" His voice broke and he cleared his throat. "She called my physician. Not the midwives."

"Mayhap that is good news, if it's not brought on the birth," Walter whispered. "It's early...

For the bairn."

There was a scream and the sound of a woman crying. The door opened a narrow space. Marioun of Ramsey, her hair wild and windblown around her white face, was shoved through the opening. Lady Elizabeth, her hands and gown spotted with blood, said, "This is no place for her." She slammed the door closed.

James grasped Marioun's arm and pulled her away from the doorway. "What happened?"

"It was my fault," the girl said around a sob. "She was so tired of being cooped inside. She ordered the guards to saddle our horses and ride out with us. I should have—done something. I should have stopped her." She used the heel of her hand to wipe her face. "When her horse slipped, she went over its head—fell so hard. Her neck was twisted..." She put a hand over her mouth, and wide-eyed she looked from the king to James and then to Walter. Her body was trembling as James put an arm around her shoulders, but she pushed away as she bent, gagging. Nothing came up and James gently raised her.

"You shouldn't be here." He patted her back as she struggled against her sobs. He tried to think who could take care of her. Where was his lady wife? Probably with the injured princess and the queen.

"Hell mend it. I must know how she is." Walter clenched and unclenched his fists. He took a step toward the doorway, but the king grabbed his arm.

"Wait." The Bruce wiped a hand across his face, looking palely ill.

A puling cry came from within—a thin wail. The king shoved Walter out of the way, stepped to the closed door, and hammered on it with a fist. *Holy Mary, Mother of God, surely the princess could not be dying in there. Please, not after what she has suffered.*

When the door opened, Master Ingram was wiping bloody hands on a towel. "Sire… I could not wait to speak to you. There was no time. The princess was already—" He shook his head. "—already dead."

Walter growled as he shoved the physician out of his way. The man hit the door with a crash, and Walter bolted into the room. "Marjorie!"

The stink of blood seeped into the landing. The king grabbed Master Ingram and shook him. "What did you do?"

The king tossed the man backward to land flat on the floor. Master Ingram pushed himself to his knees. "She was dead, Your Grace. The only way was to cut him from her body. I saved him. The queen said we must try to save the bairn."

James looked with horror at the blood soaked bed and Walter kneeling beside it.

CHAPTER 7

OCTOBER 1316

Douglasdale, Scotland

Icy rain ripped at James's face. The air smelt of oak and moss
and rain but beneath it was still the tang of long dead fire
and ash. Whatever the weather, he welcomed a respite from
the grief-stricken court. Marioun was a pale-faced ghost
whilst the king, silent and haunted, raised an army to lead for
Ireland. Grim-faced, Walter had ridden for his own lands.

Master Gautier sloshed through the ankle deep puddles
and mud to stand beside James under a bare, dripping oak.
"I'm sorry, my lord. In this weather, there is no hurrying the
work though the stones will give us a good start on building."
One of the workmen prying a stone from the rubble of a
fallen wall slipped, splattering mud and cursing. The
workman heaved himself to his feet out of the muck. The
wagon was still only half full of the stones they'd take to
Lintalee to use for James's manor.

Those had once been castle walls where James had sat
and watched his father's men marching guard, servants

carrying water for the kitchen, girls from Douglas village out of sight beyond the trees gathered giggling to talk under an oak, a man tilling a nearby field. He'd never thought to be forced to destroy it by his own hand. How hard it was to rebuild what was lost. The pieces that were missing left gaps that were never again whole.

Frigid water dribbled down the back of his neck, and James craned to look up at the slate gray clouds. The midmorning was dark as dusk. The year before the crops had been poor. This year he doubted they would be planted at all. If they were and the rain did not stop, they'd drown in the fields. It was as dire in England, but he'd have to consider raiding there. Better the English starved when he took what they had for his own people.

A gust of wind sent leaves flapping around him. *I chose a fine year to build a manor*, James thought ruefully. Rivulets edged with ice flowed downhill toward the Douglas Water out of sight beyond the trees.

"I don't fault you. Even a master mason cannot control the weather." He shook water from the folds of his cloak. The wet made his side ache from the red scar of the wound he'd taken at Carlisle, and the neck of his sodden wool cloak itched. "Do the best you can. I'd like to be in the manor by snowfall."

The man shook his head. "I fear you will not, my lord. Unless this weather breaks— And I pray that it does."

A horn sounded in the distance, half drowned by the drumming rain. "The signal for riders," James said. He took a few steps toward the road. He didn't expect the English in this weather; it was too early for the fighting to start. "Wat!" James called. "Send men out to see who comes."

Wat ran through the slush, shouting for Dauid and Johne to bring horses. "I'll see to it, my lord."

James shook the water out of his eyes. Wat had been with

him most of his life, since the day James returned to reclaim his father's lands. The man was tough as old leather, but James thought his gray hair said it was time for younger men to do the fighting. Moments later, water sprayed as the three men left at a fast canter. Wat gave James a wave as he passed.

"I could send for more men from Glasgow," Master Gautier said as he scowled at one of the men hefting a stone into the wagon. "But it won't speed the building a great deal. In this rain, even once we move the stones, mortar won't set well, no matter how many men I have."

"Send for them then. I won't expect more than you tell me that you can do, but what you can do—you must do."

Lightning sizzled across the sky followed by booming thunder. The mason excused himself and slogged through the muck to have his men stop until the weather eased. They trooped grumbling toward the line of tents. James shook the water out of his cloak again, and then turned to watch the road wondering who would be mad enough to ride out in this weather. It didn't bode well for being good news.

When riders came into sight, Wat, in the lead with several men not their own following. Wat waved an arm over his head and called, "Raiders in Teviotdale, my lord." They splashed at a canter through the mucky road, water spraying.

Thin, sharp-faced Sir Adam de Gordon climbed from the saddle, his mouth drawn like he'd tasted something bitter. "Lord Warden, English raiders in my lands. They must be from Berwick. They seized twenty cattle and captured two men to drive them." He thrust his head at the two men-at-arms with him. "There were too many for the three of us to take on, ten of them."

James gave a sharp nod. "We should be able to catch them up before they reach Berwick. They'll make for the Merse." He only had forty men in his tail, but that should be enough for a few raiders. With the king supporting his brother in

Ireland, Walter Stewart and James had been left as Scotland's co-regents. He couldn't—no, he would not fail the king by allowing such a raid.

Wat still sat astride his sturdy mount. "We'll need to move fast then. I'll order the men armed and mounted." He turned his horse toward where the men had already begun to stand from lounging beside campfires. "Wake up, you lot! We've work to do."

"Archibald," James shouted and called for his armor. Archibald buckled on his brother's hauberk and coif, his greaves and knelt to put on his boots while James buckled on his sword belt. By then a groom was leading up his black courser. It wasn't armored. James scratched his chin. Mayhap he should start traveling with armor for his horse, but it wouldn't matter for taking down a few raiders. "Get yourself armed, Archie." He swung into the saddle. "Quickly now."

Archie ran as James wheeled his mount. His men were throwing saddles on their mounts, buckling girths, checking their swords, and yelling jokes about what they'd do to the enemy. Wat shouted at them to hurry. Archie buckled his sword belt with one hand whilst he led his horse with the other. A watery beam of sunlight broke through the rain as James led them off, and they fell in behind him.

Sir Adam rode beside him. "We cannot lose those cattle. Can't afford to," James grunted. Why talk about it? Losing cattle would mean even more empty bellies. No, they couldn't afford any lose as bad as harvest the year before had been.

"Wat, send out four scouts, well spread. A small group could be easy to miss."

As they rode through the scattered woodlands at a canter, James frowned. In the distance, the hills of the Lammermuirs hunched, dappled by snow beneath smoky gray clouds. "Ten is few to take back enough cattle to feed Berwick if they're as low on food as reports say. You saw the raiders yourself, Gordon? You're sure of the numbers?"

"Aye, it might have been twelve. Of a certainty, no more."

"They've grown bold, or desperate," James said, still frowning. It was a small raid though if less than a score. James was going over in his mind the area of Berwickshire around Coldsteam as they rode along the bank of the gray-blue waters of River Tweed, visualizing the rolling hills and farmland where the raiders might make their escape. It was open country, good country for fighting on horseback. Ill if you wanted to hide. He jerked his head around at a sound above the steady rustle of the water. Hoof beats coming at a gallop. He held up his hand for a halt as one of his scouts dashed through the hawthorns and scrub.

"Not far behind me," the man panted. "A good four score and in armor all of them."

"By the Holy Rood!" Sir Adam Gordon gasped. "You're sure so many?"

"Aye. They spotted us. Rode down Ranald. They're on my trail."

"They must have been spread out to raid when you spotted them, Gordon." James wrapped and unwrapped his reins from his hand as he pictured the lay of the land. There was a stream near Skaithmuir a little way north, one that might serve as a small defense.

"Sir James!" Sir Adam pointed.

James heard shouts. Horsemen in gleaming mail came through the trees. First there were six knights. Then twelve more. Then twelve more. A double column of knights and men-at-arms streamed through the dripping, bare trees.

Sir Adam opened his mouth and made a sound, but James cut him off. He turned his horse's head in the direction of the Skaithmuir and raked it with his spurs. "Ride," he shouted.

He clearly saw in his mind the little stream and a bank

where it formed a hillock. It would be little enough defense but as a good place to make a stand as you'd find in this country. Fleeing from the English in his own country—as he had for so many years in the past. The thought of it made the blood pound in his ears.

Mud flew from the horses' hooves. He led them in a race for their lives. They splashed through the stream, icy water splattering.

A horn made a wavering call in the distance as James's mount slipped and struggled to the top of the rise. *Outnumbered.* "Plant my banner," he ordered Archibald.

Archibald unfurled it and thrust the pike's head deep into the soft ground. The white banner with its broad blue band and three stars stood steady in the midst of his men. Wat hurried them into a defensive circle, ordering them close together, for mutual protection. They were fixing their shields on their arms and flexing their sword hands on their hilts. "Do nothing but guard my back, Archie," James said. "No need to make a name for yourself this day."

He turned his horse in a circle to look over the field. The edge of the stream that half-circled the hillock was hard rimed with ice. Beyond, the ground was rolling, spotted with a few trees, but most of the land was cleared for planting in the spring. He watched as a line of men rode into view, shouting and gesticulating. A horn blew again. *Harooo.*

More men rode into view, armor catching the glimmers of sunlight and joined the mass that was forming. Their leader, tall and massive on a huge courser, rode with his standard bearer at his side, blue with a gold bend, the armorial of Sir Raymond Caillou.

Drawing his sword, James watched the man ride up and down the line, shouting. He'd heard of Caillou and tried to remember what. It didn't matter. When the leader died, most often it broke his followers. Caillou must die.

The horn blew again, and the English broke into a gallop, screaming war cries and curses as they came. Caillou waved his sword over his head and bellowed a command.

"Steady," James said. "Make them come to us up the slope." He fastened his gaze on the tall knight with the blue shield. The hooves of charging horses threw muck and icy water, the charge slowing as they labored up the rise. Then the English were upon them.

"A Douglas!" James roared. The hillock rang with the sound of steel on steel.

Two men-at-arms slashed at him. James swept his sword beneath a shield to slice one's belly. He fell, chocking and cursing. James wrenched his sword free and slashed it down on the neck of the second man's horse. He ducked a blow as the horse reared, screaming. A sword thrust at his chest. He lashed with his shield, knocked it aside, and raked his sword across the man's face. He wheeled to force his way through the chaos after Caillou.

Sir Adam was surrounded by three Englishmen. He slammed his war axe into the first one's shield, knocking it up. James took one down with a backslash as he rode past.

James glimpsed Iain vaulting free as his horse died under him. James shouted a curse and spurred his horse. It screamed and reared, lashing out and smashing a foe. He saw Caillou catch Wat in the chest with a blow, shearing through armor, blood running down in a flood. James charged, screaming a challenge.

His quarry met him with a savage blow at his head that James blocked, the shock jolting up his arm. He answered with a slash at his face that the man knocked aside. Their swords crashed together. Caillou feinted and slammed the backstroke into James's ribs, mail crunched but held. James grunted at the blow. James caught the counterstroke on his shield. They hacked at each other. Sword grated on sword.

He shoved the edge of the shield into Caillou's face. For a moment, the man was unbalanced, and James hacked into Caillou's leg. As the man reeled in the saddle, James thrust under his shield, and into his belly.

Another man came howling in rage as he jumped his horse over Caillou's body. He was checked by James's blow to the side of his head. Two more men were surging up the slope, their horses struggling in mud above their hocks. James rammed his sword into the neck of one and jerked it free. His counterblow grazed the man to his right. James spurred his horse into a rear. His foe tried to dodge, but couldn't move in the muck. The hooves crushed his head to spray blood and brains into the mud. James was screaming: *A Douglas! A Douglas!*

He looked for another enemy to kill. Three had Archie surrounded. James rode, scything his sword. He hewed the first from the back, through armor and muscle and bone. "They're done!" a voice shouted behind him. James swung his sword into the second man's neck as the knight chopped at his brother's shield. Blood splashed into the deepening rain. Archie finished the third.

"They're done," Sir Adam said, and he pointed his bloody axe toward five horses splashing through the stream as their riders whipped them to a gallop.

James ripped off his helm and jumped from his horse onto a ravaged wasteland of torn earth. He sloshed to Wat, lying face down in a pool of congealing blood and turned the body over, cradling it as he used his sodden cloak to wipe the mud that coated Wat's face. Wat. *God have mercy on him.* Wat had followed him from the first—taught James half of what he knew. He raised his head to the rain and sucked in the stinging behind his eyes. "Find people from the village to bury the English dead," he rasped to Sir Adam.

James hefted Wat's body in his arms as he stood. Richert

was bandaging a slash to Archie's forearm. Dauid hung onto his saddle, head hanging. Beside him, Fergus's lay with his throat slashed and five of his comrades sprawled around him atop English bodies. Gylys was cradling his dead brother, no mark upon him except for the red slash upon his breast where a lance's blow had killed him. As Iain led up Wat's horse and James draped the body across the saddle, the rest of the field was silent, still and dead except for a raven, cawing as it landed on a sprawled body.

"I'll take my men home."

Holy St. Bride, it was a bitter victory.

CHAPTER 8

APRIL 1317

Near Berwick-upon-Tweed, Scotland

Sea swallows squalled overhead. James walked his elegant bay courser in a tight circle, looking over the rugged green moorland and the distant snaggle-toothed rocks along the shore. "Unfurl my banner," he told Archibald. Already smoke was rising on the horizon from a nearby croft-farm his men were burning. He'd brought a tail of only two hundred men, fifty of them now busy gaining the attention of the English within Berwick—or more particularly, that of one Sir Robert de Neville, heir of the baron of Raby.

He glowered at the Castle Berwick's high gray walls, wrapped in the morning mist in the distance. The autumn before, barely recovered from his wound at the siege of Carlisle, he had been forced to make a humiliating escape by boat when their attack on the city had gone badly wrong. For now the best he could do was make life thoroughly unpleasant and hungry for its defenders. It was a rare Englishman who ventured out from its walls. But if it remained in their hands, it would be a base for another invasion. The English always used it as a base to invade since they'd dragged his father out of it in chains. Somehow, somehow he must take it—but that would not be this day. "Gylys, take two men to watch. I want good warning when Neville brings his men out."

"You think he'll come?" Archie asked as he unrolled the banner and handed it to Dauid to hold aloft, atop its tall pole. The sea breeze caught the starred banner and it snapped in the wind.

"Aye, I'm sure of it. Neville is too proud not to after he challenged me." He snorted. "There's a reason they call him the Peacock of the North. Albeit, he must have some skill to have gotten himself into King Edward's bad graces, killing Fitzmarmaduke in that duel." He circled his mount again. In the distance, the ground dipped to where silver-gray sea smashed against the rocky shore. Broad, green-leafed beeches dotted the moor above broom and grasses sodden by the summer's heavy rains. Pointing to a low hill, he said, "He'll take up a position there."

"But we'll be outnumbered, won't we? Why give him the high ground?"

"So it will be clear that I won." The returning men cantered up, damp sod flying beneath their hooves. "They're alight," Iain called.

"Dauid, I want my banner at my back." He motioned to Symon. "You at my right."

Archie frowned. "I should take your right hand as your brother."

"Not yet." James gave his younger brother a smile, although it didn't seem to reassure Archie. "When you've been at this longer. You take my left." His brother's face tightened like a fist, but James shook his head. He'd been at this too long to permit arguments with his decisions, not even from his brother. "Gylmyne, my lance." His mouth twitched as he couched it. A lance was not his weapon of choice, but it was right for such a fight.

"What fool challenges you like that," asked Sir Symon as he took his place at James's side.

"A proud one. It would seem my killing Caillou was one insult too many."

Sir Symon blew out a scornful breath as he couched his own lance. "Fool thing to do."

James fixed his shield on his arm and couched the lance Richert handed him. "If he could kill me, it would earn him his king's forgiveness."

"I don't understand," Archie said, but then he pointed to Gylys returning at a gallop, his two men spread behind him. One of the men handed Archie his lance.

Gylys pulled up his lathered mount. "Two columns. At least twelve score. Flying the banner of the Nevilles and another banner I don't know. Mostly mounted men-at-arms but six knights at least."

James stood in his stirrups and looked over his men. "Form columns," he commanded. "Be ready to make a flying wedge on my word." He clanged his visor shut.

In the distance, James heard the rumble of pounding hooves. His helm narrowed his vision, so he turned his horse to watch Robert de Neville, a red and silver banner rippling over his head, sweeping by and followed by his glittering troop, more than two hundred strong.

At the top of the hill, they pulled up, massing into a tight steel knot, bristling with lances and swords. Neville took a place at the front on a formidable brown destrier, armored and draped in his colors. Behind him flew a banner of green and silver bends, the Baron of Hylton.

Symon leaned forward in his saddle and said, "By the

Rood, look at the shields behind Neville. He has his brothers with him—all three of them."

"Take them prisoner if you can. And Hylton," James said. "That many ransoms would make this a profitable day's work."

As he walked his horse a step down the hill, Neville yelled a command garbled by the wind. His men spread out behind him, so they stretched across and down the hill on both sides.

"Wedge," James yelled. Behind him, they formed into an arrow meant to cut through their enemy. Archie took his place at his left, horse's head at James's knee to place James at the point of the arrow. Symon, on his right, shifted his shield. Saddles creaked. James's horse pawed as though it sensed the fight to come.

Neville turned his horse to face his men and his voice carried down to James, "We are the flower of England. We are rightful rulers of this benighted land. These rabble Scots will not stand before us!" He wheeled his horse hard and spurred it.

James kicked his horse to a canter. Neville was speeding toward him, and James held in a straight line. Leaning forward over his lance, Neville sat rock steady in the saddle. James jerked his horse's head, and it danced to the side just before the tip of Neville's lance scraped along the side of his helm. James's lance hit Neville's shield square and broke with a resounding crack. Neville rocked in the saddle; his horse went back onto its haunches.

His ears ringing from the blow, James cursed and threw down the stump of his lance. He snatched his sword from its sheath.

Neville juggled his lance, trying to bring it to bear on James. Instead, James turned his horse close, knee to knee with Neville, and aimed a swing at his face. Neville caught the blow on his shield, grating out, "Damn you." Neville wheeled, catching another swing on his shield, and dropped his lance as James circled him. Grabbing his sword, Neville came at him. Steel screamed upon steel.

James pressed in. Their swords locked together. They separated. Neville's eyes glared through the slit of his helm, and he hacked at James. James parried, threw Neville back with his shield and drove at him with a backslash, pressing the attack with blow after blow. Neville didn't miss a beat in their dance. Their swords clashed and clashed again. They rained blows down on each other,

James's blood sang as it pounded in his ears. They circled each other, and James pressed close, moving into Neville— slash and backslash and slash again. Chips flew from their shields. Slashing. Faster. Harder. Faster. Neville's sword caught a backslash that would have parted his head from his body. Then Neville went on the attack, hacking at James again and again. James kneed his mount, pressing the man, swinging.

"Not bad for a Sassenach," he drawled.

Cursing, Neville came at him, blade scything. His blade raked James's chest through his armor. James felt the sting and blood leaking.

He spurred his horse and drove straight into him in a stretching lunge. His sword screamed on Neville's sword, past his parry, and sank through steel and muscle into Neville's belly. The man's sword wavered in the air a moment, his breath going out with a whoosh. James slammed his shield into Neville's face and wrenched his own sword free.

Neville slid backwards from the saddle, flat onto his back. His blood gushed once and then again, weaker. Around him, it soaked into the torn and broken earth.

"Neville is dead," someone shouted. Another voice echoed the cry.

James saw that Archie had unhorsed Robert de Hylton. The man had thrown down his sword and blood dripped from his hand. James's men were fighting on the slope of the hill, sword against sword. Symon was trapped between three men-at-arms, dodging and taking blows on his shield. He reared his horse, smashing an iron-shod hoof into an Englishman's head. James shouted, "A Douglas!" and headed for the fight. But the third man wheeled his horse and spurred it to a gallop toward Berwick.

The English attack shattered like a wine flagon and spilled, racing, first a handful galloped after the first man, and then more galloped away. James spotted one of the Nevilles, a younger brother. The man gaped at his brother's body in its pool of crimson before he jerked his horse's head around. James spurred his horse, and it plunged forward. James smashed his shield into the back of the younger Neville's head. He tumbled to the ground. His horse galloped off. With luck, he was only stunned, James thought as he looked over the field.

Already crows were circling, scolding the men who kept them from their dinner. No English were left except sprawling bodies and a few prisoners. The red and silver Neville banner lay in tatters, trodden into the dirt.

CHAPTER 9

APRIL 1318

Stirling, Scotland

James awoke to dim morning light and the sound of a fist pounding on the door. Groggy, rubbing his face, he sat up and threw back the blanket.

"Sir James," Richert said through the door in a low voice. "The king has called a council."

"Saddle my horse," James replied "See that my men are ready to ride."

Megy murmured and rolled toward him when he sat up and swung his feet to the floor. He slid his hand under the blanket and stroked the warmth between her thighs. Her eyes opened. "My lord," she said in a drowsy purr.

James kissed her. "I must go. Where are my clothes?" He stood and slapped her arse. He tugged on his tunic, and she knelt to lace his breeches. "Bring me my boots." A council— That meant that the man they were expecting had arrived. He wanted to be there to see what curses were flung their way and to see if it was a matter he should take care of for the king.

By the time he was dressed, he heard snorting horses and the clatter of tack outwith the doors.

"Tonight, my lord?" she asked, smiling up at him.

"We'll see." He pulled her to her feet, gave her a quick kiss, and strode down the stairs, out into the bright morning light. He swung into the saddle and led his men toward Cambuskenneth Abbey.

When James slipped into the hall, he heard a low hum of murmurs like a hive of bees from two score lords scattered in clumps. With a secret smile, James propped up the wall with his back near a back corner of the Great Hall. This should be entertaining.

Robert de Bruce entered from beyond the high dais to their bows and lowered himself in a carved oak throne. He nodded to the herald standing beside the door. Abbot Bernard by the king's side leaned to whisper something to him.

The herald intoned, "Master Adam de Newton, Father Abbot of the Berwick Greyfriars."

James swallowed a snort as he beheld the frog-faced monk who shambled into the hall. The edge of his fine wool robe was lost beneath his three chins. Pale eyes darted from side to side to glaring nobles as he trudged toward the king. Half way he stopped and bobbed a bow. "Lord Robert, I thank you for the courtesy of a safe conduct and for receiving me."

The king smiled and waved a hand. "You are most welcome, Father Abbot. Your request was phrased urgently." A rising storm of murmurs went through the room at the lack of the king's proper address, but James crossed his arms over his chest, keeping silent behind clamped lips.

"I forgive his discourtesy. Let him speak," the king said in a mild tone.

"I have been most honored, my lord. I carry letters on behalf of the Cardinals Guacchini and Luca. Letters, my lord, they were entrusted with by our Holy Father the Pope. His Holiness is most gravely concerned about the deaths and destruction brought about by the war against England. The Holy Father has declared a two year truce between yourself and the English."

"I'm delighted to hear of the Holy Father's benevolent concern." The king gave a wry smile. "No one is more eager than I am for true and lasting peace between my nation and our neighbor."

The abbot reached into his full sleeve and pulled out a bundle of parchment secured with thick ribbons and hanging with red wax seals. "I carry letters from the Pope for you, Lord Robert." He held them out.

The Bruce motioned to Abbot Bernard who gave the king a sidelong look before he walked slowly to Master Adam. He took the packet and looked down his nose at them.

"Your Grace." Abbot Bernard's tone was icy. "These are addressed to *Our dearest son in Christ, Edward II, King of England, and to our dear son, the noble Robert de Bruce, who acts as king of Scotland.*"

"Ah…" The king nodded slowly, looking thoughtful. "I fear that there are several knights in Scotland who bear the name Robert de Bruce. It would not serve for me to accept letters from the Holy Father meant for another man. It would, no doubt, cause me to be accused of sacrilege."

"My lord…" A red flush rose from the monk's neck until it flooded his face. "My lord, I assure you, they are meant for you!"

James clicked his tongue against his teeth. *Just what might those letters contain?* Nothing pleasant, he'd wager. The king had been excommunicated for ten years. But this was a new pope. Mayhap it would be worth knowing what this Pope said, exactly.

The king smiled affably. "I have no way to be sure of that, Sir Abbot. If they were addressed to the King of the Scots, I would be sure they were meant for me. As it is, I am forced to refuse them."

"My lord, if the Pope addressed you as king, he'd be taking sides between his children. You must see he could not do that." The man patted sweat off his cheeks with the edge of a sleeve as Abbot Bernard thrust the offending letters out to him.

"Depriving me of my title is taking sides." For a moment, the king let his smile drop beneath a hard gaze. "Had you brought such letters to another king, you would have received a more savage reply."

When Abbot Bernard thrust out the letters again, Master Adam took them with a trembling hand. "Surely, my lord, in the interest of peace, you will accept the two year truce without receiving the letters."

The Bruce hesitated before he worked his face into another bland smile. "I will bring the matter before my parliament. Only they can make such a decision, but they will not meet for some months. You may wait for their decision if you like." He rose to his feet. "For the nonce, I have plans to make. The English still hold my town of Berwick. I intend to regain it."

Master Adam stuttered, "My lord... my lord..." to the king's back as the king strode through the door behind the dais. A guard closed the door with a bang. The man was panting as he turned in a slow circle, his eyes darting. "My lords." His voice shook as he nerved himself. "The Pope demands you respect this truce. You have no choice."

The murmur was quickly rising to angry shouts. Robbie Boyd marched from the front of the hall to confront the friar. "Guards, see *Master Adam* from the hall," he shouted. "He may find his own way home."

The guard at the door leaned his pike against the wall and grabbed Master Adam's meaty arm. "Come peaceably. Or I'll drag you."

In the shadowy corner where he stood, James covered his mouth with his hand.

The friar sputtered, "How dare you lay hands on me?" But he didn't struggle as he was thrust into the bailey yard.

Robbie Boyd shouted, "Be grateful you're not in a dungeon as you deserve." The room roared with shouts and threats as the door closed, but James chuckled softly.

After a few moments, he pushed open the doors and followed the cleric out into the bailey yard. Across the yard, the friar was climbing into the saddle of a beautiful roan palfrey beside his two friar companions were already on mules. Richert ran over when James motioned to him.

James turned his back to the clerics, who were clattering out of the bailey. "You and Dauid will accompany me."

"Only two of us?" Richert's eyebrows rose toward his hairline.

"Hurry. We haven't much time. We need mounts—garrons for the three of us." He narrowed his eyes as he thought. "And the coarsest tunics and mantles you can find."

James paced as he waited. Robbie paused but James shook his head and kept pacing. The others streamed grimly out. A damp, spring wind blew, sending a scatter of leaves flying. But the sun shone like a polished coin in a clear, high sky. After two years of heavy, cold rains that had drowned crops in the fields and another when famine still hovered close, the sight of the sun and of fields being plowed was welcome. The prospect of crops and mayhap taking back Berwick—the city his father had left wearing chains.

One of the garrons whickered as Richert led it up as he held up a rough bag. "I have them, my lord."

"Good." James took the reins Richert handed him and swung into the saddle. "I don't want to fall too far behind our quarry. We're on a little hunt. For pigeons."

"Whereabouts might these pigeons be?" asked Dauid, a squat bald man with shoulders like a blacksmith.

James turned his horse's head and set it to a fast walk with a nudge. "Making for the Old Roman Road and Berwick."

Richert and Dauid fell in beside him on the road as it snaked beside the River Forth where sunlight flashed on silver ripples and passed a spring meadow full of bright purple heather and yellow gorse and stands of broom in green and gold. They turned south at the bridge of Stirling, hooves clomping on the boards as the water gurgled over the rocks beneath. A cormorant circled on great black wings.

They passed a farmer taking a load of early neeps and onions to market. He nodded and pointed behind him when James asked if he'd seen a party of friars. "Asked for alms, the fine one did." The man spit. "Sounded Sassenach to me. Still I offered him a good neep, and he turned up his fat nose."

When the friars were within sight, plodding along the old road, James called a halt. "We'll wait for our pigeons to nest for the night." He led his horse from the road, and they pulled the rough tunics and mantles from the bag tied to Richert's saddle. James knelt and dug through the grass to the damp ground beneath. He grinned and tossed a handful at Richert. "You're too clean for a proper rogue."

Richert scraped off the couple of clods of dirt as he eyed James. "You're fine for a rogue yourself, your lordship." He tossed clods back.

James dodged and laughed. "Aye, there's no denying it. Royal court does that to a man." He dug out a handful of black loam and smeared it onto his mantle then ground dirt into his hands and cheeks. His men followed his example, snickering.

They tied their horses and crept through the trees until they could see a faint orange glow. The friars had built their fire off the road in a depression beside some rocks that would shelter them from the chill night wind. James and his men crawled on their bellies to within a few feet of the men they were following.

Adam de Newton was asleep in a lumpy mass under a heap of blankets next to the fire. The second sat feeding bits of twigs and wood to the flames as he whined about the damp wind. The third was the watch, staring into the darkness. James touched Dauid's hand and pointed to the one at watch. He pointed Richert toward Master Adam, asleep.

James drew his dirk and leapt down on his man. He had to admit the friar had courage, grabbing a flaming branch from the fire and swinging it at James's face. James dodged to the side as he backhanded the friar hard across the face and knocked him sprawling to the ground. "Stay down," he growled and tossed the branch back into the fire. Richert was kicking the Abbot awake. The man yelped and thrashed in his blankets.

James knelt, his dirk to his man's throat. "Keep quiet and you'll stay alive." He strode to the Abbot and jerked him to his feet. "Strip." He glanced at Dauid. "Those two as well."

Master Adam was shaking, his jowls trembling in the firelight. "You can't. We're friars. We have nothing."

James put his dirk to the man's jowls. A drop of blood ran down his fat neck. "I can cut them off you."

The man's sausage fingers shook as he knelt and fumbled at his blankets and then began to untie the cord around his waist. He looked up. "We have nothing valuable. Just take our mounts. They're all we have."

"Are they?" James kicked the blankets away. A packet of parchment dumped to the ground. He bent and picked them up, grinning. "These will be good for kindling for tonight's fire. Or mayhap some lord will pay us for them."

When he turned, the other monks were already stripped to their smallclothes, and Richert was leading up the horse and two mules. James stuck the packet of letters with their papal seal into his belt. "We're good Christian thieves. We won't kill you if you don't force us." He scooped up the head friar's robes and then took those of the other monks. Dauid picked up a bag from beside the fire. "Our food!" one of the men yelped.

"That one won't starve to death any time soon." With a nod and a wave, James led his men and their takings back into the night.

When James swung from the saddle before the doors of the Abbey, he sucked in a breath of the sweet morning air. He was tired and hungry and dreaming of a long soak and fresh bread with bacon burned black, but first he must see the king. He ripped off the filthy mantle from his shoulders and bundled it up to thrust into Richert's hands. "Well done, lads," he said, striding through the doors a guard opened for him.

James entered the council chamber, bone-tired and filthy, to find the king and Thomas Randolph bent over a map spread on the table. The king raised his eyebrows. "Holy Rood, Jamie. What happened to you?"

Thomas stared at him and brushed a hand down his velvet surcoat as though James's dirt might have infected him.

James sighed and shook his head dolefully. "I fear that I must throw myself upon the royal mercy, Your Grace. I've taken to thievery." He tossed the thick packet of letters and papal documents on top of the map. He couldn't help the twitch of his lips.

Thomas's eyes widened. "You robbed the holy friar?"

"S'truth, my lord. That is exactly what I did."

Robert de Bruce picked up the letters, sinking slowly into the chair at the head of the table. He sat staring at the packet.

Thomas's jaw worked for a moment, and he burst out, "God in Heaven, Douglas. Are you mad? If the Pope is ever to receive us back into his grace, we can't do such things."

"Then he should not send letters addressed so to the king."

"Fool!" Thomas slapped his hand on the table like a thunderclap. "We need to make peace with the Pope. We must. And you endanger that for a packet of letters."

"Peace?" James said. "There will be no peace when we aren't allowed even to plead our case. Pope Clement is from the English fief of Guienne. He hears only the English."

"Thievery won't gain his ear. Fool, I say."

"I suggest you not say so again, my lord earl," James said softly.

"Silence." The king glowered from one to the other. "Both of you. Master Adam cannot say who took his letters, I take it, James."

Thomas gave James a cold look. "He will guess."

"What matters a guess?" James crossed his arms across his chest and smiled when the king pulled his dirk from his belt and slit the seal on the letters. He shot Thomas a triumphant look and received a glare in return. "He did not know me, Your Grace. I give you my oath on it."

The Bruce flattened the parchment, reading the words under his breath. "I never received this," the king said at last. He held up a parchment affixed with the ornate Papal seal. "I am excommunicated."

James snorted. "Again?"

"A truce now would leave Berwick in English hands and yet gain us nothing. Here, the Papal bull demands we restrain from any attack upon the English, all English prisoners and hostages to be freed, upon pain of the entire nation, including both of you by name, being excommunicated. Jamie is right we need to know as much as we can of the English schemes, and I have no doubt…"

A rap on the door silenced him. A guard peered in and said, "Pardon, Your Grace."

Robert de Keith, James's good-father, pushed past the man. "An urgent matter, sire." He looked over his shoulder at the young knight behind him. "You tell the king about the letter, William. It came to you." The young knight looked at the king with eager blue eyes. He pushed shaggy, sweat-soaked hair, as red as fire, from his eyes.

"Sire, I received a letter in secret carried by a farmer who'd sold—" He bit his lip, looking shamefaced. "He'd been to Berwick and sold food in the market. They pay so much for food, aye?"

James grunted. He'd have a word with his men about food making its way through his blockade.

The king nodded for the Keith's son to go on. "We have a cousin in Berwick married to an Englishman, Syme of Spalding. He's in charge of part of the city wall." He pulled a much folded and sweat-stained letter out of from his sleeve and held it out. "He paid the man well to sneak the letter out and bring it to me. I rode as fast as I could from Galston to bring it to my lord father."

The king held out his hand. "Here, Sir William, let me see it. This is an entertaining day for letters." The king unfolded it, and his eyebrows rose as he read. "You did well to bring it to me, Sir William. If you'd taken it to my lord of Douglas, Randolph would never have forgiven you." The king gave a wry chuckle. "And if you'd taken it to Randolph, Douglas would have been wroth."

"Your grace!" Thomas Randolph exclaimed. "You wrong me."

James laughed. "I fear that it's true, sire." He held out his hand to Thomas. "Peace, cousin."

Thomas eyed his hand and then clasped it. "I still say you were wrong—but..." He grimaced. "...you are the only man I know who would have so much grit in his belly."

James twitched a shrug. He supposed that many might have done the same for the king if they'd thought of it.

"Now about this letter." The king handed it to Thomas to read. "Keith, do you know this Syme of Spalding?" he asked the Lord Marischal.

"No, Your Grace. And his wife, I've not seen her since she was a lass. A distant cousin, the daughter of my father's cousin."

Thomas looked up from the letter. "So as far as we know this could be a trap. Though if it is the truth..."

"What does he say?" James demanded.

"He says he will help us enter the town over the section of wall that he guards," Sir William said. "I—I don't think it's a trap, Your Grace."

"I can't send an army on one man's word, one none of us knows. It's too great a risk."

"Can we afford to miss such a chance?" James said. "Nothing else has worked to take Berwick, but this might. The man would want a reward. Let me meet with him... I'll know if he speaks the truth."

"That would be as great a risk as sending an army," Thomas said. "If you were captured, Douglas, what would be the cost?"

James raised an eyebrow. "Winning requires risks. I don't begrudge them."

Later the Same Day

A high, clear voice warbled a tune.

As I was walking all alone,
I heard twa corbies makin a moan;
The one unto the other say,
"Where shall we go and dine the-day?"

The voice stopped, as well it should. That was not a song for the king's court, but a child's squeal followed and a piping demand, "Sing more."

James snapped his fingers at his shaggy-coated deer-hound that had stopped to nose the scent on the wall. "Mac Ailpín, come." He rounded the corner of the tall, thorny hedge into the palace's pleasure garden. The air was redolent with summer roses and violets, and a clump of rue gave up a spicy scent. William again demanded, "Sing more," hanging on Marioun of Ramsey's arm as Princess Maud sat pulled the blossoms from a wallflower and dropped them into the grass where a maidservant sat nearby.

Marioun. A perfect rose in the midst of the garden, and he had never before seen it. Golden-haired Marioun. Wide-eyed Marioun. She was slender, straight as a blade, with a radiant face. No longer a child, she wore a wife's sheer veil bound by a golden circlet and a silken gown that shimmered in the sun. He stared at her as she laughed down at his son. There was joy in her face.

"Lad, you mustn't pull so on a lady," James said.

The lad turned loose and looked up. "Father!" And then his eyes widened. "A dog..." he said in a rapt voice.

Marioun sent James a look that barely hid a smile. "Greet your lord father properly, William."

William gave a good try at a bow. He slid a look at Marioun from the corner of his eye and frowned fiercely. "My lord father," he said.

James squatted and held his arms. "Come. Let me see if you've grown whilst I was away."

William ran to fling himself onto his father's chest, wrapping his arms around his neck. "I'm very big now. Did you bring me something? I want to play with the dog? Is it yours? May I have one?"

"It depends on what I hear of you." But a clear-eyed examination from his son showed the lad remembered James never came without a toy. Ruffling the lad's hair, James couldn't help beaming. How did he grow so fast? Had that much time truly passed? In two years, he'd be of an age to take a place as a page. And James had to wonder how he had gotten so old. He hoisted the boy up as he stood. "Has he been practicing his courtesies with you, Lady Marioun?"

She wrinkled her brow as she pretended to frown. "He talks a great deal, my lord. Even sometimes when he should be silent." James looked into her wide, blue eyes, and it was as though she could see right through his eyes into his depths. But her frown dissolved into a smile.

William's lower lip was trembling as he looked at Marioun as though she'd betrayed him.

"But he behaves not too ill," she gave in. James sank onto the stone bench beside her and sat the lad on his feet. He patted William's bottom. "Play with Mac Ailpín and mayhap I have something for you before I go."

The hound settled with a resigned sigh at James's feet as William eagerly tugged on its ears. "Come look," he commanded the Princess who'd apparently tired of destroying flowers and wandered over to try to catch the dog's feathered tail.

"Prince Robert isn't with them." The health of Marjorie's son was a delicate subject. "Is he unwell?"

"He..." She lowered her voice. "He tries so hard to keep up with the others. But he still limps and yesterday he fell. He hurt his leg, so he's abed." Marioun twined her long fingers together. She ducked her head and swallowed.

James rested his hand on hers to stop the twisting. "It

can't be serious. Sir Walter would have said something if his son were badly injured."

"No, but it's hard to see him try and try. And the other children aren't always kind."

He glanced at his son. No, he might not be kind to the lame lad, and young Robert would face such things for all of his life. When William was older, he'd talk to him about protecting his cousin. "But the child is healthy except for a limp? Or so his father says."

She chuckled. "He's healthy. And determined to outstrip the others, hence his falls."

"The king dotes upon him." When she nodded, James said, "As does his father, but when we depart tomorrow Sir Walter rides with the king."

"Robert will miss his father. He's been much with us of late."

One day when he was a page, William would be much with him, James decided. If he could, he'd take the child into his own household. William had straddled the big deerhound like a horse. The dog rose with a surge, sending him tumbling into the grass. He looked up and scowled at the indignity. James reached into his purse and brought out a top painted in stripes of bright blue and red. "I don't suppose anyone might want this?" he asked.

"Mine!" William exclaimed. When Marioun shook her head at him, he said, "Thank you, my lord."

Marioun rose and held out a hand to the Princess and said William. The maidservant rose to follow meekly behind. "I married this spring, my lord—to Cuilén MacDougall."

"I know." He was still staring at her. She led the children to the entrance through the gateway, but she paused to give James a last look.

"I wish you might stay longer," she said. Then she was gone.

CHAPTER 10

LATE APRIL 1318

Berwick-upon-Tweed, Scotland

Douglas bobbed his head to the guard. "Neeps is what I'm bringing in. Early from the ground and fresh." He gave a tug on the mule's bridle. The animal brayed.

"A couple of bags. Hardly worth letting you through the gate." The guard's hard black eyes squinted at him.

James reached grimy fingers into the rough purse at his rope belt and pulled out two pence. "It's all I have, sir." With the other hand, he scratched the itch at the back of his neck and wondered if he'd managed to get lice along with his disguise. That should make it convincing. He dropped the coins into the guard's palm.

The man grunted. "Aye, I suppose. We need all the food we can get. Even damned turnips."

A second guard pulled the gate open, and James hauled on the mule. "Come on, you son of the devil." Tromping, head down, into the cobbled street, he stopped below another guard, leaning against the parapet, watching out over the wall. "Hoi, friend. You know Syme of Spalding by chance? His wife's a cousin, and I promised I'd give 'em some of my neeps."

The man spit. "I heard he'd married a dirty Scot."

"Aye, well..." James frowned at the man but shrugged off the insult. "Know where I might find him?"

"Up the street a way. Be about your business before I have you tossed out."

James led the mule, hooves clattering, into the strangely quiet town. No dogs barked. No chickens scratched at weeds. All eaten, he suspected. The reports he'd received from the few spies who'd gotten in had been right that it was town gnawed by famine, and the same spies had said that the guards had been shorted on their pay. A church bell tolled the Angulus, and some guard shouted a command, the sounds echoing off city walls. "A few masts bobbed above the roofs but few for so large a port. In the midst of the city, Berwick Castle rose, gray and grim. The Cross of St. George snapped in the wind over its high walls. Taking the castle would not be easy, James thought, even once they had the town that surrounded it. But with no access to that port, it could be starved into submission.

He tossed a pence to a lad kicking a stone who was happy enough to lead him to a little thatch-roofed cottage, the stones covered by peeling whitewash, shutters firmly shut.

When he hammered on the wood plank door, the man who opened it was brawny with red-brown hair tumbling around a wide forehead. "What is it?" the man demanded.

"You're Syme?"

"Aye, and what's it to you?"

"Our cousin in Galston asked me to bring some neeps for your good wife." James untied one of the bags from the mule and hefted it over his shoulder. "It's been a dry walk..." He smiled and waited. The mule crunched at a patch of weeds by the doorstep as Syme looked James over. At last, he nodded and held the door wide.

James dropped the sack with a thud onto the rough plank table. He nodded to the thin-faced woman stirring a pot that gave off a scent of onions and thyme. "For the pot."

Syme sat on the bench and leaned an elbow back against the table. He motioned for James to have a seat, so James straddled it beside him. "There are rewards to be had for a king's man, I've heard tell," James said softly.

Syme looked at his wife. "Woman, some ale for the two of us. We have man's business to talk on."

She drew two cups of ale from a little keg in the corner before she picked up a basket piled with clothes. She ducked her head at James and went out the back way.

Syme looked thoughtful as he buried his face in the mug. "So a king's man would profit?"

James swallowed a gulp of the dark ale to wash the dirt of the road from his throat. So far, the man had a better feel than he'd expected. "I've heard there are lands in Angus and silver merks—if Berwick should fall." James put down his mug and rubbed a hand over his beard. "But I want to know why you'd help us. Convince me. If you do, I can speak for the king."

"Why shouldn't I help you? We're half-starved. Months go between ships with supplies and never enough supplies when they come. Most of it goes to the soldiers when it does. Then I married Elspet. Well, she's a good lass and came with a dowry. A good wife. Why should I care she's a Scot? There's been naught but trouble since. Dung thrown at her. I beat one of the bastards bloody. But there's no end in sight for any of it." He slammed down his mug. "So if your king will do right by me, I might can help him."

"How?"

"I have a turn every week for a night watch at the Cowgate. Someone might scale the walls there unnoticed if the watch looked the other way." The man gave a sharp nod and drained his mug.

James leaned close to Syme and said softly, "You'd be well rewarded. But make no mistake, if you betray us, you will not live long enough to regret it. One way or another, I'd see to it."

Syme reared back, face flooding red. "I'm not after betraying you, man. I just want someplace where I can take care of Elspet in peace, have our children, and not always be waiting for supplies that don't come."

James silently looked into Syme's face before he held out his hand. "Then you're our man, and you won't lose for it." After Syme gave his hand a hard clasp, James reached into his tunic and pulled out a small leather purse, heavy for its size. He bounced it in his hand so the man could hear the clank of coins before dropping it onto the table. "To show the king's good faith."

Syme picked up the purse. His eyes widened when he spread the drawstring to peer inside. "I'm your man right enough."

"Good. Now what night of the week is it that you have watch?"

"Tomorrow. And again in a week."

James rubbed his hands together thoughtfully. It was enough time. Thomas had a goodly tail of men with him and James would have ample time to bring his own from Douglasdale. The main army would be the king's, and those were already gathering. "My men will be outside the walls on the eighth night then. After nightfall, light a torch and drop it over the parapet as a signal."

Syme snorted a short laugh. "I saw one of those rope

ladders the Black Douglas uses. Canny things they are. Those what you'll be using?"

James gave a wry smile. "Help me bring in those bags of neeps, and walk with me to the Cowgate. I want a look at the wall on my way out." He stood and clapped Syme on the shoulder. "You'll not regret helping us. That I can promise."

* * *

Motionless as a stone, James crouched on a knee beside the wall. He'd left off his helm because it limited his vision, and his shield was slung on his back for the climb. Low clouds scurried across the crescent moon, sending flickering pewter light onto Thomas's face as he stared upward. James could see dark shapes hunched on each side as their men, eighty of them, waited. They needed no command. Each knew what he must do.

At the signal of a burning brand tossed over the parapet and tumbling to earth, they went to work. James stamped out the torch's flame as hooks at the ends of their rope ladders were hoisted to catch on the edge of the walling. The hooks clanked softly as they caught. James loosened his sword in its sheath and worked spit into his dry mouth. They had all done this many times, but it was always new, climbing into the darkness to face foes who might wait at the top. He patted Thomas's shoulder and put a foot on the first step. He climbed, foot over foot on the narrow boards fixed between the ropes. With a grunt, he threw himself over the coping and rolled onto the parapet-walk. Four or five figures were already there, silhouetted by a fire in a small brazier, and he jerked his sword free. But the light flickered on his own stars on the breast of one of his men, and he sighed in relief. There was a constant low clatter of weapon and armor as their men clambered over the walling. Beside him, Thomas crouched, sword in hand as he watched.

"Shhh…" Syme hissed. "It's two hours until my relief."

"Good man. Now hie you home unless you want a hand in this fight," James whispered.

"I'll receive my reward?"

"I gave you my word. Now home with you." James gave the man's shoulder a push toward the stone stairs to the street. "Sir William," he said, trying to make out faces in the wavering light of the tiny fire.

"Aye."

"Take your men through the streets. I want every street to the castle warded. And quietly as you may."

It took several minutes of whispering names and clanking steel before Sir William led his men away. "To the gate then," Thomas said.

"Dauid,Lowrens, keep watch up here. No way of knowing which way someone might come."

James hunch ran down the steps to keep from showing a silhouette. He swung his shield off his back and slid his arm through the straps. "Two hours until his relief."

"We'd best put a watch," Thomas said. Two streets opened onto the gate like dark mouths. He sent two of his men to watch down each.

As he pulled his sword from his sheath, James knelt. "This is the gate my father was dragged out in chains after Long-shanks broke his oath to him."

"Is it?"

"You cannot know how long I've waited to take this city back." He shifted his knee on the hard cobble of the street. "It was a holy vow, to regain all he had lost—all the English stole. There are few things on earth that will give me more joy than taking Berwick."

A wind that smelled of the salt sea rustled weeds. An owl's shriek made James flinch before he saw it soar in the moonlight on wide, pale wings. The moon turned the shadow of the parapet into teeth that slowly ate their way across the cobbles.

Suddenly, there was a distance scream and shouts. A tongue of orange and red flashed into the air. James leapt to his feet, cursing, as Thomas drew his sword. A tumult of shouting rose. "Scots!" someone shouted. "Scots within the walls!"

"Hell mend them." James spat. "They've started looting. I'll see someone hang."

"I hope you live long enough," Thomas said. "Backs to the gate!"

The watch Thomas had set ran back towards them, swords raised. A tumult of footfalls were like hail on the cobbles. "On them!" someone screamed. Other voices flung shouts of "Damn Scots!" From both streets, a crowd of guards surged out. The four on watch went down under the surge of chopping blades. The crowd surged forward.

"To me!" James shouted to the handful of men they had left. He had his back to the gate, feet spread, Thomas beside him shield raised. The first guard reached him swinging his sword wildly, two handed. No skill, James thought as he slashed under a swing into his belly, and a welter of blood and guts splattered. He kicked the fallen body away. Thomas was slashing left and right, holding off three men. James saw one of their men go down under the onslaught.

"A Douglas!" James screamed, hacking about, slaying, and gave himself over to the madness. "Scotland!" There were shouts everywhere. *There are too many*, he thought and chopped into a foe's neck. Another came at him and died.

Someone went to their knees in front of Thomas and

shrieked until Thomas swung, taking his head off. But more came.

Suddenly, from the gaping maw of the street, there were shouts of, "A Keith! A Keith!" And screams of "Run. We're trapped."

James dove into a gap between two of men, scything his sword in huge arcs. He smashed another's head with his shield. Beside him, Thomas was shouting, "Randolph!" as he hacked right and left.

James raised his sword, raging, but there was no one left to kill. "My lords," Sir William gasped. "We returned as soon as I could rally my men."

James lowered his sword and gazed around him. Dauid and Richert were at the top of the stone steps, a pile of bodies leaking a rivulet of crimson onto the ground, Dauid mopping blood from a slash on his face. The four men of the watch sprawled amongst the dead in pools of blood. One of Thomas's men slumped against the gate, armor slashed to pieces. Iain had died holding his belly as his life leaked away.

James sank onto the bottom step. He was red to the elbow and his face splattered with flecks of blood and gore. "We owe you our lives, Sir William. It's not a debt I'll forget."

The young knight just shook his head. "No debt, my lord. And I had to kill the two men who started the looting. There was a sally from the castle, but they retired and raised the gate." Within the city, the lights of flames still raised and flickered, fanned by the sea wind. "The fight here is over. Take your men. See what you can do to put down the flames. And find out who began the looting. I'll hang them myself."

Trumpets sounded on the road outside the gate. Voices were shouting commands. Horses neighed and he heard the steel clamor of armor and weapons.

"Open for the King of the Scots!" a herald outwith the gates shouted.

"Open the gates for the king," James said as he stood. He sheathed his sword and stared up at the castle with no doubt it would soon be starved into submission. "I've more pleasure greeting him in Berwick than I would at the gates of Paradise." Berwick was theirs.

CHAPTER 11

OCTOBER 1318

Dunfermline Palace, Fife, Scotland

The bailey yard of Dunfermline Palace was chaos and clamor. Hundreds of sumpter horses were being unloaded of bags of grain and beans, of coin in ransom payment for James having spared Richmond and Hartlepool, bags of jewelry, of silver ewers, of crucifixes, church plates, candlesticks, and rich vestments. A line of men, laughing and calling for warm food and ale, carried bags inside to the storerooms to be added to Abbot Bernard's accounts. Dozens of finely clad prisoners, held for ransom, were being gently herded toward the palace doors. Horses were being unsaddled and led toward the stables. Snow flurries blew in the chill autumn wind, and everyone was in a rush to be within doors.

Cold wind blurred James's vision, and he ducked his head. His men, the thousands he'd led as he'd swept like a storm through Northern England as far as York, were too many for the palace to hold so with him were only a hundred of his men, the rest on their way to Douglasdale. He longed for home, for the manor he'd barely seen since it was completed. For now, on the bracken-covered slopes outside, his men would have to make do with rough tents. Tomorrow he'd lead them home as well, he hoped.

Richert was dismounting with the prisoners and James called out to him, "See the men are camped as well as may be. Find me if there is any problem." Richert bowed.

James strode into the palace, stripping off his gloves and shaking flakes of snow from his hair. The palace chamberlain met him, saying that the king awaited him in the Privy Chamber. And so the chamberlain opened the door and bowed him in.

The Privy Chamber was richly furnished, and if much had once been in English hands, that mattered not. Moorish carpets covered the floor. The walls were hung with Belgian and French tapestries that shimmered with gold, silver, and silk threads. A side table bore silver flagons that give up a scent of mulled wine and were surrounded by goblets.

Snow splattered against high arched windows edged with lions and falcons twined into vines. "Lord Douglas," William de Soules greeted him, holding out a hand. "I have been most anxious for your return. There is little time to prepare for the dedication of St. Andrew's Cathedral."

"Then your anxiety is relieved," James said as he tried not to flinch away from the feel of the man's soft, sweaty hand. "As you see, I am here." He brushed by the man to cross the room and bow to the king who stood by the windows talking to Bishop Lamberton. The bishop, still stooped and thin, although he was much recovered from his many years in an English dungeon, pressed James's hand as James bent to kiss his ring. "I hurried back as best I could, Your Excellency."

"I was sure you'd return in time, Jamie." The bishop's eyes

were shining with pride. "After a hundred years, St. Andrews Cathedral is complete, and the entire world will know it, including the Holy Father."

The Bruce nodded. "It will say to all that once more Scotland can resume its rightful place as a kingdom of Christendom."

"I leave tomorrow to complete the preparations for the dedication. It—" Lamberton's voice faltered for a moment. "It is the culmination of my life's work. I feared I might not live to see it finished."

"Nonsense, my friend." The king gave Lamberton a stern look. "You're not old enough to talk so. No more than four years my senior."

"I'm not as strong as I once was, Your Grace. But God is good and… it is done."

"You summoned all the nobility for the celebration?" James asked.

The king squeezed Lamberton's shoulder and took his place at the head of the council table. "I did and all the burgesses and freeholders who are able to reach the cathedral—all of the community of the realm. This is an occasion the like of which we've not seen for many a year—a reason besides battle for our people to celebrate."

Thomas Randolph had poured a goblet of wine and sat down near the king. "It will be an opportunity to show the people that we are strong again, or regaining our strength. That Scotland can once again be a shining beacon of Christendom."

"Oh, they know that." James grinned as he helped the bishop to his seat. "Since Bannockburn no one has questioned it."

"Ruling a kingdom is more than battle, Jamie," the king said.

"I stand corrected, sire." James slid into his place. "When

do we leave for St. Andrews? I would like to lead my men home."

"There isn't time, so your sergeant must do that for you. You know the court moves slowly. Women and children can't be rushed nor do I wish to do so. We'll do this well—as it should be done." His brows rising toward his hairline, the king stopped as the door was silently opened.

Sir Roger de Mowbray, tall and rawboned, stood in the doorway, his beaky face covered by purple and green mottled bruises. Behind him, eyes wide and not daring to enter, was a great keg of a man in battered armor. After a silent, echoing pause, Mowbray limped to the king's side and dropped to a knee.

"Your Grace," he said in a hoarse voice. "Your brother... The king of Ireland is dead. In battle at Dundalk."

The Bruce closed his eyes for a moment, the color draining from his face in a tide.

"Sire?" Mowbray said.

"Dead..." The king's chest heaved as he sucked in a breath. "Grievous news, but for a knight it is not the worst death—" His voice broke and he made a strangled noise. "What happened?"

James remembered his king's face the day they brought the news that three of his brothers had been tortured to death on an English scaffold: hanged, drawn—their guts ripped out whilst they still lived—their bodies beheaded, and quartered. The king had near died of it. But Edward's death in battle would surely be easier to bear.

Mowbray's face was pale under the patches of bruising. "It was a slaughter, Your Grace. We begged him to wait for reinforcements, but he wouldn't have it. We were outnumbered by ten times our number. At the last, we begged that Gib Harper be allowed to wear his surcoat. But he was picked out by his crown and cut down along with everyone with him."

"How many?" the king grated out. "How many of my people died?"

James dug his fingers into his knee hard enough to bruise. The pain would help him keep his silent. Thomas glanced at him, raised an eyebrow, and then shook his head.

"Philip de Mowbray escaped the slaughter, but sorely hurt. The rest..." He took a deep breath. "John de Soules, Sir John Stewart, my cousin Philip, Alexander MacRuari, Gib Harper, all the two thousand who accompanied him. A handful of small folk escaped. All else in the first column died." Mowbray slanted his head toward the man still hovering in the doorway. "John Thomson was leading the last column—the men of Carrick. The few of us who escaped the slaughter were able to reach him in time that he could retire."

The king scraped his chair back as he jerked to his feet. James pushed his chair back and stood as quietly as he could and all the silent men in the room did as well. None would sit when the king stood. The Bruce strode to glare out the window at white blotches that hit the glass and disappeared. "He was a difficult man—hasty and impulsive. We argued often. But he was my brother. My last..." He turned to glare at Mowbray and grated out, "And you left them to die."

John Thomson took a hesitant step into the council chamber. "I swear to you, Your Grace, they were past rescue. Sir Philip barely escaped as he was being dragged away. He told me, albeit he was injured past helping, that he saw your brother cut down."

The king bowed his head, and after a few moments said in a milder voice, "You have brought my brother's body home to us."

"Sire..." Mowbray licked his lips.

Sir John took a step back, his ruddy face paling. James felt his heart give a thud. Thomas gave him a quick, thin-lipped stare.

"Your Grace," Mowbray stuttered. "The English took his body after the battle—only his out of the thousand who died. They—they quartered it. Beheaded it. Sent pieces across Ireland—his heart and one quarter to be nailed over the gate at Dublin. The head to be sent to King Edward in England."

"Defiled," the king whispered. "How... how could anyone..." Turning, he grabbed up the silver flagon, wine sloshing as he drew back. He dashed it against the wall. Wine covered the wall in a dripping crimson splotch, and the flagon clattered to the floor. "When Gilbert de Clair died invading my kingdom, did I defile his body? Did I? Have I ever treated their dead so?" He turned to glower at them but slowly the anger drained. He groaned. "My brothers... All of my brothers..." He stepped to his chair and gripped the back, his knuckles whitening with the force of his grip.

"Your Grace," Soules said. "He died an honorable—"

With a roar, the king hefted the chair over his head and smashed it down on the table. It broke to pieces. Shards showered across the room. The surprise of the crash sent James stumbling a step back. The Bruce lifted the broken piece of wood still in his hands, staring at it as though it were from some strange and foreign land. He lifted his gaze though it went through them. "Out," he rasped. "All of you. Leave me. Now!"

How could he leave the king so? But the others backed toward the door, and Thomas grabbed James by the arm and jerked him after them. With a last look at the white-faced man, who stood grieving, James closed the door.

He leaned his shoulder to the wall and rubbed his hand

across his mouth. He had disliked Edward de Bruce always, been sure that one day his stubborn impatience would come to disaster—but this?

"*Deus misereatur nostri,*" Lamberton said softly. "How Thomas died... At least Edward..."

James preferred not to think about how hard Thomas de Bruce must have died on that scaffold. Even after these years, the thought of the dreadful death of his friend was a stone in James's chest.

Lamberton shook his head absently, his eyes distant. "They were all wild as colts as lads. Took after their mother, who was a woman like no other I've known. Dear God, how they laughed. There was no jape they might not try, and Robert in the lead." James saw the bishop's hands were trembling, his voice thin. "Prayers. The king will want prayers for the repose of his brother's soul." The bishop's face was whey-white.

"You must stay strong for the dedication," James told the prelate. "Seeing to the prayers for Lord Edward—he'll be no less dead if you rest first."

"It is not seemly—not kingly for him to act so," Mowbray said with a look at Soules.

Thomas Randolph glared at Mowbray. "He grieves. But we can't stand about like women, wringing our hands. The queen. I'll go to her. She—" He slid his eyes toward the door, and they listened to the silence from beyond it. "She must be told."

"John Stewart. Dear Holy St. Bride, Walter at Berwick must be told his brother is dead," James said. "Who else?"

"One of the queen's ladies in waiting, Marioun, her husband was there. Surely we should leave that to the queen," Mowbray said. "I brought the news to the king, but I'm no servant to run errands, delivering messages."

This was no time for them to come to blows and the usually patient Thomas Randolph was glowering at Mowbray as though he might do just that. James frowned at the group of whispering servants huddled at the end of the corridor. He motioned to the florid-faced chamberlain and called to him. "Find a page to aid his reverence to his chamber, and then send my brother, Archibald, to me. Quickly, man." He nodded to Thomas. "My lord earl and I will seek out the queen. My brother will take the news to Walter Stewart." He gave Mowbray a considering look. "As you say, Sir Roger, you have done your duty. You're still injured, and no doubt you want to find your chamber."

"The matter of the succession can't be ignored," Soules said. "This leaves decisions which must be made. The only heir must not be a lame child."

"Not now, man," Thomas Randolph barked and turned to the chamberlain. "Is the queen in her solar?"

"She is, my lord earl."

James nodded to the men and made for the stairs, Thomas on his heels. They passed alarmed servants. The news of disaster always spread quickly though they might not know what the disaster was. Or perhaps Mowbray's servants had already spread the nature of his news.

* * *

The queen sat down heavily, a hand on her rounded belly. "His grace has been told?"

James swallowed. "Roger de Mowbray brought him the news."

Elayne sat beside the queen and glared at James as though the ill news were his fault. Lady Mary, the king's sister, slowly rose to her feet, her face drawn into grim lines. Her sister Christina put an arm around her and whispered, "God rest him." Marioun had dropped her needlework into her lap. She slowly raised a hand to press to her lips.

Thomas caught James's eye. James wondered for a moment how she had felt about her husband, who must have left with the forces of Carrick soon after they wed. But now was a cruel time for such thoughts. He shoved it into a corner of his mind.

"My lady," he said and dropped to a knee beside her. "I'm sorry. Sir Edward's entire force was cut down. All were killed."

He reached for her hand and squeezed it. She held his hand for a moment, returning the pressure, but then jumped to her feet. "I can't—" She whirled and hurried to the window to stare out at the bleak sunshine that peeked through the clouds and flurries of snow. "What do I do?"

Lady Elizabeth rose and went to Marioun, put an arm around her shoulder. "Child."

Marioun made a muffled sound that might have been a sob or a gasp. She rocked a little as the queen stroked her shoulder. "I should be weeping." She looked up at the queen. "Why am I not weeping? He was my lord husband."

Lady Mary's lips were in a thin line. "There will be time for tears after. There always and always is time for tears."

Another's comfort would be better than his now. James rose to his feet and rubbed his temple. As ill-timed as Soules's comment had been, indeed, the succession would have to be discussed soon. Would the king still want to leave for St. Andrews on the morrow? This would mean another parliament. And there was news he had yet to give the king about the proclamations he had found whilst in England— the new anathema from the Pope upon King Robert that added both James and Thomas Randolph. If he'd smiled that his own name had joined the king's in the Pope's fulmina-tions, the king would not take the matter so lightly.

"Your Grace," he said after what had seemed like a long silence, "the king is... much grieved. Should you go to him?"

"I will give him some time, Jamie." She ran a hand over the bulge of her stomach. "He'll come to me when he is ready for comfort. We have our own grief here."

CHAPTER 12

DECEMBER 1318

Scone, Scotland

The refractory of Scone Abbey was crammed with men. With the parliament to be held the next day, nearly every member of the Privy Council had made the harsh winter trip to have a voice in the decision. Some James would have been well satisfied had they not done so, and that included Sir William de Soules who had him cornered, fiercely gripping his arm in a damp hand. "A child as the heir is unthinkable, I tell you," Soules said. "And, worse, a cripple. We dare not risk such a pass."

"Yet the king's nearest male heir *is* that child," he said keeping his tone mild and courteous, "and a lusty lad in spite of his limp."

James pulled his arm out of Soules's grip and threaded his way through long benches to where Robbie Boyd stood by Thomas Randolph near the carved oak throne at the head of the room. "I see you made it through this foul weather,"

Thomas said. "Not a time I would have chosen for a parliament."

"It is not so dreadful as that. Besides, the king gave me little choice." James shrugged. "He commanded my presence."

Robbie Boyd snorted. "With Soules whispering in everyone's ear, it's not a bad thing."

"Whispering what?" Thomas asked. "He keeps a good distance from me."

"I wish he did from me. He's saying that there shouldn't be a child heir," James said. He gave the man across the room now with his head close to that of Mowbray as they talked. "I cannot like the man, and does he not know that young Robert is a cousin? Fool."

"There are those around him who are not." Robbie frowned as he watched the two men conferring.

"Mayhap not." James moved to stand at the bench directly in front of the throne as Abbot Bernard entered the room, followed by Bishop Lamberton, leaning on the shoulder of a page, and Bishop David of Moray walking beside them. The three men took a bench reserved for the clergy advisors to the right of the throne. There was a rustle of movement as all stood when the king strode in accompanied by Gilbert de la Haye.

The king took his seat and gave a brusque wave for the assemblage to take their places. He nodded to Abbot Bernard.

The abbot stood and went to stand at the king's left hand, his lines scored deep around his mouth and forehead. "My lords, the king has called you to consider two matters, both of great weight. The Cardinals before they left England proclaimed an anathema against Lord Robert, our king. Such has been done before, however unjustly. However, they added all of his grace's followers in this new proclamation, including his lordship the earl of Moray and

Sir James, Baron of Douglas, who were named most particularly."

James leaned forward, his elbows on his knees as he listened. He had not expected this to be brought up in the council. What was there to be done about it? The Pope refused even to hear their pleas for justice, and James was right glad to join his king if that was his fate.

Bishop David rose and said, "If I may speak, sire."

The king nodded. "With my good chancellor's permission."

"Our primate of Scotland, Master Lamberton, has not accepted this excommunication, based as it is upon lies by the English to the Holy Father. No priest, cleric, or friar in Scotland will obey it. Moreover, I continue my call to treat any fight against invasions by the English of our lands as a holy crusade. But we must consider how to take our argument to the Holy Father. We are being damaged in the eyes of other kingdoms whose rulers may be loath to trade or negotiate with his grace or his representatives in the face of papal ire. So I would call upon Abbot Bernard to gather a group to write to the Pope. He does not receive our representatives, but I am convinced he will read such letters.

We clerics of Scotland must make our case as must the nobility in separate letters. But most important must be a letter—a declaration—from the community of the realm of Scotland as a whole. Thereafter, good men must be found to brave the risks of a trip to Avignon to carry the letters, which I have no doubt the English will try to prevent. And they must present them for the Pope's consideration."

Maol of Lennox stood. "We've made our arguments to the Pontiff year after year. What makes you think he'll listen now, especially this Guyenard. The French and English influence at Avignon is complete."

"With all respect, my lord earl, our arguments have not been made. As long as our king is excommunicated the Pope will not receive his representatives, but there is no such objection to letters. They must be carefully written by men who know what is acceptable to the Vatican as well as knowing the history of our people. Such will not be an easy task. I freely confess it."

As soon as the earl of Lennox resumed his place, James stood up. "As long as my king is an excommunicate, I am pleased to be so, as well. But for the good of the realm and the heart's solace of my liege lord, I believe this effort is worthwhile." He'd seen time after time grief it gave the king from the fulminations against him by the Pope, even if his own bishops were faithful. "Though I know nothing about matters of the Pope, can such letters do any harm?"

"Is the council agreed?" Abbot Bernard asked. At a general murmur through the room of agreement, he said, "Now on to the main matter of the council. The matter of the succession—"

He bowed when the king broke in to say, "This is a matter of the greatest concern. No man can be certain of the future, not even the morrow and especially so in this Scotland of ours. Nor am I a young man."

"Your Grace..." James broke in as a muttering of protest went through the room, but the king silenced his interruption with a glare.

"I have not spent a life of ease. The day will come, only the good God knows how soon, when I must have an heir. We have seen too well what will happen if the succession is not established. Our enemies would pounce upon our poor land. That King Alexander did not was a disaster beyond measure. How many thousand upon thousand have died because of a great king's one mistake? The succession must be settled. From my Privy Council, I only ask advice on who to name. My will is fixed that I will have it done."

There was a pause and then Thomas Randolph said, "Surely, there is no question, sire. Your grandson Robert must be declared your heir presumptive. He is the only male in your line."

"I cannot agree, my lord earl," William de Soules said softly. "The risk of an infant heir is too great, and the Bruce line is not the only royal line in Scotland. Until the child reaches his majority, another more able to rule should be declared heir."

"What are you saying?" Maol of Lennox jumped to his feet and spun to face Soules. "Who would you have? The Balliols? The line of Toom Tabard? Never."

Angus Og shouted, "I'd spit him on my sword first."

"The line of King Alexander had many branches besides the Balliols. That must be considered."

"And risk another battle over the crown?" someone shouted. James craned around to see who, but everyone was craned and scowling at Soules.

"That's madness," Boyd said.

"My lords!" Gilbert de la Haye shouted, stepping forward. "This is a counsel, not a brawl. Remember yourselves in the king's presence."

Angus glowered at Soules for a moment before he resumed his place. Maol gave Soules a hard look before he did the same, and there was an uneasy silence. James glanced at the king's rigid face and back at Soules.

Soules raised his open hands. "Sirs, I suggest nothing so drastic as recalling the Balliols. I only remind you that a child is not our only choice."

"The king is in good health," Robbie Boyd put in. "But if he should be killed, God forefend, we have strong men to rule for the child. Guardians of the Realm must be named."

"What is the advice of the council?" Abbot Bernard said.

"Is there another name put forward besides the king's grandson?"

Soules turned, staring at the angry faces around him. "No. I have none," he said and sat down. *Who was it whom he would have named?* James wondered. But the man said nothing more. Soules's grandfather had made some distant claim to the throne, but surely Soules did not think they'd accept him in place of their rightful king's heir. *Impossible...*

"Then is the counsel's advice to put forth the name of Robert Stewart, son of the High Steward, to the parliament to be declared heir presumptive to the throne?" Abbot Bernard asked.

"It must be the king's grandson," James said. He watched Soules from the corner of his eye. The man sat with eyes downcast, saying nothing more.

Maol of Lennox said, "Boyd is right. The Guardian of the Realm cannot be left in doubt. It must be someone who can be trusted."

The king held up a hand. "Both of you are in the right, my lords. A Guardian must be named, but with the lad's tender age, I'd have two guardians. My nephew, Thomas Randolph, earl of Moray, was named in the previous act. I believe he should be named again. But there must be a second for a child so young. I say that should be the good Sir James, Lord of Douglas. There are no two men in the kingdom I trust more."

James closed his eyes and sucked in a deep breath. Holy St. Bride, to be Guardian of the Realm? True, he'd been regent briefly whilst the king was in Ireland, but he'd never dreamed of being named after the king's own nephew.

Lennox was nodding. "That would be wise. I agree to it."

There was a shout of agreement, although one or two held their tongues, and Soules was frowning. "Your Grace, what if the child dies?" he asked.

Walter Stewart jumped to his feet and took a step toward Soules. "My son is a strong lad. He will not die. I pray God that his grace has a son, but if that is not God's will, we've named my son as his heir."

"Sir Walter," Soules said, "I meant no ill. I'm merely concerned that the succession be made clear—for the good of the realm."

Walter's jaw worked as he continued to glare at Soules, but James stood up and put a hand on his shoulder. "Let it go, Walter," he whispered. "The thing is decided."

The Bruce stood. "And the succession will be made clear, Soules, at the parliament on the morrow. I thank you for your advice, my lords. Tonight we will resume the celebration of the birth of my daughter as a respite from these weighty matters."

Near Berwick-upon-Tweed, Scotland

Moonlight flickered through the leaves. The whisper of a warm summer breeze through the branches mixed with a whicker of horses, the clank of steel, and the metallic slither of mail. A company of men, silhouetted in the moonlight, stretched beyond sight on the road. James stepped into the open. "Sire," he said.

"What did you learn, Jamie?" Robert de Bruce asked.

"The city is surrounded, as we feared. I looked for myself, though winning through was no easy matter. Lancaster arrived yesterday to join the king."

"How many?" Gilbert de la Haye said from where he sat ahorse beside the king.

"Many thousand arrived with Lancaster in addition to at least four thousand that were already with King Edward. And even worse news—they brought siege engines and a host of men versed in using them. They have ships in the harbor with siege engines, as well. One of my men sneaked through with word that Walter beat off a sea attack yester-day. But it was a close thing."

Archibald led up a horse, and James vaulted into the saddle.

"There is no way of cutting our way through?" Thomas asked.

"They have two lines of earthworks behind palisades of sharpened stakes all the way around the city. No. They intend to have Berwick again. I found no weakness—no way through."

"And what then if we did?" the king asked. "We'd be trapped. Walter is well-provisioned and garrisoned, but they can only hold for so long if we cannot relieve them. Jamie had the right of it. You'll have to draw Edward away."

"He can't be sure," Randolph said.

"I had word from more than one of my spies that she's there."

"They'd use Berwick—"

The king cut Randolph off with a brusque, "I know, but if the queen is at York, then attacking them there will draw Edward off. If Jamie's wrong, then you'll be forced to press south. For London or as close as you can reach. Even if she slips through our fingers, a threat to Queen Isabella will bring Edward running. Her brother of France would take her capture most ill, and he would blame her husband. With Edward's troubles at home, he cannot afford that."

"And I've heard that the lady is bountiful in her atten-tions." At Randolph's protest, James sputtered a quiet laugh. His interest lay with a sweet lady of their own court and nowhere in England, but Randolph was easy to bait. "She is at York, my lord earl. That much I am sure of, and Edward can't count on Lancaster. It's well known that Lancaster hates him. Or more likely, Lancaster cannot count on Edward. They will fall out. All we have to do is help that along, and if we don't, we've lost Berwick. I know what you were going to say, my lord earl. You're right. Of a certes, they'd use Berwick as a base to invade. We can't let that happen."

The king said, "Lamberton had news of a gathering of churchmen at York, as well. Archbishop William de Melton and the Bishop of Ely have called a chapter, it seems. That may speed Edward when he learns of your movements. You must gain their attention as you sweep south. Haste you."

"Might the churchmen want to make some donation to St. Andrews, do you think, sire?" James asked, grinning.

Even in the moonlight, James could see Thomas's scowl. "It is no matter for japery, Douglas, attacking a woman and priests."

"There is no need to attack the churchmen, Thomas," the king said. "The threat should move Edward—threat toward his queen or his churchmen. But if you should take the queen as a hostage, it would force him to the peace-table. That is worth bending that pride of yours."

"How many men do you give us, sire?" James asked.

"All except my own tail—two thousand. I'll take a hundred men to return and move the court to safety. But you must make all haste, or it will be to no gain to us. Draw Edward away from Berwick and avoid Lancaster if he tries to cut you off on your return. Once you cross the border to England, burn every farm and town that you pass. You're to leave naught but smoke, ash, and cinders. Any who resist—."

Thomas Randolph was tight lipped but he nodded. "As you command, Your Grace."

The moonlight caught on mail like ripples in a dark river as James called a command to move forward. A breeze swirled around them, stirring their cloaks and ruffling their banners as they turned south toward England.

CHAPTER 14

Near Myton-upon-Swale in Yorkshire, England

Nicholas Willelmi sank onto the grass and litter of blown leaves, a splotched carpet still wet from the morning rain, and leaned back against the trunk of an oak. The Englishman's eye was a slit, half his face misshapen from swelling and purple with a bruise. James hunkered beside the man. "What happened?"

"Tinnicokes let himself to be caught as you ordered. I was watching York Castle when they dragged him in." He gingerly touched his fingers to his face, wincing.

"You think your partner was alive?" Thomas asked with a hint of his disapproval in his voice. He could not seem to relieve himself of the belief that spying was dishonorable, but James didn't expect him to have dealings with the matter. Spies were his own province.

"Aye, my lord, he was alive. The last I saw he was. Not even bad hurt, though I don't know what they'd do to him. He knew his part was to resist a bit, and then to say if they'd spare him being put to the question, that he'd tell what he knew. By dawn there was a fair to do in the Castle. Men shouting, horses being harnessed and saddled, horns blowing. The church bells in the city were ringing, priests running about. There was a whole flock of fat, pompous clerics, the bishop of Ely and the archbishop both with hundreds of squawking, clucking followers and burgesses shouting for their men. I knew I needed to bring you word, so I made for the gate, but it was closed. I went over a low place in the wall."

"And they objected?" James smiled.

"One of the guards came at me with a club as I went and was about to drop. The funny thing is it helped me get away since I dropped like a rock and rolled down the hill."

"The queen will be fleeing south soon if she isn't already," Thomas Randolph said.

"There was never much chance that we'd take her. The king knew that." James pulled a handful of silver merks out of his purse at his belt and put them into Nicholas's hand. The job they'd done was worth high pay. "Lancaster must already have news we've burnt all the way from the border. He won't be pleased to sit whilst we do it nor any of the northerners. But we have to make sure the threat brings them running. The threat to the bishops will do that."

Thomas blew out a breath. "They can't be so stupid as to fight."

"If they don't, tomorrow we'll pursue the queen and burn the rest of the way to York. For now, we'll put the fields here to the torch. A smokescreen will not be a hurtful thing." James rose to his feet and threw his gaze over the rolling, oak and birch covered hills. In the distance, he could see crofters' cottages, golden fields of wheat ready for harvest, and the River Swale, a silver-blue slash in the land though the stone bridge across it was out of sight beyond a gently rising slope. "Sir Symon," he called. "Take two score men. Once you have the fields and houses fired, watch the bridge and sound a trumpet in good time if the English decide they want to fight. Let them cross and then hold the bridge behind them."

"There can't be any large number of fighting men left in York. They're all with the king," Randolph said. "The sheriff's men and a few militia, but they can't mean to give us battle with so few. With priests? Burgesses?"

James shrugged as he shouted for the sergeants to ready the men to form a schiltron.

"At least you pay well, my lord," Nicholas said, carefully levering himself to his feet. "I'll let you know if I have word that would interest you." The man ducked an awkward bow and limped into the trees as James watched, rubbing a hand over his short beard.

"Why are you so sure they'll face us?" Randolph said.

"Because they don't think that we'd lead a full army south, whilst Edward is besieging Berwick. The word my man took them was that I have a few men to sneak an attack on the queen." He grinned. "And catching the Black Douglas in his own trap would be a braw thing, would it not, if you were an Englishman?"

"You can't be sure that he told the story the way you meant him to."

"No, but I pay well, and the story Nicholas brought sounds exactly as it should."

Thomas shook his head. "So you've tricked them into fighting. Holy Jesu, Douglas—"

"We'll not kill them if they surrender," James snapped. "You know that. The Archbishop of York and the Bishop of Ely would make superb hostages to force Edward to the peace-table, if not as good as the queen. But we'll burn all to York if we must in order to save Berwick."

Archibald ran up leading their horses, and James swung into the saddle. Thomas turned to mount, his face stiff with displeasure, but James knew that he would do his sworn duty. That was Thomas; however much he might hate the duty he was put to, the king could count on him. So James stood in his stirrups and scanned the hills for sight of Symon's men. On a hilltop, he saw a roof of thatch catch, orange flames leaping into the air until the cottage stood against the sky bathed in fire. A field caught and then another, billows of smoke coasting above their heads. A torch arched, tailing a long tongue of flame, into a haystack. The smoldering hay added a gray ribbon that drifted toward them. The sky darkened to slate as farms and fields were consumed. Reeking strands drifted and wrapped around his men.

A long blare from a trumpet climbed up from the river to tell him that the English were approaching to enter his trap. It blared again. For a moment, he felt pity for them. They were fools if they resisted, but being a fool should not cost a man his life. But in war, often it did.

"Into a schiltron," he said. The sergeants shouted, echoing his orders and the sound mingled with the rattle of armor, the scrape of pikes being hefted, along with curses and feet pounding as two thousand men ran into place. Thomas drew his sword, still looking glum, but he nodded to James and turned his horse to ride along the lines of jutting pikes. He spoke quietly to the men as he went.

Turning his horse in a circle, James looked over their men. There were two ranks of pikemen formed into a square. His eyes stinging and watering from wafting tendrils of smoke, he saw his banner unfurl as his brother shook it out. Further down, flapped Thomas Randolph's yellow and purple banner.

Suddenly, through the swirling smoke, James glimpsed the first of the English, riding over the top of the rise. In the lead was a white-robed friar holding aloft a massive gold crucifix. "Do they think to defeat us with that?" Randolph said in a tone of disbelief.

"Look." James pointed at two men both in glittering, bejeweled vestments on high-stepping, white palfreys, the archbishop and bishop, but the men had maces in their hands. Around them ranged a motley army of priests and brightly dressed merchants all with shields and swords and pikes of every description. Some wore helms or rusty mail hauberks, but many were bare of armor, in white priests robes.

"Jesu God," James muttered.

The English boiled over the rise, more of them and then even more. James sucked in a breath. There were thousands of them. Three thousand? Four? In the smoke and their disorder, he couldn't be sure.

He kneed his mount and rode out a few yards. "Surrender," he shouted. "You'll not be harmed."

The English broke into a run, shouting curses and prayers as they came.

For a breath, James hesitated, but then he called out, "On them!"

His men moved forward in a wall. The archbishop reined and turned his palfrey shouting words James couldn't make out over the screams and moans. The man tossed down his mace. Prayers and curses turned to screams as the leading wave of English were scythed down like summer grass. James put his spurs to his horse and called out, "Take what prisoners you can."

The English reeled back under the onslaught of the slashing pikes. Men fell, dying under the murderous assault. The bishop in his finery came hard past his superior, knocking into his horse in desperate flight.

James saw Richert catch a burgess, with gold chain about his neck, full in the chest with a pike, splitting him from neck to crotch. It was already a route as the English flung down their weapons and ran.

"Break the schiltron," James bellowed to be heard in the chaos. "To horse. To horse! Take prisoners if you can." As his cry was repeated down the steel hedge of the schiltron, his men tossed away their pikes and dashed to the horse-line, throwing themselves into their saddles.

James wheeled and spurred his horse after the fleeing enemy. The rider with the crucifix was using it to beat his mount to a faster gallop, splashing into the river. The horse was belly deep and then swimming. The archbishop paused in his flight before he lashed his horse and plunged ahead. A knight wearing gilded chain mail turned his horse as he guarded the archbishop's escape. James charged.

His quarry met him with sword raised and aimed a swipe at his throat. James dodged as their horses rammed together, his black going back onto its haunches. He slammed the sword aside and smashed his shield into the Englishman's helm with a sickening crunch. As the man reeled, James gave him a vicious blow with the flat of his sword and freed a foot to kick him in the side and knock him from the saddle. The Englishman was on the ground, rolling out from under his horse's stamping hooves as James drew up, his black snorting and dancing. "Yield or die."

The man rolled onto his back. "I yield, my lord." He dropped his sword from his hand.

When James turned his horse in a circle, the battle, such as it was, was ending. He saw Symon dismount at the edge of the bridge with a kneeling priest at sword point. The archbishop's horse was heaving its way up the far bank of the Swale. As the archbishop galloped away, a friar crawled out of the water and knelt heaving. But the water of the river was solid with white—the white of priests' and friars' robes floating in deep water, drowned in escaping their fool enterprise. Here and there the pall of white was broken by a splotch of color from a burgess who had died with them. Wisps of smoke crawled over them like worms.

The sound of hooves coming up from behind him made him turn. Thomas reined up, shaking his head. "The mayor wouldn't surrender. Made me kill him. Damn, what a day!"

James scowled down at the prisoner he'd taken—some member of the king's court from the look of him. At least his ransom should be profitable. "The best prisoners got away, too. But if this doesn't bring Edward and Lancaster on the run, I'll surrender my spurs."

"Which of us has to describe it to the king?" Thomas turned his head to gaze at the mass of floating bodies and the scattered, bloody corpses on the field. "How many do you suppose drowned?"

"The Chapter of Myton." James snorted a pained laugh. "We need to be sure that Edward and Lancaster are on their way, and we'll swing west to make for home. In the meantime, by the merciful God, have our men fish them out and see if any still live—and claim any treasures they have on them for the king. Mayhap we should roll for the doubtful honor of telling him this tale."

Randolph shook his head.

CHAPTER 15

Dunfermline Palace, Fife, Scotland

It could not truly have been the most weary three months of his life, James was sure. But the snow that swirled and blew into his face from the drear ravine of Pittendreich as they rode up the palace hill seemed colder than he'd ever known, and his body more worn. A gloom of clouds covered the sun and the woods were coated with ice. White flakes speckled his horse's black mane, and behind him, he heard one of their honor guards coughing. James shook himself out of his lethargy as the king turned his horse to ride beside them. "How did you fare? You were forced to kill fewer clerics this time, I pray."

"We killed none, sire," Thomas Randolph said. "There were few men we killed of any sort as they did not resist us."

"We carried out your commands most particularly." James knew his tone was sour, but he couldn't help that. "We burnt the whole of Gilsland, except the grain we sent back. We slaughtered the cattle because they carried the murrain.

Fired the houses, the barns. We marched as far as Borough under Stanemoor in Westmoreland, burning as we went, and laid all to waste. Then we passed through Cumbria still burning. We raided Holm Cultram Abbey, took all the beans and grains from the storehouses, sparing only the abbey itself, and returned home."

The Bruce was silent for a moment. "Are you unwell, Jamie?"

Startled, James turned from staring ahead. The king was examining him oddly. "Pardon, my liege. I'm weary… Only weary. Of fire and smoke and ash and laying waste and too many weeks in the saddle." He shook his head and managed a wry chuckle. "Once I would not have felt so. I fear I'm getting old."

"He's been prickly as a blackthorn bush for the past weeks," Randolph said as they rode into the palace bailey yard.

The king was silent as he swung from the saddle. He stood gauging James, frowning, his eyes narrowed. "I put much upon you, James. I always have. Do you think I don't know that?"

"Forgive me. You know I'm your man. I remember my oath. In life or in death… or so weary I feel I could die of it." James slid from the saddle, too tired to worry if it showed. He tossed his reins to a stable boy and turned to the king, forcing a smile. "I need to rest and to see my son." He might hope to see Marioun as well though. The sight of her face made him remember why he did this. "That's all. Whatever you ask of me, it's yours." If he hoped the king might not ask anything of him for a while and that Marioun might be glad to see him, that was his own affair and not to be mentioned.

"Good," Thomas said with one of his half-smiles. "Then you'll stop chopping my head off at every word I say."

James craned his neck to look at the slate sky and blacker

clouds moving in from the sea. But they'd be dry soon with wine warming their bellies. A wry chuckle worked its way out of his chest. "As though you gave any notice of my foul temper, my lord earl."

"Aye, but it's not like you," Randolph said as a guard threw open the door. Sir Symon was ordering the men to the stables with the mounts and Archibald was grumbling as he followed his brother inside.

James strode into the Great Hall covered in the dirt of the road and unshaven for days, past tapestries of feasting and great hunts into ease and laughter. High above, halfway to the vaulted ceiling, two minstrels strummed lutes in the gallery. A servant placed a flagon on wine of a long table at the side of the room. Elayne talked with Lady Elizabeth and Marioun before a roaring fire in the wide hearth that gave off a pleasant scent of pine as a retainer knelt to pile on more logs. Andrew de Moray, lean and blond and so like James's memory of his father it made him blink, stood laughing with one of the king's sisters.

Roger de Mowbray swaggered to meet them at the door. "I see you found them, Your Grace."

Elayne turned and a frozen smile moved over her face. "My lord husband, welcome back. Praise God you are safe."

"You look well, my lady." James brushed by Mowbray to cross the room and leaned down to buss her cheek. Over her shoulder he saw color rush up from Marioun's neck and stain her cheeks as she swept him a curtsy.

Behind him, he heard Christina de Bruce greeting her nephew, but he couldn't tear his gaze from Marioun. He took her hand and kissed it as she rose. "Sir James, we've missed you, so little have you been here these past months," she said.

Andrew joined them with Lady Christina's hand on his arm. "A welcome addition to the court. I'm pleased that you're safely returned."

"We were in little danger." James smiled at Marioun before he tore his gaze away and smiled at Andrew. "But it's welcome to see something more pleasing than the smoke of burning villages and men in filthy armor."

"You'll find few and few in filthy armor here," Christina said. "Especially Sir Andrew who wears finer clothes than any woman in the court."

It was true that Andrew was finely clad. James knew that the Moray's of Petty had long been as rich as Croesus, though much had been lost in the war with the king of England's special enmity for the family. But Andrew was in blue velvet with stars embroidered in silver thread on his tunic and a finely worked silver belt held his dagger. "I wear armor at need," Andrew said with a laugh. "When there's no need, I prefer wearing my best."

Lady Christina laughed at him. "Gilded armor even finer than the king's is what you wear to fight in."

"Mayhap he means that we women of the court do not look our best and should spend more gold on our clothes," Marioun said with a smiling glance at Moray.

Lady Christina tilted her head and pursed her lips. "Why that is an excellent thought. I believe I shall take his advice." She was still a handsome woman though she had lines deeply scored about her eyes and gray streaked her blonde hair.

The king took his sister's hand, grinning. "I beg you do not give her such ideas. My sister is already trial enough upon my purse."

"You'd think a king would speak truly. Why I hardly spend any merks at all," she replied with a perfectly straight face, although she ran her hand down her silk gown.

"Moreover, any man I propose for her to marry, she turns up her nose and refuses. What am I to do with such a sister?"

"Let me do as I please, Your Grace, though I still say I'm little trial upon your purse. You should thank me. "

Thomas was laughing, and even Elayne managed a smile as the king shook with laugher and wiped his cheeks. Marioun's lips twitched in a droll smile.

Christina made a fluttering sound with her lips. "Why only last week I refused a merchant who offered a sumptuous—"

She was interrupted by the footsteps of two men and the chamberlain bowing. "Your Grace's pardon," the man said, "but there is a friar with a letter from Bishop Lamberton. He says the message is urgent and insists he must put it in your hands."

The chamberlain bowed and stepped aside for the brown-robed friar, sturdy and broad of face with a tonsured head. The Bruce greeted him pleasantly and held his hand out for the letter. The chamberlain led the man away to the kitchen for ale and a meal as the king broke the seal of the bishop of St. Andrew with his thumb.

Holy St. Bride, James thought, *let it not be bad news.*

Within was another letter. The king read the outer, frowning and then he unfolded the second. He stared at the letter, seemed to read it once more, and barked a triumphant laugh. "They want a truce. Clerics brought letters from Edward for Lamberton to forward to me. They're asking for a truce for two years."

"A truce?" James stared at the king. "A truce…"

"Isn't that what the Pope asked for?" Andrew asked, and Mowbray's eyebrows climbed.

"Before we took Berwick, aye. Then such a truce would have been a disaster. Now we hold all of Scotland, and Edward is admitting defeat—for now. It's not the peacetable, but it gives us time, time we sorely need."

Thomas Randolph was nodding thoughtfully. "Time for letters to the Pope, it seems to me."

"Two years." Mowbray crossed his arms, looking thoughtful. "There is much that might be done in that time and much that might be changed."

James stared at the man. Why would Mowbray speak of changes? James had no interest in changes except to rebuild their strength and to enjoy being at peace—for the first time in his life.

* * *

When James stepped out of the tower doorway onto the snow-covered parapet walk, two small figures wrapped in thick cloaks darted ahead of him, one limping behind the other. William giggled and pressed his hand to his mouth. James smiled. What were the lads up to? There was a command shouted from below. The two paused to watch drilling in the bailey yard. In boiled leather and mail, squires grunted and cursed as they swung staves and wooden swords under the severe gaze of Sir John Thomson.

William shrugged and crouched dashed to the wall of the next tower. He threw himself flat and motioned his cousin down. Young Robert squirmed onto his stomach, and James heard a giggle before William shushed him.

Mischief. That was clear. James softly clicked his tongue to his teeth. He'd told William to take care of Robert, not to teach him how to find trouble. He should put a stop to whatever to do they were about, but instead he crossed his arms and leaned against the icy stone of the tower doorway and ruffled Mac Ailpín's ears as the deerhound sat at his feet. A smile twitched his lips. The holy God knew he'd done worse, poaching the French king's forest, than any trouble they could find.

William waited until the guard on the next parapet marched in the opposite direction. He jumped up and fumbled at his lacings as his cousin was still pushing himself to his feet. He was no sooner unlaced than James was striding toward the two. A second yellow stream splattered on the yard below.

William stared down as he pissed and yelped in surprise when his father grabbed his arm. John Thomson was shouting, "You imps from Hell!"

James shook both boys by the arm. "Lace yourselves," he ordered as he desperately swallowed a grin.

"I thought it would freeze. I wanted yellow icicles," William said, blinking up with a look of practiced innocence. "Icicles make good spears."

"Lace yourselves, I said." James shook them again, although it wasn't a hard shake if he were to admit the truth. They were both lacing as fast as they could. "I arrive and seek my son to find him acting a villein. You'll both make your apologies to Sir John for pissing nearly in his face." He gave them a push on the napes of their necks. Holy Mary, he dare not laugh. Yellow icicles...

He followed the two as they trudged dolefully down the stairs. In the yard, one of the squires sniggered but bit his lip when Sir John gave him a sharp look. "That will be all," Sir John told the score of squires he was training. "This afternoon you'll work at the quintain. Any one of you that eats dirt will spend the rest of the day cleaning tack in the stable."

As the squires hurried through the yard to the armory, James said, "You have something to tell Sir John."

William flicked his father a glance, and James frowned at him. "I'm sorry, Sir John." There was a quiver in the middle, but no tears.

James nodded and squeezed his shoulder as he nudged the king's grandson. "Robert."

The lad echoed his cousin, looking stubborn, just like the king did at times. James ruffled his hair.

"They have spirit," Sir John said crossing his arms over his barrel chest. "But a daily birching would not be amiss to teach discipline."

William's mouth had dropped open, and he stepped behind his father's hound for protection.

"I'll think on it," James said in a serious tone. He prodded both lads toward a side door and waited until they were out of hearing of the irate master at arms. "I suppose you might still have the gifts that I brought, though I'm sure neither of you deserves them."

"Truly, my lord?" Robert asked, beaming up hopefully. "Gifts?"

"Your lord father gave me something to bring you as he cannot leave his duties."

"Me too?" William asked in a forlorn voice. "Please..."

The lads were being pampered by the women beyond reason, James thought, as he shook his head. William's wheedling was too practiced. Not that he'd deny the lad a gift —the look of him, so like James's own father made him dote upon the lad himself. But he would speak with the king. Both were too young for taking up duties as pages, yet mayhap it should be considered. They had heavy duties to grow into and sooner than anyone would want. "Aye, you may have it." The wooden knights with their swords that worked by a lever might interest them enough to reduce the mischief— for a few days. He chuckled. "Come, you imps. They're in my chambers."

He took each lad's hand and slowed his step to Robert's pace, but the lad's limp did not seem to reduce his speed when it came to finding trouble.

* * *

It was too seldom that he drank uisge beatha, James decided, as his listed and caught himself on the wall. Robbie snorted with laughter. "I always could drink you under the table."

James straightened and gave Robbie a dignified look. "I am not under the table." He grinned. "Albeit my legs don't want to cooperate in walking straight."

They both laughed and James leaned back against the wall. When Robbie belched, they both roared. James wiped his cheeks with the heel of his hand. It had been a better night than James could remember having in many a year. Peace. He hadn't known it could be such a joy. They'd drunk deeply and talked of the battles they'd won and ignored the ones that they'd lost. "Do you need a hand up those stairs?" Robbie asked him. "It would be a shame to fall and break your neck when we're not fighting for once."

"No, go find that lady wife of yours though she may kick you out of her bed—coming to her stinking of drink."

Robbie waggled his eyebrows, no mean feat in his condition, James thought. "She is not so particular how I come to her as long as I do. And..." Robbie's fond smile sat oddly on such a war-worn face. "I'm happy to go to her, whatever my state."

"Pah! You're getting to be a sentimental old man." James gave him a shove toward the corridor. "I'm fine to reach my chamber without you playing nursemaid."

"There are worse things than living to be an old man, Jamie." He punched James's arm and turned to swagger away, listing into the wall and then straightening. James smiled, shook his head and rubbed his stinging arm. Getting to be a sentimental old man or not, when Robbie gave you a thump, you felt it. And there were worse things indeed than living long enough to have peace. James had gone three steps up the narrow stairway when someone whispered, "Sir James."

A skinny, red-haired lad in the livery of a king's squire motioned to him as he hugged the wall, one of the Campbells, Lochloinn by name James thought. "My lord, I come from a certain lady with a message." Eyes glittering with delight at the intrigue, Lochloinn held out a folded and sealed letter.

James took it and, bemused, watched the youngster tip-toe away before he used his thumb to slit the seal. It was hastily written, or perhaps the lady did not have a fair hand, but James smiled, intrigued. He knew the place she had set for a meeting, a bower outside the walls where in summer a noble might have a quiet meal. Marioun had only asked him for a few moments to speak privily, but he was never for a moment alone in her company. Even that day in the garden they had not been truly alone.

If he'd had a taste too much of uisge beatha, that no longer mattered. He took the stairs two at a time, whisked on his fur cloak, and closed the door quietly behind him so as not to waken his snoring squire. She'd asked for discretion, so he took the winding back stairway and went through the kitchen yard, past the well and dark outbuildings. At the postern gate, a guard nodded to him as he passed, breath fogging in the icy air. He strode through a pleasure garden where the snow-covered bushes made strange white shapes in the flickering moonlight. A building loomed before him and a shape in the doorway, outlined by the light of a fire.

"My lord," she whispered.

He took her hands, icy in the chill night, and closed the door behind them. "My lady." He smiled. "No need to whisper, I think. No one is near and the palace was silent. You have nothing to fear."

She was looking intently at his chest. "Don't I? Alone with you here." She gave a trembling laugh. "I think I may have much to fear even though it's my own fault."

"From me? Marioun—" James chafed her hands between his to warm them. "You're freezing. Come closer to the fire."

He led her nearer to the flames on the small hearth. He'd thought so many times of being alone with her like this, dreamed of sending her such a note. But it was she who had a warrior's courage to do what he'd only dreamt of. For how long had the thought of her made his heart try to beat its way out of his chest? Courage, he thought, was easy in battle. Not so much so in matters of love.

She pulled her hands free and held them toward the fire. He felt her shivering even though the room was no longer so cold. She shook her head. "I never thought I'd play the wanton, not for anyone."

He grasped her chin and turned her head to make her look at him. "You're no wanton. I know that." When she didn't try to turn away, he rubbed his thumb along her soft cheek. "We've neither of us had a choice..." He paused, swallowed, and started again. "Marioun, I've few soft words for wooing. I'm better at battle than courting, but since that day in the garden I've watched you."

He bent to kiss her, but she turned her head, so he pressed his lips to her cheek, not letting her go.

"Why? The Douglas—the great friend of the king—you can have any woman you want."

He captured her mouth for a soft kiss. "They wouldn't be you, Marioun. Kind, gentle, beautiful..." He kissed her again and she opened her lips for him so sweetly.

But when he released her mouth, she turned her face away to press it into his shoulder. "But I need more than that you—want me. I want… more."

"You think that I don't, as well? Marioun. I want everything there is. I've loved you. I don't know how long, your beauty, your sweetness, but what we have is only this. Would I could change it." He kissed her hair and her ear and her cheek.

"Love? Truly?" She pushed back from him to look up into

his face in the dancing firelight. "I know that men want me. My husband did. Other men. And you. But love?"

"Dear God, Marioun, my love for you has kept me alive. Lust? For that, there are others. A coin in the street takes care of lust. You don't want to know, but I'm no better than most men." He gave a wry laugh. "Worse than many, but what love I have left in me. That is for you."

She slid her arms around his neck as he pulled her gently to him.

"James... Sweet God..."

He bent to kiss her and slowly pushed her cloak from her shoulders and shrugged off his own. His mouth and his tongue claiming hers, she tasted of wine and berries, and her fingers trembled as they threaded through his hair. He tugged at her gown and was on his knees tasting her soft breast, trailing kisses over her belly, as she bent over him and pressed her lips into his hair. She was on her knees, and he knew not how or when. He was lost in her, but their cloaks were warm and soft to receive them. His hands glided along her sides, a sweet smoothness.

A million sparks lit his senses on fire all at once, his shudders, her fingertips on his back, the sound that she made when he licked the hollow of her neck. He burned at her touch. It sent his senses soaring, wild, tethered only by her arms around him, by her lips murmuring his name to guide him back.

CHAPTER 16

MARCH 1320

Newbattle Abbey, Near Edinburgh, Scotland

The king's chair scraped as he rose, his face knotted with anger. James leapt to his feet as the others around the long refectory table stood. The king furiously paced past Bishop Lamberton, Bishop Sinclair, Bishop Moray and Bishop Cheyne, as well as his chancellor and a half score of noblemen. He strode back, threw himself into the chair, and slammed a fist down upon the table. "This is beyond enduring. Demanding the presence of our bishops in Avignon and threatening interdict on the entire kingdom. Now they address the papal letter to 'Robert de Bruce, governing the kingdom of Scotland'! At least in the letters of two years ago, the Pope admitted I was *acting* as king. That is..." He sputtered to a halt, shaking his head. "It is not to be borne."

"And yet, we do bear it," Thomas Randolph put in to receive a glare from his uncle.

"We must respond, Your Grace." Abbot Bernard laid his

knitted hands atop several parchments covered with writing. "He must be made to see that he is hearing only lies and calumnies from the English."

"Sire," Lamberton said softly. "You've borne this burden, and it weighs on you. We all see that. But now with this truce is the time to act. We shall have our voices heard in Avignon." Lamberton tugged on the crucifix that hung on a chain about his neck as he often did when he was thoughtful. "Winning messages past the English will be a challenge in itself. And they must be carried by someone we could trust and who would be well received by the Pope. I await word from France. If the French king agrees to it, if any man can reach Avignon with letters and be well received, it is Odard de Maubisson. But whether the French king will agree? I have hopes that he will. Sir Odard was eager for the commission."

"Wait," James held up a hand. "Before we talk of *sending* letters, should we not have such letters? Or have a plan for them?"

Abbot Bernard breathed a soft laugh through his nose. "Lord Douglas, such letters have been written. Three: one to be sent by King Robert, one from the bishops, and one from all the community of the realm of Scotland to be signed by the nobility and leading freeholders of the land."

James raised an eyebrow as Abbot Bernard shuffled briefly through his documents and slid a parchment toward him, covered with writing in a cleric's script. He looked at it and twitched a wry smile. "My Latin is not so good as all that."

Lamberton reached across James for the letter. "I'll translate the main portions for you. We've discussed it much in the writing, so parts I can abridge. The letter begins with the history of the Picts and Scots and how Lord Robert came to be king. It then lists the perfidies of Edward Longshanks in betraying our trust and his sworn word and the suffering, bloodshed, and degradation our poor nation has endured at English hands."

The bishop rose and went to the window, tilting the letter to catch the sunlight. "From there, it comes to the main part:

But from these countless evils we have been set free, by the help of him who though he afflicts yet heals and restores, by our most tireless prince, king and lord Robert. He, that his people and heritage might be delivered out of the hands of our enemies, met toil and fatigue, hunger and peril, like another Maccabaeus or Joshua, and bore them cheerfully. Him too, divine providence, his right of succession according to our laws and customs, and assent of us all have made our prince and king. To him, as to the man by whom salvation has been wrought unto our people, we are bound both by law and by his merits that our freedom may be maintained, and by him, come what may, we mean to stand.

Yet if he should give up what he has begun, and agree to make us and our kingdom subject to the king of England or the English, we should exert ourselves at once to drive him out as our enemy and a subverter of his own rights and ours and make some other man who was well able to defend us our king, for, as long as but one hundred of us remain alive, never will we on any conditions be brought under English rule.

The bishop paused for a long look at the listening men before he continued reading.

It is in truth not for glory, not riches, nor honors that we fight, but for freedom—for that alone, which no honest man gives up but with life itself."

The room was silent. James swallowed and blinked back an odd sting behind his eyes.

Mowbray eyed Lamberton with a smile that seemed almost insolent. "Moving words, your excellency. Such a letter might be most timely to the Holy Father."

Strangely put, James thought. He cleared his throat. "It would be an honor beyond words to put my seal to it."

"Some of those words indeed will be well-timed in Avignon." From across the table, William de Soules offered his hand to James who had to repress a shudder at the cool, moist grasp. "I will join in signing it most gladly."

"And for me," Randolph said.

Robbie Boyd was nodding vigorously. "And I."

"I will." "And I." The agreement echoed around the table.

"All the earls are needed to put their name and seal to it, and as many barons as we can gather. I have sent for certain leading freeholders so that the Pope will know it is all of Scotland that speaks." Abbot Bernard leaned back, smiling with satisfaction. "We'll need Scots to travel with Sir Odard to Avignon. Master Alexander Kinninmonth had much influence in drafting the letters and…"

James sighed. It was never as simple as merely agreeing to a thing. The clerics always insisted it must be discussed—at length. His mind wandered to the king's agreement that both William and young Robert should begin their service as pages in the summer. There was yet to be made the decision of whom they should serve. In the court, he wondered if they would be doted upon too much by the ladies. He would rather the lads served him, but did he truly have time to begin a household of pages when they'd soon be once more be at war? If there were some way…

He blinked when Abbot Bernard said, "Do you agree, Sir James?"

With a bland smile, James replied, "Of course." He wondered what he'd agreed to. No doubt it was something the bishops and abbot had planned. But the meeting was over. The king walked away, talking with Abbot Bernard. James nodded to the others and made for the door. At least this Privy Council had been less tedious than most. Words echoed in his mind like a clarion: *for, as long as but one hundred of us remain alive, never will we on any conditions be brought under English rule...*

CHAPTER 17

JULY 1320

Dunfermline Palace, Fife, Scotland

It was full night outside the tall, arched windows. Torches gleamed against the polished metal of the sconces, filling the Great Hall with light. James sat on the raised platform at the high table beside Andrew de Moray a few places to the right of the king and queen. Squires in livery were filling the wine cups. Thomas Randolph and his wife and Maol of Lennox were next to the king. The Great Hall of the palace was rich with the smell of venison stewed with red wine, rich spices, and fresh baked bread.

"Where is the music? Let it begin," the king called to the gallery filled with pipers and harpists and drummers. A piper took up a tune.

To James's side, William was looking a little doubtful as he offered a basin, his third day serving as a page. James gave him an encouraging nod and held out his hands. One of the squires, Lochloinn, poured warmed water from a silver ewer, a job a page wouldn't be trusted with. But his son held the basin steady below to catch the spill. "Well done," James whispered, and William smiled as another page dried James's hands.

Marioun smiled at James when he extended his cup to her. Across the long room, Elayne tilted her chin and gave them a frosty look. James just smiled. What point was there in incensing her further? Since she did not want him in her bed, why should she be wroth when he went to another, he wondered. She turned her head to smile fondly at the squire who served her, and James shook his head.

The chamberlain stepped past the screen and announced, "Your Grace, Sir Muireadhach of Menteith begs to be allowed to approach." Menteith's appearance was planned, of course. He'd been in England since long before his father's death in a dungeon there. If he was to make his peace with the king, he was expected to make a show of it and rightfully so. Young as he was, perhaps he might be forgiven his tardy return, though James would want to see proof of his loyalty first.

James watched closely as Menteith strode through the tables. He was the picture of a bluff knight: a square, plain face, dark hair, a heavy build good for wielding weapons, but James would not make any bets that he was good with wielding his wits. It was over quickly, the knight kneeling and begging to be taken into the king's peace and grace and the king accepting him. More had done the same act than James could count.

Once the knight took his place at a lower table, an old man brought in his dancing bear. After, a minstrel in the gallery sang some outrageous ditty and the king, in high good humor, called him down. He tossed the handsome, lanky youth a coin.

"God's blessings upon you, Your Grace." The minstrel gave a deep bow, but he looked at the guests with a bold look.

"Give us the blessings of more music, lad." The king chuckled. "I like your songs. Amuse my guests with them."

The lad grinned. "I'll sing something to do you honor. Shall I sing a lay of a brave knight?" When the king waved permission, he drew a plaintive note from his harp.

As I was walking all alone,
I heard twa corbies makin' a moan;
The one unto the other say, oh,
"Where shall we go and dine the-day? Oh,
Where shall we dine the-day?"
In beyond yon old turf dyke,
I wot there lies a new slain knight;
And none do ken that he lies there, oh,
But his hawk, his hound and his lady fair, oh,
His hawk, his hound and his lady fair.
His hound is to the hunting gone,
His hawk to fetch the wild-fowl home,
His lady's taken another mate, oh,
So we may make our dinner sweet, oh,

The king threw his head back and roared with laughter. James made a face. Across the hall, Mowbray gave a sardonic smile and bowed. James lifted his goblet to the man and wondered what the smile might mean.

Ye'll sit on his white neck-bone,
And I'll pick out his bonny blue eye;
Wi' one lock o' his golden hair
We'll thatch our nest when it grows bare, oh,
Many a one for him makes moan,
But none shall ken where he is gone;
O'er his white bones, when they are bare, oh,
The wind shall blow for evermair.
The wind shall blow for evermair.

James shuddered. The man was singing something that resembled too much his own likely death. There was a silent pause, but when the king tossed the minstrel another coin, shouting his approval, the hall joined in, laughing and applauding.

"I like me a bold minstrel with the grit to sing more than pap. I'd take you into my court, but I have no need for another. Now my good Sir James has no minstrel in his household, I'm told. He'll take you on." The Bruce bared his teeth in a wolfish grin and raised his cup to James. "Will you not, Sir James."

And it was clearly no question, so James bowed to the inevitable. He dug a coin from his purse without looking to see what it was and tossed it to the smirking youth who caught it mid-air. "My household has more use for swords than harps, Your Grace, but he is welcome in it." To his chagrin, the sour tone was met with waves of laughter, except for Elayne who looked through him as though he were not even there. James frowned at his new minstrel. "Though I suggest never singing that particular lay for me."

The king laughed at him again as the chamberlain waved in two stilt-walkers each juggling a half dozen colored balls. James shook his head, watching after the new member of his household as he slipped from the hall. There was no news from the ship carrying their letters to the Pope at Avignon, was of more interest than adding a damned minstrel to his household. It was too soon, he knew. Would they hear while the truce yet held?

James drained his cup as the server put before him a pastry wafting a scent of partridge and onions. Where was Lochloinn with his wine? He toyed for a moment with the pastry, plunging his knife into its center and letting out a gust of fragrant steam. He offered Marioun a bit of the tender meat from the point of his knife, and she took it delicately between her fingers to nibble.

The pipers and drummers had taken up a loud piece, and

the guests raised their voices to a shout to be heard. And James needed more wine. The noise was crashing like a wave in the crowded hall; his head was beginning to throb in time with it.

He held up his empty cup and turned. A squire at the king's table did not leave a guest's cup empty. As he looked over his shoulder, there was a sound of retching and gagging. James shoved back his chair. Lochloinn clutched a silver flagon to his chest, slopping wine down his chest like blood and gasping.

Marioun stood up. "What's wrong with him? Help him."

James grabbed the flagon from his arms and pounded his back. "He's choking." Lochloinn tried to say something, but only a gabbling sound came out. James thrust the flagon into Marioun's hands and grabbed the lad as his legs collapsed under him. His body was cold as a snowdrift in the warm hall.

The king stood as well. "Master Ingrim!" He shouted for his physician at one of the lower tables.

James jerked loose the neck of the lad's tunic and lowered him to the floor. What should he do for him? He'd never seen anything like this. Lochloinn's bowels loosened, and a brown puddle spread beneath him. Marioun made a choking sound as the stench spread.

He had never seen such a sickness. He looked up as Master Ingram shuffled toward them and pushed him aside. He knelt by the lad who lay limp, his eyes darting frantically. Drool rolled from the side of his mouth. Sweat beaded and rolled down his face as he made a horrible sucking sound. His body arched off the floor.

"God in heaven..." The physician looked up. "Touch no more of the food or drink!" He grabbed James's arm. "See that no one touches the food."

He has been poisoned, James realized. He jumped to his feet.

"Take the king out of here!" He spun to find Gilbert de la Haye. "Gilbert! OUT!" Against all courtesy, Gilbert grabbed the king's arm and shoved him toward the doorway behind the dais. For a moment, the king stood stubborn, but then he looked at Lady Elizabeth and hoisted her before him to safety. Marioun was still holding the flagon as she backed away. James snatched it from her hands. "Go," James told her. "There's nothing you can do here. Go!" She whirled and fled.

Chaos raged through the room as most rushed for the door, but a few shoved their way forward to see what was happening. Muireadhach of Menteith pushed his way through, and stood staring. The man's mouth opened and closed as the color drained from his face. James watched Menteith for a moment until the knight turned and elbowed his way into the press.

James spotted the Keith and shouted for him. "Have the guards clear the hall."

The Keith bellowed for the guards and shoved guests for the doors, not seeming to care whom he was pushing. People were fleeing, gagging, white-faced. At last, the doors slammed closed.

Lochloinn was making wet, choking sounds, his eyes wide and rolling with terror. His body jerked and trembled and his feet hammered upon the floor. Master Ingram pressed a spoon down the lad's throat, but after a time he went still.

Master Ingram held fingers to the lad's neck for a moment, shook his head, and stood, grim-faced. They stared at each other. "Merciful St. Bride," James whispered.

"What did he eat? Drink?"

"He shouldn't have done either. He was at his duties, but squires..." James looked down at the flagon he'd taken from the squire. "Most likely he sneaked a taste of some dish or a cup of wine. He was serving this." He felt the hair on the back of his neck prickle. "If it was poisoned, surely it wouldn't have been only him."

"If the poison was slipped into only one flagon..." The slender, gray-haired physician raised his eyebrows. "He was serving this to you, my lord?"

James nodded, feeling as though the flagon of wine in his hands had turned into a viper. He looked at the poor dead lad still on the floor. What a horrible death—in the king's own household.

Master Ingram took the flagon and sniffed it. "The way he died, it was much like he was dosed with monkshood. A large dose kills fast." He dipped just the tip of his finger into the wine and then rubbed his fingers together. He touched the tip of his tongue to the dampness. Then he nodded. "The numbness of monkshood is there. It is strongly dosed. I'll test it on an animal... But, yes. I fear he was poisoned."

James slowly sank into his chair, pressing his hand to his mouth. Muireadhach of Menteith had a strange look on his face, but surely they all did. Such a thing would leave anyone shocked, even a more seasoned knight than Muireadhach. It had to have been someone who could get at the flagons, yet that might be anyone's servant—even the newcomer? The two men looked for a long moment at the pitiful body stretched out on the floor.

James stood. "His body must be tended. And we must speak with the king."

* * *

James felt a bit green when he looked at the goblet of wine and thrust it away.

The Bruce thrust his hand through his hair. "My taster sampled it, Jamie."

James felt chilled though he thought it was more the idea

of poison than the cool of the night. The Privy Chamber was round and formed the first floor of the East Tower, a thick structure built into the wall of the palace where it overlooked the ravine of Pittendreich. Banners covered the walls, and there was a round shield and crossed axes above the hearth. He went to hold his hands out to the small fire. "Why would someone try to poison me? It makes no sense. If I were gone, another lord would just take my place."

"Mayhap it was meant for the king," Thomas Randolph said thoughtfully.

"I questioned the squires." Abbot Bernard leaned forward, elbows on his knees, hands steepled. "They all agreed that the lad had asked to serve you, Sir James, and had bribed the others to leave you to him. But he wouldn't have poisoned himself."

"Does Muireadhach have a squire?" James asked.

The king raised his eyebrows. "You suspect him?"

"It's a small thing, but he looked—strange. He approached the lad as he was dying. Was white to the lips and had a look about his eyes…"

Thomas made a noise in his throat that was almost a laugh. "I may have had a strange look as well."

James nodded slowly. "As I may have, but the look on his face nags at me. His look was almost… knowing? Aye, I thought I saw knowing in his face. And fear."

"But if he has a squire, he was not serving at the table," Abbot Bernard said. "I spoke with them all. There was so much bustle and to-do that no one noticed if someone touched the ewers, but I believe they would have noticed a stranger moving about."

"How could they have known if I would be served from that one ewer? I served too many meals as a squire to think that a good scheme. That would be a mad way to try to kill someone. It could too easily go wrong."

"As it did," Thomas put in. "Unless we think it was meant for poor Lochloinn."

The Bruce leaned back in his chair and the firelight gleamed on his gold hair that was well streaked with gray. The firelight showed the deep lines about his eyes and his mouth. "So it is someone who didn't care if it went wrong. Or it was too important for them to try even if it might not work."

James strode fast around the room and back again, rubbing his neck. "I swear to you that Muireadhach knows something about the affair. If he is not guilty, he knows something." He turned and stood spread-legged as though for battle. "Bring him here. I want to see his face when I press him with it."

The king stared into his face for a moment and nodded. "Very well. I agree that it is suspicious that he returns the very day of such a foul murder." He looked at the chancellor. "Have him brought before us."

James breathed a soft laugh as he picked up his wine cup. He gave it a faintly suspicious look and made himself drink. It went down warm and helped to calm the riot of horror and anger in his belly. Thomas was grinning at him. James shook his head. "You'd not be eager to drink either, my lord, if there'd been such a devil's brew in your wine."

"No." Thomas's face sobered and when he shook his head it was accompanied by a shudder. "I will never forget the look... I've killed many a man in battle, but I pray I never again see such a death. And of a young squire."

James downed the wine and stared into the fire. As Abbot Bernard went out the door to have the guards seize Sir Muireadhach, James watched the leaping flames, wondering. What would have been gained by his death? For whom?

The Abbot took his time about it or perhaps Muiread-hach was hard to find. An hour had passed by the time a guard knocked and threw open the door for the robe-clad abbot and the scowling knight.

"Your Grace," the guard said, "you wish to see Sir Muireadhach?"

"I do." The king waved the man away. "You're dismissed."

Muireadhach bowed. "Your Grace, guards were not needed if you wished my presence."

"And yet you were not easy to find," Abbot Bernard said as he took a seat. "In fact, I found you returning from the bailey yard."

"I wished to speak to—to a member of the court. I went seeking him." Menteith flicked his open hands to the side. "I am here. I was not in hiding."

James walked to look straight into the man's face. His eyes met James's gaze for a moment but flickered to the side. He shifted his weight. James nodded slowly. "You killed him. Or you had him killed."

"No!" Menteith took a step back. "He was poisoned? That's it. It must have been. I thought..." He looked at the king. "I swear by the Blessed Virgin and all the saints. No. I wouldn't even know how to do such a thing."

James refilled his wine goblet and took a sip. The others watched him, but Menteith still had his eyes fixed on the king. "It could be that you only know who did." James tilted his head and looked the man up and down. He could believe that he wouldn't know what poison to use though even James had heard of monkshood. And Menteith's squire would not have found it easy to slip something into an ewer. So... "Who was it whom you were seeking tonight? And why —so late at night and after such a dreadful event?"

"Dear God," Menteith muttered. He closed his eyes for a moment, his sunburnt face pale. "Your Grace, it may be I should have told you when I first came to your peace—that he had written to me whilst I was in England. He said that

Scots were ready for a new king, one with a better claim to the throne."

Robert the Bruce tilted his chin at a haughty angle. "A new king... So with this treachery in your mind you took your oath and accepted my peace."

James clamped his hand into a fist as Gilbert de la Haye stepped to the king's side. Only Haye as Lord High Constable carried a sword and the hand on it was white with its tight grip.

"No! I meant my oath. I'd had enough and more than enough of the English since my father died in one of their dungeons. I replied to his letter. Told him..."

"Who!" James exclaimed. "If the plot wasn't yours, whose was it? We'll have a name."

"Roger de Mowbray. He then seemed to withdraw what he had written and claimed he was merely testing my loyalty." Menteith turned to face James. "I don't know that he was the murderer, but when I saw that tonight—I was afraid of what I might know. Of what I was thinking. I went to find him, and he and his squires were gone."

James growled deep in his throat. "Damn you, man. You take your time to tell such a tale when we should already be seeking him."

The king nodded to Gilbert who ran for the door, shouting for the guards to search for Mowbray. The door slammed behind him and in the corridors was the sound of thudding feet of running guards as they scattered for the hunt.

James frowned. "Then the poison must have been meant for the king, though..." He shook his head. "I don't see how."

"I don't think so, Douglas," Thomas Randolph said. He looked at the goblet in his hand and shuddered. He sat it down. "Think on it. If they mean to kill the king, they must kill you first. Me, as well. The Stewart. We would all die before we accepted a usurper. He'd have to go through us to reach the king, and Mowbray knows it. He would not meet us in battle, but poison or a dirk in the night may kill the hardiest knight. Easier to kill the king once we were out of the way—or at least some of us."

James crossed his arms and examined Menteith. "What else did Mowbray say in these letters? Who else did he name? I can't believe he acted alone. And how was the king to be changed? Who did they mean to crown?"

"Soules. He named Soules. But they gave me no details. They certainly did not mention murder." He looked from one to the other. "I swear it, my lords. I assumed they were thinking of Balliol. Who else could it be? But it seemed only talk when he said that it was merely pretense."

The king slammed a fist down on the arm of his chair. "Soules is in Berwick, governor there, holding the castle. My lord warden, how many men do you have with you?"

"Only twenty, sire," James said. The king was right. Guarding Berwick and putting this down was his duty as Lord Warden of the Marches—and his craving, as well. The betrayal was like acid in his belly.

"You'll need more so take two hundred of my men. At first light, you'll ride. You seize him and anyone with him."

The door was flung open with a crash and a thrashing woman, her silk gown awry, was held by the arms by a panting Gilbert de la Haye. James let his mouth drop open at the sight of the struggling Johanna, Countess of Stathearn. Gilbert pushed her ahead of him into the room. "I caught her in the bailey yard, ready to flee."

The king raised his eyebrows. "Riding so late at night, Johanna? Why so?"

She shook her long, gray-streaked hair out of her face and glared over her shoulder at Gilbert. At the king's nod, he released her. Her eyes widened when she saw Menteith. She darted looks all about the room. Her hands started shaking, and she clasped them before her. "It was nothing to do with me," she said, her voice thin with fear. "Mowbray and Soules came up with the plot with the English. They'd crown Edward de Balliol, and he'd give them wide lands. I only listened. I had nothing to do with..." She gave James a wild glance. "I had nothing to do with it, only listened. It was the two of them began it."

"Began it? There were others then," James said.

She shrugged. "David de Brechin, John de Logie, Gilbert de Malherbe, Walter de Barclay, and Patrick Graham were part of it. I was there when they talked. But I had no part in it."

"Merciful Jesu God! Brechin? I thought him an honorable man. A crusader." The Bruce jumped to his feet and strode furiously to stare into the fire. He turned. "If you had no part, why did you not reveal the plot? How long has this gone on?"

"Since... since before Mowbray returned from Ireland. I know there were letters and payments from the English." She threw herself down on her knees in front of the king. "Sire, mercy. I did you no harm. I never lifted a hand to harm anyone."

"Which is why you were fleeing," James said. He felt hollow at the extent of the treachery. "I say throw her in a dungeon where she belongs."

As she gaped up at James, the Bruce shook his head. "No, it's not fitting to put a woman in a dungeon. Gilbert, have her locked in a tower room with ample guards. Send a message to her son that I expect his attendance. I pray to God he had no part in this. I cannot believe it of him."

Gilbert grabbed her arm to pull her from the room. She dragged her feet and writhed. "I beg you..." But Gilbert wrestled her out the door, and it slammed behind him.

"Thomas, take your men and hunt down Mowbray," the

king said. "He can't have gone far. James, have them in Scone in two weeks hence. Hold them incommunicado until then. They'll be tried before parliament, so it must be called."

James was clasping and unclasping his hand. He wanted his sword in it and his men at his back. "Keep Gilbert by your side, sire. And taste nothing that another has not tried for you."

Randolph gave a sharp nod.

"I'll ride at dawn." After a quick bow, James dashed to gather the men he would need. By the light of dawn, he would be on the road for Berwick.

CHAPTER 18

TWO DAYS LATER

Berwick-Upon-Tweed

His banner whipped in the wind. It was near noon under a bright summer sun as he galloped through the Cowgate into Berwick-upon-Tweed. "Welcome, my lord," a guardsman called out to him, but James slashed his courser to a faster pace.

"Make way for Lord Douglas!" Richert shouted. "Make way! Make way for the Douglas!"

A woman jerked a barefoot girl in a ragged skirt out of their path. One of the horses barreled into a cart. It tipped its load of hay onto the cobbles. The man-at-arms cursed as his horse reared, but James kept going, his men thundering after. Barefoot, a throng of boys in an alley shouted and hooted as he galloped passed. A burgess in gaudy silk pressed his back against a wall, and a brindle dog ran after their horses, barking furiously. Then up the sloping road to the castle, his horse's hooves striking sparks from the cobblestones.

He bent over his horse's neck and slashed it. They had to

be within the castle before Soules knew he was in the city. Sweat dripped down his face, and his ribs as the courser surged its way up the long sloping road.

"It's the Douglas," a guardsman called as he reached the barbican. "Find Soules."

They were through the tunnel-entrance like thunder. "Archie," James shouted. "Take the gate." Archie threw himself from his horse and ran with a dozen men up the parapet stairs, swords drawn. A score of his men threw themselves from their horses and spread across the bailey yard. Richert and Dauid ran for the keep door and three guards with their pikes in their hands. "No one has permission to enter," one said.

James leapt from his horse. He cut down the first guard as he turned to jab at Richert. His men hacked into the others. "Get the door before they can bar it," James yelled at Richert. Another guard ran from across the yard shouting. James ducked under the guard's spear and cut his leg out from under him, felt his sword cut through the bone. Richert was struggling with the door as men inside tried to hold it.

James grabbed his horse's reins and vaulted into the saddle. He spurred it at the door. Richert jumped back as it reared, hooves lashing. The edge of the door splintered as it flew open. He was through the keep door, and Soules lay on the floor, crab crawling upon his back. A guard ran at James. With a backslash, James cut him across the face, and he went down in a welter of blood. A squire died under Lowrens's sword whilst one huddled whimpering in a corner. James's men dashed through the door after him, knocking over the tables and flinging benches out of their way.

James pointed his sword at Soules. "Bind him," James ordered Richert. Sir David Brechin ran into the middle of the chaos. James knew him slightly from the days since he'd returned from France. A tall, thin man with silver-gray hair,

James knew he was a braw knight. No one would have thought him a traitor. "Yield or die," James said and pointed his bloody sword. For a moment, James thought Brechin would fight, but his shoulders slumped. He held out his hands whilst Iain wrested his sword from its sheath.

"Search the castle for the traitors. Find me Logie, Malherbe, and Patrick Graham if they are here."

CHAPTER 19

AUGUST 1320

Scone, Scotland

The refectory of was silent except for Soules's words and the indrawn breath of hundreds of knights and lords as they listened to him recount his treachery. Seven men, Soules in the middle, stood dressed in plush velvet suitable to their rank but heavy chains clanked when they moved. At the side of the room, a screen hid the Countess from view as was fitting. To the other side was a black draped bier where the body of Roger de Mowbray lay, dead from a fall from his horse down a crevasse whilst fleeing Thomas Randolph.

On the dais, Gilbert de la Haye stood close by the king's side and guards stood, pikes in hand, at every door. Abbot Bernard de Linton, the king's Chancellor, stood behind the throne. On the other side of the dais sat the bishops of Scotland, led by Bishop Lamberton.

James sat on the long bench reserved for the Privy Council between Thomas Randolph and Walter Stewart, both set-faced and grim. "I would I could have brought the traitor here alive," Thomas muttered before he clamped his mouth shut in a thin line.

"There are lines more royal than yours," William de Soules said. "The Balliol line should govern. Edward de Balliol has returned to England. The reward for helping restore him to the thrown would be great." A rumble of protest went through the room but was silenced when the king demanded to hear Soules's words. "His father was crowned, and he should be king. You are excommunicated and have no right to rule in any kingdom. He is not. It is Balliol who is the rightful king." He gave the Bruce a scathing look.

Robbie Boyd jumped to his feet. "And how much English gold did you receive for this loyalty to Toom Tabard's son?"

Gilbert de la Haye pointed at Robbie. "My lord, did I hear you ask for leave to speak?"

James saw Robbie's chest heave, but he shook his head and sat down.

Maxwell, thin and balding and grim-faced, stepped forward, chains on his hands and his feet clanking. "I would speak." When the king nodded, he glanced at Soules. "All that I would confess is that Mowbray was my friend. I swear that I took no part in conspiracy. I'm no traitor. Yes, he said that he opposed young Robert as heir, and some other should be sought. I told him I had no complaint. I'm a knight, not a cleric to worry on such matters." Maxwell looked toward James. "Sir James will testify that I was not with Soules and his men in Berwick. I was in my own lands. So I am told were Barclay and Graham."

Sir Patrick Graham who had been staring at his feet, lifted his eyes and said, "That's the truth, Your Grace. They may have named me, but I had no part in this plot of theirs. Soules sent me a letter carried by that squire, Richard de Broun." He tilted his head toward a black-haired squire James had captured at Berwick. "And Logie was close to him and with him ever. Him and Mowbray."

"What did this letter of theirs say?" Abbot Bernard asked.

"That they wanted to meet to discuss changes in the realm. It said that Brechin would be there, but I was busy with my own lands. This truce has meant that I had time for rebuilding. I had no use for such talks and told Broun so. On my honor, I tell you they said nothing about a plot against the king."

There was a tense silence when Graham finished speaking.

"I confess that I knew," Brechin said in a booming voice. "I will not dishonor myself with lies. Mowbray told me their plans. Mowbray was a friend, a valued friend. I would not, could not, act against him. I told him I would take no part, but I swore to him that I would not betray him."

Robert de Bruce leaned forward. "So instead you betrayed your liege lord."

"But I swore…" Brechin broke off in the face of the king's glare.

James gripped his fists. This needed to be over, though mayhap Graham was not guilty. But Brechin? No, he was as guilty as Soules. James knew what must be done, but having seen it done before formed a stone in his chest. He closed his eyes and tried not to hear William Wallace's scream as he had died those years before. Yet these men had earned such a death. He rubbed his fist on his thigh. They would do what must be done but no more.

Gilbert de la Haye said, "Are there any others who would speak?"

"Would it matter what we said? You've decided our fate. Get on with it!" Malherbe shouted.

James rose to his feet. "My lords?" The king waved his permission, and James said, "Graham and Maxwell spoke the truth when they said they weren't taken captive with the traitor, Soules. Nor was Barclay. They were in their own lands and made no flight. It is no crime to be friends, even with a traitor." He frowned and worried at his lip for a moment. He didn't like speaking for these men, but only those he was certain were guilty should be sent to an unspeakable death. "I propose that we vote that these two are not proven guilty."

There was a slow and obviously reluctant assent through the room.

William de Lamberton rose. "My lords, God is merciful, but I fear that we cannot be. We are at war with an implacable foe. They would defeat us with treachery if they cannot defeat us with steel." He met James's eyes, and James knew this cost the bishop much. "It is a terrible death we speak of, but this evil of treachery must be stamped out."

Sir Ingram de Umfraville jumped to his feet. "Not Brechin. The Flower of Chivalry and a hero of the crusades, and my friend. He must not be put to death." Hawk faced and with silver hair, Sir Ingram was a striking figure as James pondered him. An Englishman by birth, it was becoming clear to James where his true loyalty lay.

Sir Ingram said, "He did not take active part. Punish him. Imprison him for a time. But do not put him to death."

Randolph rose slowly to his feet with a drawn and solemn face. "I cannot agree with Sir Ingram. There are two we must spare, I fear, though I have no pity for them. We cannot condemn a woman to the scaffold. And Soules bears royal blood in his veins. If we execute him, it will be said it was because we feared his blood and this must not be. The others..." He shrugged. "As the good bishop said, such treachery must be stamped out."

"Wait, my lords." Gilbert held up a hand. "The penalty is not for us to decide. That is his grace's decision. We must declare their guilt or their innocence." His face tightened. "My vote is for guilty."

"Guilty!" James shouted. The refectory was a tumult of shouts. "Guilty!" "Guilty!"

The king held up his hands for silence. It took a few moments as the Master at Arms thumped his staff.

The king's face was haggard, the lines deepened in the past weeks. He voice was stern and even as he said, "I thank you for your verdicts, my lords. Maxwell and Graham shall be released from their chains and restored to their estate according to your verdict." He paused and seemed to draw a deep breath. "William de Soules and the Countess of Strathearn should die. But because she is a female and he…" The king paused before he nodded toward Randolph. "My nephew spoke truly. I will not have it said I killed Soules because he was of the line of King Alexander. They both shall suffer imprisonment in the Castle of Dunbar for as long as they live."

A scream and sobbing came from behind the screen. Soules seemed stricken mute.

Beside James, Randolph nodded his head in agreement, but Robbie had a frown. James wasn't sure how he felt about this doubtful mercy. If it were him, he would rather die. They deserved whatever fate their liege lord decided. James was glad it wasn't his decision.

"Malherbe, Logie and this Broun are guilty of the most heinous of treason. They would have turned the kingdom over to chaos and war once more. And for what? For the son of a man who gave up the throne? They would have given Scotland over to the English. And for their own profit? I have no more mercy upon them than they would have upon me, my followers or upon Scotland. Their lands and titles are forfeit to the crown. They will be dragged to the place of execution to be hanged, drawn and quartered this day."

Logie moaned and sagged to the ground, but the rest of the room was silent.

The king inclined his head toward the bier. "I will not sentence mutilation upon a dead man. Too often my own family has suffered such a fate. His lands and titles are forfeit. I turn his body over to the church for burial, and may God have mercy on his soul."

"Sir David de Brechin." The king looked at Brechin and the lines in his face were even more deeply graven. "It is a sad day to sentence a knight honored for his courage fighting for the church. But he put his loyalty to a friend above his loyalty to his liege lord. He would have seen Scotland go once more into fire and chaos and lifted not a hand to stop it."

Brechin held his head proudly high as Robert de Bruce continued.

"I sentence him to be dragged from this place to be hanged and beheaded like the traitor he is."

"No!" Umfraville jumped to his feet. "This is wrong. I tell you, you must not do this. Not to Brechin. Withdraw your words. Show him mercy."

The king's face hardened. "Sir, you heard my sentence."

"This is the act of a villein, not a king. To kill such a man. I will not stay to serve someone who would send David de Bruchin to such a vile death."

"Then you have my leave to take quit of my realm. I will not hinder you." Robert de Bruce looked quietly around the room. "I require loyalty of my nobles. We have no room in Scotland for traitors. Not if we are to survive."

CHAPTER 20

JULY 1322

Near Carlisle, England

For four days they had ridden, burning as they went. Behind them they had left a swath of destruction. For miles, fields were burnt and trampled, the trees of the orchards blackened hands that grasped at the sky. Behind them they left villages empty, shops plundered. The people ran into the hills and the forests, and James let them flee.

The land around them was an anthill of riding men. A hundred trampled a field, whooping and laughing, driving a herd of lowing cattle before them. Another field was alight. Further up the stream at the edge of a beech copse, a forester's cottage had logs piled high ready for burning. His men surrounded it, throwing torches into the wood and onto the roof. Flames shot into the sky as trees around it caught.

The air reeked of smoke and ash. James leaned and spit the taste from his mouth. *But what would it take to cleanse the taint of ash and burning from my soul?* He felt his mouth tighten. Perhaps he would carry it with him to Hell. So be it.

In this life, he had his duty. "How many do you think men do you think King Edward has raised?" James asked.

Robert de Bruce grunted a response and watched as Gawter tossed a torch, its flames trailing, onto a thatched-roof cottage. A raven went flapping into the sky. "More than they had at Bannockburn. Can't your spies tell you a number?" The flames caught and began to dance across the roof, blowing in the wind.

James snorted a laugh. "They don't count that high, Your Grace. I have only heard that the line of it stretches far out of sight."

"I always said that Lancaster was a fool." Randolph coughed as a thick wave of smoke blew over them. "Now he is a headless fool."

James knew that Randolph was still provoked that he had convinced the king to involve them in Lancaster's rebellion against King Edward, but anything that hurt the English king could only be to Scotland's benefit. Lancaster might have taken the English throne had he been smarter, and at the least, until he was captured by Harcla and had his head chopped off, he had been a distraction. Now it seemed that Edward was so swollen with pride that he would try another invasion of Scotland even as the Scottish army put the north of England to the torch.

"Is King Edward truly so witless? All of the English? That they can't see…" James let his horse drop its head into the blue-green trickle of water to drink. "All they have to do is come to the peace-table."

The two men didn't answer because there wasn't an answer to a question the Scots had pondered for eight years.

Walter Stewart trotted up, Andrew de Moray behind him in gilded armor. "There's another herd of cattle beyond the hill." Walter pointed to the east.

"They should have already been taken" the king said. "How many?"

"A hundred mayhap. Enough to speed up trampling the fields."

The king climbed from the saddle with a tired sigh. "We'll camp here whilst our men finish their work."

James slid to the ground. A camp would be little more than cook fires and cloaks to wrap in, even for the king. He watched their men gallop across the field of golden grain. Torches spun through the air as they were flung. "Richert," James shouted. "Send men for those cattle Sir Walter spotted. And have someone bring wood for a fire."

He led his courser across the pebbly finger of a stream. There would be water for drink and use in their bannocks, and the men could spread along the stream with their mounts. "Three days to finish burning Carlisle."

Randolph nodded and flung himself onto the grass, stretching out his long legs. "Next we burn Scotland before them."

Dauid came to lead their horses to picket. The king looked around but there was nothing to serve as a seat. He grunted as he sat on the bare ground. "I'm getting old for this."

"Lothian. We must burn as far as the Firth of Forth," James said. One of their men was carting an armful of wood and dumped it onto the ground. James snorted. "I must burn it. In the March, the duty is mine. And Edinburgh must go. What about the court at the palace, Your Grace? They'll be in danger, surely. Should they be sent north?"

"I'll think on it, but... let's see what Edward of Carnaefon does first. When we return, the fiery cross must be carried across Scotland." The king nodded. "It is as you say, Jamie. Thomas and Walter and Andrew, I shall send to carry the fiery cross and raise all the powers of Scotland, of the Highlands, of the Isles. I shall hold at Culross and send a force to hold Stirling, but everything below the Forth will be left bare —of man or beast, of crop or habitation. That I leave to you."

James drew his dirk and tested the tip on his thumb. The king would also expect the spears of Douglasdale and all of his lands. But first more burning.

CHAPTER 21

SEPTEMBER 1322

Edinburgh, Scotland

When he shimmied up to the highest branch that would bare his weight, James could see the castle rock rising into the sky topped with a rubble of boulders left from the slighting. The tall marble spires of the Abbey of the Holy Rood were nearer. Below the foot of the rock, broken chimneys poked up through the trees. Burnt roofs clustered along the edge of the Firth of Forth, and dozens of wooden piers thrust into the blue-green water. No ships were tied up, and single fishing boat bobbed in the waves. He bent further out and the branch wavered beneath him. Hundreds of thin curls of smoke rose from cook fires. There was movement on the shore, but it was too far to see what. He bent, grasped the branch and dropped to the ground with a grunt.

There were no earthworks around the city. That would make things easier as they scouted. He must know if the enemy had any food left. How near to starving? How near to retreating to their own land?

Behind him was desolation. Villages, cottages, farms, fields, and barns, if it would burn, he and his men had burnt it, whilst all the people of the Lothian fled, herding their animals and dragging scant few possessions into the hills and the broken lands. On the night he led his men out of Edinburgh a month ago, the flames of the burning city had leapt so high that the water of the firth itself had shimmered as though it were on fire.

James squinted up at the sun. "Dusk is the best time to sneak in," he said to Archibald.

"What if we're questioned?"

"You sound like a damned Sassenach. You'll pass as one of them. Just say we're looking for our companions."

Archie glowered at him. "You sound like one too when you want to."

"I don't want to—unless I must. You do the talking."

Without waiting for an answer, James pulled out his dirk to drop on the ground, kicked some dead leaves over it, and walked off. His sword could pass for that of any well-armed soldier. They were both wearing unmarked leather brigandines studded with steel such as a man-at-arms in any army might wear. He scrambled down a steep braeside, using brambles as handholds. Archie stomped behind.

The sun had fallen behind the tops of the trees and dark would be upon them soon. James sniffed. "I smell smoke."

"We burnt the town and there are cook fires. Thousands of them most like. That must be what it is."

James grunted skeptically. "Follow behind me." He darted away, silent in the thick padding of leaves. He used the widely spaced trees, slipping from one to another in the shadows. As they grew closer the reek was strong, fresh smoke from something larger than a cook fire and more recent than a month old. There was little he'd left for the English to burn.

At every tree, he paused to listen. At the fifth one, he heard the hooves of hundreds of horses and men's voices. And the stink of smoke got stronger. He'd fired too many buildings himself to mistake it. They'd fired something. But little was left unburnt except the Abbey of the Holy Rood.

A hawthorn thicket shielded the way ahead on the edge of the city. By the time he reached it, the lavender tint of dusk had darkened to black, but a fire lit the shells of cottages he could see through gaps in the branches. He twisted through, the thorns tearing at his hands and face.

He stepped boldly into the open and gave a jerk of his head as Archie forced his way through. They had to blend in with the crowd of soldiers laughing and jeering as flames wrapped around the Abbey. James's heart sped up and tried to rip its way out of his chest. He'd spared many and many an abbey and church in England. He knew they couldn't expect the same of their enemy. Flames wrapped around the magnificent spires.

"Most of it won't burn..." Archie mumbled in an undertone.

James gave a sharp nod. They'd removed all of the treasures for safekeeping, and the friars had fled like the rest of the city. But the burning of such a place... He gripped the hilt of his sword and turned to dodge around the edge of the crowd toward the town proper. There was naught he could do here, and Archie was right. The damage would be shameful but would be repaired. A wind blew off the firth and threw sparks high into the sky as James put his back to the flames and strode into the remains of the city.

Well beyond the burning abbey, a line of guards in mail stood leaning upon pikes around pavilions as large as houses. Banners flapped from tall poles driven into the ground. On one James could make out a hint of red and gold in the flickering light from a campfire. The other was paler, perhaps blue and white. They might have been the banners of the Plantagenet king and John de Warenne, earl of Surrey or mayhap it was that of the earl of Richmond, but in the dark of evening, he couldn't be sure. Beyond them between burnt out cottages, tumbled stones, and blackened foundations, the common men camped in the open or in crude tents squatting helter-skelter like mushrooms.

James grinned at his brother and sauntered up to one of the guards. "Damn lords. They'll have ale. But none for the likes of us."

"They have fine wine." The guard glanced around for listeners before he hawked and spat. "Though not more beef than the rest of us. I hear Warenne is having horsemeat for his dinner. At least he has that. And the rest of us not having more than beans for dinner in weeks—if we were lucky."

James elbowed his brother. "Whose horse did they eat? I'll wager it wasn't that of my lord Goddamn earl."

Archie laughed and punched James back, and they both laughed hard when the guard joined in. James wiped his face with the heel of his hand.

"Nae, it's cart horses they're slaughtering." The guard motioned with his head and James stepped closer. "I heard we're breaking camp tomorrow before the war horses are so thin they can't make the trip."

"About time," Archie said.

"Hoi!" A voice cut through the night like the edge of a sword. A compact man, hard and spare, stomped toward them. "What's to-do here? You're supposed to be on guard, not gossiping like a henwife." He glared at James. "And who are you?"

"James of York," James said, tugging his forelock. "Meant no harm. Just stopped to pass the time of night."

"Be on your way," the sergeant said sharply.

James gave the guard a wry smile and sauntered away just

as a party of knights and men-at-arms thundered up. A tall man in azure silk and a white satin cloak threw himself from the saddle, cursing. "That was the most expensive beef I've ever seen, I swear it. We found one lame cow to feed the entire camp."

Out of the corner of his eye, James saw someone throw back the door covering of the largest pavilion. He decided it was time to keep walking.

"Wonder how long it's been since a ship got through," Archie whispered.

"Whist. Talk about that later," James said as he wended his way between men lying wrapped in cloaks, tents, and cook fires. He hadn't seen a dog since they'd entered the town, so he raised an eyebrow when one of the men squatting by a fire stuck a hunk of meat on the tip of his knife into the flames. The camp was quiet for so many men. They sat huddled about their fires or crawled into their crude tents with feet sticking out. A snore grated the air. He heard someone in the distance bellowing a curse. He passed horse lines, quiet except for an occasional stamp or whicker. The air reeked of horseshit and men with a hint of hunger and sickness beneath.

When he came to the shoreline, they strolled until the night was ink black. Not a single ship was at anchor nor a light anywhere in sight on the firth.

"I've learned what I need to know," James said.

"You mean you'll attack—"

James gave him a thump on the back of the head. "Watch your tongue."

"I thought I was supposed to do the talking," Archie said.

James chuckled and shook his head. "I changed my mind." His brother was loyal, but it would be nice if he had sharper wits about him.

CHAPTER 22

Hambleton Hills, England

Kneeling on the soft sod, the Bruce thrust a finger at a spot on the map. "You're certain he is at Rievaulx Abbey?" Even kneeling, Robert de Bruce was a tall man with long legs and massive shoulders, his arms were thick and corded with muscle, but his once golden hair was now streaked with gray. Lines were carved deep around his eyes and his mouth.

"My spies say with few of his forces, Your Grace." James snorted. "And his queen. By the time the dysentery finished with his army, it was broken, and Warenne left for his own lands. John of Brittany's joining him stopped my advance." Thick smoke from a burning field wrapped itself around them, and James rubbed his stinging eyes.

"Such modesty, Douglas," Thomas Randolph said. "You don't mention the beating you gave his light cavalry at Melrose."

James shrugged. "They deserved it. I was—angry. Bad enough that they burnt Holy Rood Abbey but to burn

Melrose Abbey as well." He ran his finger along the line of Humberton Hills on the map before them. "Here." He stood and pointed, sweeping a long line toward the dark and tree covered brae, hunched like a whale back. "John of Brittany has formed a line and holds the way all along the crest of Sutton Bank."

Iain Campbell, Ruairi Macrauri, Hugh of Ross, and Gilbert de la Haye rose to their feet and spread out, frowning, doubtful looks between them.

"We could go by Helmsley. But..." Thomas Randolph shook his head. "We'd lose King Edward. It is too long a way, and he'd be warned that our army has joined Douglas. Moreover, it would mean showing our backs to John of Brittany and risking his attack on our rear."

Walter Stewart peered through the drifting smoke, squinting. "A frontal attack will not work. Not up such a steep slope."

Andrew de Moray grunted, still kneeling next to the map in his shining, gilded armor. "I thought Harcla would be lured out by the burning. I'd not let an army burn my lands before me as Douglas did when he passed through Carlisle."

"Harcla has other plans. He will treat with me," the Bruce said. "Already does, in fact. My Chancellor has exchanged letters with him. He knows that's the best way to end this madness. Strange, it seems to me that for men who are so different, in this King Edward is truly like his father. He both hates and covets Scotland. And he will not give up."

James twitched a smile. "And he sits at Rievaulx Abbey only fifteen miles hence. If we could reach and capture him, then he would be of a different mind."

"So... Is there some way for us through these hills, Jamie?" The Bruce stared at the smoke-hazed reaches. "You know them better than any of us. The map is useless. Tell me about the lay of the land."

"Obviously, John of Brittany knows that I'm here." They all joined him in laughing. He wiped tears that were more from smoke than laughter. "Whether he has spotted your force, I cannot be sure. I think not, hidden by smoke and with his attention on my own men. To the north, Humberton Hills runs into Cleveland Hills, and there is no good route through. To the south, the bluffs are steep and easily defended. West, as Randolph said, there is Helmsley, but it is a full day's ride. There," he said, pointing straight ahead to a steep, heathery path up the braeside that was dotted with bilberry bushes and bracken between thick beech and oak woodlands, "there is a path up to the crest. John of Brittany holds that in force."

"So he may think he faces only your small army," the Bruce said. "And that gives us an advantage when we attack."

"A battle then, sire?" Andrew de Moray grinned up at the king from where he knelt.

"Aye, a battle. But we must move swiftly," the king said in a voice of quiet satisfaction. "The English will be forced to the peace-table. Whatever it takes. If it takes full battle in their own lands, so be it. And if we capture Edward, so much the better."

"I'll lead the attack, sire," James said. It might be suicide to fight their way up that sharp slope. Probably, it would be. Today, in truth, he thought he didn't care if it would end this: the day after day, the year after year, of blood and burning and ash, hunger and suffering, and death. If it would leave his lands and his son and Marioun and all of the rest in peace, it was worth dying for. "He holds the way, but I'll lead my men up the escarpment to cut our way through if you give me the word."

"First, tell me about the land around this pass. I'd have you live through the battle, my old friend. I'll not throw your life away." The king came to face him and gripped both of his shoulders for a moment. "Are the flanks to the north and the south so high that Highlanders couldn't climb them?"

"I don't mean to throw my life away—though if that is the price..." He blew out a breath and turned, narrowing his eyes as he pictured the way, blanketed now by waves and eddies of smoke. "They could climb the bluffs on the flanks, though they're steep and wooded, but not as steep as their Highland mountains." He laughed grimly. "Not as steep as where they defeated us at Dail Righ, but he would throw all his men against them."

"Sire!" Andrew exclaimed. "They'd be slaughtered. They're fierce fighters, but he has too many." Many of the Highlanders were his.

"Not if Douglas has already made a frontal attack. Richmond has to expect Douglas to try to fight his way through, either to raid or to try to capture the king. So we give what he expects. Jamie will draw the English to him, so when they're attacked from both flanks, we'll have them in a trap." He turned to Walter Stewart. "The main of the chivalry are yours. Be ready to ride with them for Rievaulx Abbey once we've cleared the way. Campbell, the left flank is yours to lead. Ranald, the right flank is yours. I will hold the reserve with the rest of you."

James chewed his lip as he thought. "I'll take seven hundred of my own men of Douglasdale to form a schiltron. It'll be sore fighting. I trust them to hold hard and not break while the flanks are attacked."

"Are there more fields to be fired?" Thomas Randolph asked. "Let's keep the English attention on your men and make sure they can't see that more have arrived."

"I'll send a troop to see what they can find," James said. He blinked tears from his stinging eyes. "I'm not sure we really need more."

"Hie you then," the king said. "An hour and we must be ready for the attack."

* * *

James's men were massing as Archibald shook out the Douglas banner. A blanket of thick smoke hugged the ground.

Archibald scowled and coughed. "I wish you'd use another banner bearer so I could fight more."

James threw him a hard look. "You'll have chance enough. Is your sword sharp? That banner will draw them to you." He had no time for foolishness and drew his sword. The king's forces were out of sight beyond the woods and twisting columns of smoke. James wondered if the king had begun the movement of the Highlanders. He'd have to trust they'd reach their place in good time. "Get your pikes into position. Stay close together as we move or they'll have us," he shouted. He spotted Thomas Randolph strolling their way, helm under his arm, trailed by two squires who led their horses.

Randolph ducked his head and smiled, looking embarrassed.

"Does the king know you're here?" James asked.

"Not exactly, but he did not forbid it."

James snorted a laugh through his nose, and then he threw an arm around Randolph's shoulder. "It will be a good dance. You're welcome to join." He gave Randolph a friendly shove and turned back to the bristling hedgehog of steel that was forming behind him. James swung into the saddle and turned his courser in a tight circle. He stood in his stirrups and shouted, "We'll take the brunt of the fight. We're outnumbered and we'll be fighting uphill. But if we die, it's for Scotland and King Robert. We'll teach the Sassenach how we fight in Scotland!"

Thomas was grinning and James raised an eyebrow. "You give an encouraging speech. You could mention the possibility of winning or that it will be a good fight."

"They know that." He looked over his men to be sure they were in position and then called, "Lowrens, blow the advance." The trumpet blared. Smoke and ashes swirled through the air.

James led his men into the path. As Randolph rode beside his he made his sword sing with wide swings. On the other side, Archie still grumbled as he carried their waving banner. Plants they trod underfoot gave up a green scent. Suddenly, a red grouse whirred out of bush crying *Goback, goback, goback*!

The ground rose in a steep slope. At the top of the hill was a vast host, thousands strong. Archers arrayed themselves in a line to the right. James gave them a worried glance. If Richmond brought them into play before the Highlanders attacked, it could mean he and his men died on this slope. To the left, hundreds of knights on heavy barded horses were massed together. James saw Richmond's blue and yellow checky banner unfurled. Dozens of other banners fluttered above them. Even from a distance, Richmond was splendid in a cloak of cloth of gold and polished steel mail inlaid with gold and plumes of blue and yellow atop his helm. But James had never heard that Richmond was a great soldier and shining armor did not win battles.

Between the two lines, a thousand pikemen formed long rows, sun glinting off their blades.

Behind him, James heard the rumble of his men's feet as they marched. They were halfway up the slope, and sweat was dripping down his face and into his eyes, already stinging from smoke.

Archie waved the starred banner over his head. "A

Douglas!" he shouted. The hundreds of men behind them picked up the cry. "Douglas! Douglas! Douglas!"

"We may be bait, but they'll choke on us," Randolph muttered beside him. James hoped he was right. He nodded. His men were experienced and well armored, with good pikes in their hands and sturdy brigandines on their bodies, but fighting uphill whilst being cut down by English archers… Good pikes and armor might not be enough.

He had no more time to think on it. The English horns blew. *Haroooo* The drum of hoof beats was like thunder. The Sassenach broke into a gallop, shouting as they rode. James smiled as he realized that rather than use his archers, Richmond was leading his knights against them. They were upon him in a flood of shields and lances.

James saw horses shy as they charged into the pikes. Pikes ripped into others, slashing into their necks. Knights went down as horses died under them. Randolph was surrounded by three knights. His horse reared, lashing out its hooves to smash the first man's head as Randolph took the second in the face with a backslash.

A knight came hurtling toward James, his lance couched. James danced his courser to the side. His foe was tall and heavy with a lion on his blue shield that James did not recognize. As he wheeled to charge again, James aimed a slam of his shield at his head. The tall knight dodged and wheeled in a circle as James rode around him, keeping too close for the lance, hacking at his shield and arm. He threw his lance aside and scraped his sword free. "Pour Notre Dame!" he screamed as he chopped. James shoved in close. Their blades locked and James leaned in hard, baring his teeth in a grin. James wrenched his sword free. They swung at each other, stroke and counterstroke. Fragments of shield flew, but the knight's swings were slowing. James slammed his foe across the side of his helm so hard that it rang. The knight reeled in the saddle. With a twist of his sword, James locked their blades. A jerk sent the knight's sword flying and then another slam spilled the knight onto the ground. He rolled onto his back as James's horse danced around him. "Yield!" James yelled.

The man lay limp, his hands open in submission.

"England!" a voice bellowed. "For England and King Edward!" John of Brittany came thundering toward him, swinging a sword. James spurred his courser. They slammed together.

Arrows pattered around them like rain, onto English and Scots alike. Randolph slumped in the saddle, an arrow through his shoulder. One bounced off an English knight's helm. Where were the damned Highlanders, James wondered as he hacked at Richmond's shield. Two of his men fought back to back. The schiltron was broken. It the Highlanders did not come they would die here.

"A Douglas!" he shouted. An arrow hissed past his head. He hauled on his reins and his courser reared. James hacked down on Richmond's hand, and the man screamed, but again he swung weakly at James. Blood dripped from his hand. "Yield, damn you," James said. He slammed the man in the face with the flat of his sword, all the weight of his body behind it.

John of Brittany jerked his reins, trying to turn his mount as he lurched in the saddle. James slammed another blow across his back. "Don't make me kill you," James screamed at him. The sword slipped from Richmond's hand, and he slid from the saddle to kneel in the dirt, pressing a hand to his wound.

James looked around for Randolph, but the man had ripped the arrow from his shoulder. Blood dripped down his arm, yet he was still in the saddle, hacking at a pikeman. Randolph shouted, "Macruari's men!" Shouts of rang out.

Like scythes, the Highlanders with their long axes were cutting into the archers.

James spurred his horse toward another knight. His men were raggedly shouting, "Douglas! Douglas!" and "Scotland!" James lopped off the end of the knight's lance and then his arm at the elbow. A pikeman in a studded brigandine ran at him, and James turned his horse to circle him. He drove the point of his sword into the man's back so hard he lifted him from his feet. He kicked a foot free from his stirrup, and grunted as he kicked the body loose. He rode past Richmond's banner, planted listing in the dirt, and chopped it off with a swing.

A knight rode out of the chaos, to chop at him with a two-handed sword. Randolph galloped up from behind and took him in the back. James spurred his horse. He slashed at one knight and then another who threw down his sword, so James spared him. "A Douglas!" he shouted. His sword was red and his gauntlet dripping gore. A pikeman fled from him and James ran him down.

And suddenly, James realized he was at the top of the hill. Below, back to back, the remnants of his men hacked at a few knights. He saw that Ranald MacRuarie's men were strung across the hills as they pursued the archers and pikemen. Pikes and bows were strewn where they'd been tossed away amongst the bodies. Crows cawed as they circled and landed.

Trumpets sounded and sounded. Walter Stewart's chivalry swept up the path, scattering the remains of the battle like leaves. Five hundred knights thundered past, sunlight flashing off their armor. The blue and yellow Stewart banner rippled over their heads as they galloped.

The fever of battle leaked out of him; James threw a leg over his saddlebow and slid to the ground.

* * *

The thin archer screamed when the pikemen dragged him before him. James didn't say anything, just pointed his sword to the ground. One sat on the archer's legs while Gawter sat his chest and held down his arm. "No. Please! I'll do anything," the archer shrieked. He tried to thrash.

"Struggle and I may miss," James said. He brought the sword down and felt it cut through flesh and bone. Blood spurted from where the archer's thumb had been.

Gawter stood and tossed the archer a rag. The man rolled onto his side, whimpering as he hugged his maimed hand to his chest. "Better use the rag before you bleed to death," Gawter said. He turned and stomped off.

James nudged the archer in the ribs with his foot. "I'm done with you. Be grateful it wasn't your neck."

The rattle of hooves made him turn as the king cantered up with Haye and Andrew de Moray by his side. As they swung from the saddle, Moray said, "Torture, Douglas? What point for only an archer?"

"Say policy, rather. Every English archer has ten Scottish lives that hang from his belt. I either kill them or make sure they take no more Scottish lives."

The king grunted and waved away the topic. "I understand my nephew joined you. I'll have a word to say to him about that, albeit a fine victory for the both of you. But how dear was the cost?"

"Randolph took an arrow in his shoulder, sire. He's with your physician, so I pray you'll not be wroth with him. Otherwise—" James frowned. "—the cost was dear enough. I lost more than half my men. But we killed more of them than they did of us, and we took more than a few prisoners."

A squire in the Stewart colors rode up at a fast canter and threw himself from the saddle to give the king a deep bow. "Sire, Sir Walter bade me bring you news. He chases on the heels of the English king. He fled with Lord Dispenser and others riding for York, my lord believes. But behind them, they left much. Sire, I have never seen the like!" The squire's eyes were wide with excitement. "Sir Walter left two score guards to hold the Abbey until you could claim it. Such booty —silver plates and goblets from the English king's own table, horse trappings with gold inlay, bags of coins, immense piles of treasure. But sire, Sir Walter said especial to tell you that they left behind something else."

James was shaking his head at a king he truly could not understand, when the Bruce said, "On with it, lad. What else?"

"On a table there was a gold seal—big as a platter and jeweled. He said it was the Great Seal of the kingdom of England."

"He left—" The king stopped, apparently struck speechless. After a moment, he nodded to the squire, "Well done and I think you. Shortly we shall ride for the abbey and examine what the English king values so lightly." He turned back to James. "If any can catch him, I trust Walter to do it though it sounds as though they may have had a good start on him. Now you had other news for me?"

James cast a last glance at the archer who hunched, rocking against the pain, with a bloody rag wrapped around his hand. He pointed down the braeside to a cluster of knights seated between two spreading oaks and surrounded by guards.

"Here are some who did not escape, Your Grace." He walked with the king toward the prisoners. Strands of smoke still drifted like ghosts across the grass and the air stand of ash and blood.

John of Brittany, earl of Richmond, watched them, surrounded by a dozen other men, crouched or sitting on the ground. One stood proudly to watch as they approached. Richmond's golden cloak and silk tabard were dirt and blood streaked, his hand wrapped in a bloody bandage. He was a cousin to the Plantagenet kings but in no way resembled them. Instead, he had stingy brown hair streaked with gray and a long nose that seemed nearly to touch his knobby chin over thin lips. But his eyes were sharp and shrewd as he stared at Robert de Bruce. He bowed stiffly.

"So." The king's face was set, his voice cool. "Would you care to repeat to me, Sir John, the words you said to my lady wife when she was a prisoner in Edward Longshank's hands? Have you the courage? Or is it only a helpless woman you would give affront?"

"I did nothing to Lady Elizabeth." He blew through his lips. "I had no interest in her, except for her lord father, the earl. It's not my fault if she took something I said ill. What do you expect of a woman?"

"You contemptible coward," the Bruce growled. The Bruce turned his back on Richmond as the man sputtered. "Who are these other prisoners, Jamie?"

James flashed a smile and motioned over the tall knight he had fought. "Your grace, Sieur Henri de Sully, Grand Butler of France."

Sully, a tall, imposing man with a strong nose and hooded eyes, strode over and bowed low to the king. "Your Grace, your Sir James—he defeated me in honorable combat. It was a privilege to cross swords with so formidable a knight, although I would have wished to meet you not his prisoner."

"You came here a guest of Edward of Caernarfon?"

"Indeed, Your Grace. On the command of my own liege lord in France, we were sent to visit our king's sister, Queen Isabella." He shrugged and motioned toward two knights watching nearby. "When our host was faced with battle, of course, I considered it my duty to aid him, even against such renowned knights as yourself and Sir James."

The Bruce laughed. "Naturally. I know your reputation

for gallantry, Sieur Henri. And you surrendered your sword to Sir James?"

Sieur Henri rubbed the side of his nose. "If I am to speak the truth, he took my sword from me before I could surrender it. A truly fine knight. The finest I've ever crossed swords with. Though my ransom may be high, it is an honor to pay it to someone I so respect." He looked over his shoulder. "And these, my companions as well surrendered to Sir James."

"Nonsense, Sieur Henri. Your liege lord is a friend, and I hope soon to be his ally. You are my guests and not prisoners if that is agreeable to you. All of you from the French court."

Sully's hooded eyes widened. "That will be a heavy cost to Sir James."

James waved his hand. "The cost is no concern to me."

"Nor should it be." The king's eyes gleamed, and he looked down at his right hand, big and spotted with freckles with massive gold rings on two of the fingers, one a wide band set with an enormous emerald. He tugged if off. "I will make up the lack. Sir James, let me see your hand."

James stared at the king for a moment before he held out his right hand. The king pushed the heavy ring onto the main finger. "A token for the charter I'll gift you with in repayment." The king beamed. "It is in my mind to give you full freedom from knight fees and other taxes for your baronies of Douglas and Lawder, the royal forests of Selkirk and Jedburgh that you hold for me and of all your lands. For you and your heirs."

James felt his face flush as he knelt and took the king's hand. "My liege."

"Excellent, Your Grace," the French knight exclaimed. "We accept your gracious hospitality. What a pleasing change in our fortunes and a fitting reward to the finest knight in all of Christendom."

"Gilbert," the king called to Gilbert de la Haye. "I will have the earl of Richmond held most closely, and I bid you keep him out of my sight. I shan't soil my hands with blood of such a wretch. Some of the other prisoners have hurts to be tended. See that they're given any aid that we may." He nodded genially to his new French guests as James rose. "Come, sirs. As you know, Rievaulx Abbey is but a short ride, and I have business there. It will be more comfortable for all of us. Jamie, I'd have your company."

CHAPTER 23

JANUARY 1323

Lochmaben Castle, Ayrshire, Scotland

Their horses' hooves sloshed through the thin covering of snow. A cold wind was blowing out of the north, whipping their cloaks. The breaths of their horses and men, steaming, fogged around them. Over their heads flapped their banners, the royal lion of Scotland and the yellow of Randolph and the starred blue of Douglas. An occasional curse at the cold and the creak of saddle leather were the only sounds from the score of guards that rode behind them.

The Bruce rode between James and Randolph, his gray shot hair stirring in the wind. He had a serious look to his blue eyes as he swallowed down a cough. The loch shimmered white under the drifting flutters of snow and reeds poked through the covering. Little remained of the great castle of Lochmaben except fire blackened stones and the hollow shells of stables and outbuildings. The gatehouse still stood beside a square entry in the half demolished wall.

It was an uncomfortable place for a meeting, but it would

be secret, as Harcla had pointed out in his letter. No one would expect the King of the Scots to be in this forlorn place in the midst of the Yuletide celebrations and a chill Scotland winter. In the weed-overgrown bailey yard, a dozen horses were tied to a couple of fallen boards.

There was a shout. In a corner of two broken walls, ten men in studded brigandines stood up from a small fire. Another with a hard, scarred face walked toward them. "It's them his lordship is expecting," he said.

James jumped from the saddle and took the king's bridle. "Gather wood and build another fire," he said to the sergeant. "And keep yourselves to yourselves." He stamped to warm his frozen feet as the others climbed from the saddle.

Randolph shoved open the door to the gatehouse with a creak like a scream, and a gust of warmth rushed out. The room was alight from logs piled into a roaring fire. James jerked off his gloves and rubbed his hands together as the feeling returned to his fingers.

A man faced them, a thick fur cloak about his shoulders, brown hair lightly salted with white and a broad, bony face. Andrew de Harcla, earl of Carlisle gave them a cool, measuring look. After a moment he bowed deeply, "Your Grace."

"Sir Andrew," the king said, nodding. "It has been a long time since you were our guest."

"And I prefer it thus. My ransom cost me more than you can know," Harcla commented dryly as he motioned to a flagon of wine and cups beside the hearth. "I crave your pardon for bringing you so far unseasonably. At least I can provide the comfort of wine. Warm yourselves." His smile was sardonic. "But not so warm as Sir James makes my poor lands of Carlisle."

The wine curled pleasantly in James's belly. Harcla was right It was unseasonable to be about. He'd choose a warm bed with Marioun or even working up a sweat with his men in the bailey yard to talking treason with the earl of Carlisle. Treason he had no doubt that it was.

"Your letters were secretive enough." The king drank down a long swallow and James frowned. There was nowhere for the king to sit, and they didn't want any Englishman to know that something was wrong. James didn't know what it was, but the king was not well. He had grown thin and gaunt these last months, and his cough never truly went away.

"So what is it that you want of the king?" James asked.

"It is not what I want, my lord. It is what I can offer." He took a drink of his own wine before he continued, his voice thinned with bitterness. "Do I need to tell you how bad our case is? It was you who burnt all the north of England. Took the cattle. Ruined the crops. And we have a useless king. He can't defeat you, but he won't treat with you. He leaves us to starve. Does not come to our defense or make peace with someone who should not be our enemy." He snorted softly. "He summoned me to defend him before the Battle of Byland, when you defeated John de Brittany, but wouldn't come to the man's defense himself. He ran." His mouth grew hard. "Ran like a craven."

Harcla cleared his throat. "My presence here might be treason, but when the king will not act then someone else must. Things in England worsen by the day. There no depths the Despensers will not plumb, especially the younger. That he is a sodomite is the least of his crimes. All added to the shame of the king's flight, the shame of the Despenser abandoning the Great Seal, I am sure I can raise the support I need in the north."

"For what? What is it that you propose to me because in rebellion against your liege lord, I tell you I will not give aid."

"Not for rebellion," Harcla said bluntly. "To join together

to force the king to take the action he should have years ago and go to the peace-table. But if he will not be forced, then I am ready to swear my allegiance to a king who gives some care to his people."

"And why would I trust a man who would betray his own liege lord?"

"It is my liege lord who has betrayed *me*! When I made my oath to him, did he not make an oath in return? To protect me and mine? Have I not protected him, even against Lancaster who was my friend? And when has he protected the north?" Harcla looked at them and James found he couldn't meet the man's eyes. "When?"

James picked up the flagon and filled the king's cup and his own. Randolph shook his head at him, looking grave.

"Forgive me, Your Grace." Harcla held out his hands to the fire and seemed to forget they were there for a bit. When he continued his voice was calm. "I am no coxcomb. I'm a simple soldier raised beyond my station, a Cambrian by birth, and I tell you the north is ready to rebel if something is not done. And no one is ready to do what must be done except me.

"I tell you, Your Grace, that Edward of Caernarfon will never make peace with you. No matter what you do, were you to raid London itself, he would not make peace. So what I propose is that with other lords from the north, I take a proposal to him that he recognize you as King of the Scots and Scotland as a free kingdom in return for terms you give me." Harcla continued to stare into the fire. "He will refuse them, no matter what they are though I ask that you name terms that should tempt any sane king. And when he refuses, I will raise an armed revolt in the north."

He was speaking in deadly earnest, James realized. He was talking open rebellion in England.

"I've given terms—more than fair ones. I would even pay

reparations for the damage of our raids into England if he will do what is right and give up his claim ," the king said.

"Harcla is right." Randolph broke his long silence. "Nothing will induce Edward to recognize our right to our own kingdom. But I ask who would rise with him against their own sworn lord? " He looked directly at Harcla. "Can you truly promise such a thing?"

"A number of lords are ready to take action. The Despensers have driven many to the point they will join me." He turned to face them. "The earl of Lancaster's brother, Henry for one is bitter at his brother's death and at being deprived of the titles. The Dispensers have stolen the lands of Thomas of Norfolk. He will certainly join to put down their tyranny. Edward has denied Edmund of Woodstock his rightful lands. Now is the time for a throw of the dice."

James shrugged. "All that is true, Your Grace. But whether it means they will join Harcla—that I do not know." It was all very well for Harcla to claim that Henry of Leicester would rebel. He had no doubt the man hated the English king, but it was Harcla who had turned Leicester's brother over to the Despensers for execution. So who did Henry of Leicester hate most?

When Randolph caught his eye, James suspected he had much the same thought.

"They are all enraged with the Despensers and know the only way to rid themselves of him is to crown a new king. And there is one other I have not named."

"Ah," the Bruce said as James realized whom Harcla meant. The queen.

"She hates her royal husband. And even more, she hates the Despensers. They say that young Hugh raped her, though I don't know the truth of that. She would be glad to see her son on the throne. Young Edward is his old Longshank's true grandson, much like him and in his tenth year. With a new king, if you offer such inducements we can make peace—peace we both need. But first we must throw off Edward of Caernarfon."

The Bruce frowned. "I will not involve my kingdom in an English civil war."

"But you could aid us. That is all I ask. Give me terms to present to the king, and if he refuses, give me aid when I lead a rebellion. A raid to distract them whilst I take London for our new king."

James's mouth twisted into a smile, but he kept his voice even when he said, "And you'd have the king put that in writing."

"On the aid I will take the king's word. Just give me a letter to present to the king offering terms for peace. And leave the rest to me until I send you word."

The king gave a sharp nod. "I have no clerk with me, but in secret I'll get you what you want. And if you can raise a rebellion with such a following, I will send my Lord Warden of the Marches with his men to your aid."

Harcla raised his cup in salute.

"When the day comes, I shall come to your aid," James said gravely and returned the salute. *If,* he thought. *If the day comes...*

CHAPTER 24

Lintalee, Scotland

James crumpled the letter in his hand and nodded his thanks to the gaunt, sharp-faced gray-robed friar who had put it into his hands. "My thanks. Will you stay? The winds are still chill, and you're welcome at our table. My chamberlain will find a place for you."

The man's sturdy dun palfrey pawed the cobbles of the bailey yard. "For the night, my lord. On the morrow, I must leave for Arbroath."

James sucked in a lungful of the crisp spring air. No doubt the man carried a similar letter for the abbot. The church was responsible for much of the news they received from England. That they were excommunicated and under interdict was a detail that many friars managed to ignore. But this was news he must carry to the king himself. He couldn't leave it to others. Harcla had paid harshly for his treachery, but if the other news was true as well, perhaps they would profit after all.

Behind him, the yard rang with the sound of the whacks of wood upon wood. "Hoi," James called to a stable boy. "Take the good friar's mount." He watched after the man as he went through the manor doors. Yes, he owed the friar at least a good meal and a night by a warm fire.

Six pages were drilling, heavily padded in quilted linen gambesons that went to their knees, clouting and walloping at each other. Sir Symon, who'd taken over duties as master-at-arms, grunted and said to keep their swords up.

William was the largest of the pages, tall at eight years but as round as a barrel with the padding. Robert was puffing as he whaled away with a wooden sword. William caught each blow on his own. He answered with a counterstrike that smacked his cousin hard on the arm. The smaller lad staggered, but William had sweat dripping down his face. He was tiring. Robert yelped as he managed to slide the point of his sword hard into William's belly.

"That's the way!" Young Lowrens hooted. The other spectators yelled out advice.

"They're improving," Marioun said.

James gave her a lazy smile. Over the noise he hadn't heard her approach. "Not very much but they have time." He took her hand and kissed the inside of her wrist.

Sir Symon called a halt and led the lads to the practice dummies on the far side of the yard to practice their strokes.

"Will you keep them with you?"

From beyond the wall a little skylark rose like an arrow into the sky higher than the tops of the trees, beating its wings furiously as it poured out a melody. James cocked his head and let it flow over them before he said, "If I can."

"They love it here," she said, watching the pages as they listened to Sir Symon's instructions. "As do I, though I would miss being in Dunfermline when the queen has the babe."

"Dunfermline." He looked down at the letter crumpled in his closed fist.

"What is that?" She frowned at him, making a line

between her brows that he was fond of, especially when he kissed it away. "I saw the monk. Did he bring news?"

James smoothed the parchment and folded it to stick into his belt. "Aye. Though it may not be as bad as I had feared. Tomorrow we'll leave for the palace. I must take the news to the king."

"Aye," she agreed. "I suppose if there is news then we must, albeit I'd rather stay here. Like the lads. Why won't you tell me the news?"

He looked back up into the high blue spring sky. The lark was gone and later, in spite of its sweet song, it would fight for its home. "Because it is grim." He sighed and wound his fingers with hers. "The English have executed Andrew de Harcla. Horribly as they do with anyone they consider a traitor." He ran his thumb over the back of her hand. "But Henri de Sully and the other French knights were on their way home by way of London. I think Harcla's treachery convinced the English king that he needs space to deal with his enemies at home. Sully is negotiating a truce."

"A truce?" Her eyes found his, and he could see how deep the hope went. "Peace. At least for a time."

"A long one. The talk is of thirteen years. If it is that long a truce, than I can safely keep my pages here with me." He turned her to face him and held both of her hands in his. "And even a lady."

CHAPTER 25

MARCH 1327

Cardross, Scotland

James gripped the king's hand and bowed to kiss it, trying not to frown at his liege's thin face, his hollow cheeks. "Are you well, sire?"

"You know that I'm not, Jamie, nor have been for some time. The years of lying out the cold have left me with this cough, and food has no taste to me." The king's voice was hoarse, but he smiled at the Queen sitting in the afternoon sunshine with little Prince David banging on the ground with a wooden knight. James bowed in her direction from beside the king, and she smiled. James thought her face looked full and she seemed rounded again. But surely she was past the age to give the king yet another child, especially since the long-looked for son had been born two years before. Beside her step-mother on the stone bench, Princess Margaret scowled as she poked her needle into her sewing.

The king's voice was hoarse and scratchy, and he cleared it. "The queen insists that I eat, but it gives me no strength, so I go on as I must."

"What does your physician say?"

The king laughed around a cough. "Did you think I called you here to physick me?"

"No, Your Grace." He shrugged and looked around at the king's new manor house on the banks of the River Clyde. Huge beeches, green with spring leaves, overhung its white-washed walls. The roof was thatched, and threads of smoke rose from a dozen chimneys. Gardeners dug as they readied the pleasure garden for planting. "But I was glad that you called me to you. I wanted to see your new manor since it's finished."

"You brought William with you?" the king asked as he continued to watch his wife and the two of his children. "His company would be welcome. Robert has been desolate since his father died. The lads have always been close it seemed to me."

James shook his head. "Walter. Holy St. Bride, that was a shock. There was no sign of sickness in him when I saw him last, and then he was dead."

The king patted James's shoulder. "Walk with me down to the water. I want to speak with you privily."

Purple mountains rose in the distance beyond the glistening inlet where the king's pier thrust into the water. The single mast of a long berlinn bobbed tied up to the pier. "How many oars does it have?" James asked.

"Forty." The king grinned and James laughed. A birlinn so large could stand against to anything in the Irish sea. "I'm having an isthmus dug between the lochs at Skipness to Tarbert to give our galleys quicker passage." The king threw his head back, and eyes closed, took a deep breath. "I've always loved the smell of the sea. If I'd been born a MacDonald instead of a Bruce, I think I would have made a good sea captain."

James smiled faintly. He'd never liked admitting the sea made his stomach roil and he'd emptied it into the waves more than once. "I'm glad that you were not, sire. I'd not have enjoyed following you to sea."

The king laughed until he started to cough, throwing an arm around James's shoulder. "It was neither of our fates, Jamie, but I would have you follow me to sea anyway. I have in mind to sail to Moidart to test my new galley, and you'll go with me."

James smiled but more serious thoughts drifted in. This was not what the king had called on him for. "Soon?" he asked.

"Mayhap I'll test it nearer for now. I have other tasks for you first." The laughter soured in the Bruce's face. "Donald of Mar has returned to beg for my peace and my aid."

"I knew he had returned." James flashed a wry smile.

The Bruce's strode furiously down to the reeds at the shore and spun to face James, his cheeks flushed though his face was still pale. "He would have me help rescue his beloved friend, Edward of Caernarfon. He has abdicated. Edward is no longer king and is a prisoner in Kenilworth Castle."

James blew out a long breath and watched as a kestrel spread its wings and let the wind lift it high in the air. It flew into the bright sunlight, and he lost sight of it. "Our truce was with Edward, so that is ended."

James nodded his understanding. When word had come that Queen Isabella and her lover Lord Mortimer had landed from France with an army at their backs, he'd known this day might come, but it was sooner than he had thought. "Have they crowned the boy already?"

"They have. My nephew is on his way here with Donald of Mar." The king gave James a sour look. "I shall forgive Donald his ten year delay in returning home and return his earldom to him."

James rubbed the back of his neck as he tried to think through the path that would be best. "Isabella and Mortimer may not have the hatred for Scotland that Edward had, though I don't count on any of the English to lack his greed. Still, it may be possible to push them to the peace-table. The question is how." He raised his eyebrows at the king. "We will attack England again?"

"They have hired the Flemish heavy cavalry under Jean de Hainault." He snorted. "Even whilst sending messages requesting to renew the truce, they began to send commands to raise the English levies for an attack. They think I'm a fool!"

"So it's open war yet again."

"You and Thomas will lead your men into England whilst I attack the English in Ireland."

James gave the king a skeptical look but the king frowned. "I'm not so old or so feeble, yet that I cannot lead an army."

CHAPTER 26

JULY 1327

Stanhope Park, England

Rain dripped down James's back and through his short beard. He scraped his hand through his hair, pushing it off his forehead as he spurred his horse across the frothing stream. Beside him, Donald of Mar gave his heavy cloak a shake, cursing the weather. The rain was light but steady, soaking through cloak and armor alike. Mar would have to learn that war wasn't a soft life as he'd had in the English court. Up ahead a horn sounded. "Richert," James said. "Good. They are keeping proper watch."

When James glanced over his shoulder, the score of men who rode with him were hunched on their horses but in good order, in a close march. It was midafternoon, but the slate clouds made it dark as dusk. James wove his way between massive oaks and past rocks and dark bogs until he spotted the fires of their camp, hundreds of them in a flicker ribbon of light along the south banks of the River Wear. Picketed horses formed on one flank and beyond them a herd of cattle milled and grazed under guard—a *gift* from their English hosts.

At the sight of the camp, he set his heels to his horse's flanks and cantered down the ridge. A stone bounced down dislodged by a passing hoof, and his men hooted and shouted in relief at returning. The wind was blowing wet and heavy as they crossed the valley and rode double file through camp. James turned in the saddle and shouted, dismissing his men to picket their horses. The air smelled of damp and men sweating, and meat cooking over the fire. There were cook fires all along the river amongst the trees and rocks. Many of the Scots hunched beside the flames, warming their hands and pulling bannocks cooked on metal plates from the fire with a stick. Others sheltered beside rocks of lean-tos made of hide. At one fire a man was sharpening the blades of pikes and tossing them into a pile. At another two squires hacked at each other with dulled practice blades and grunted when one landed a blow.

Five plain canvas tents huddled together next to the river. James flung himself to the ground, tossing his reins to a guard. His feet sank into the sloppy muck of the ground. Thomas ducked under the low opening of his tent. "Any sign of them?"

James shook his head. "I found a good spot I'll keep in mind though if we want to move camp. If the pup king and his fancy army ever show up. No sign of my brother either."

Mar climbed from the saddle, pursing his lips as his stepped into a puddle. "It's only been three days since Archibald left."

"Three are enough." James bit back a curse. He'd long since given up on teaching Archibald what he'd learnt himself in a hard school.

"We'll have to send scouts further afield," Thomas said. "Somehow we have to find them."

James snorted in amusement. "Patience, Thomas. They'll find us soon enough, and I like it here."

Thomas looked around the muddy camp and sighed.

"I don't understand," Mar said. "Why?"

James shrugged. "I'm hungry." He strolled to the fire that blazed in the middle of the square formed by their small tents. A hide still damp from skinning formed a rough pot. His stomach grumbled at the meaty smell. He pulled his dirk from his belt and poked into the simmering mess until he stabbed a hunk of beef. After he kicked a chunk of log closer to the fire, he sat down and gnawed on the meat. Mar stared at him, eyes narrowed. James knew he shouldn't poke at the lad. Well, Mar wasn't really a lad any more, but hell mend him if he didn't seem like one.

Thomas chuckled as he poked around in the pot for a piece of the stewed beef.

"This is a good spot for a fight, Sir Donald." JamesHe wiped his mouth with the back of his hand. "After burning our way here, we shouldn't be that hard to find. By the Rood, it makes me wonder if they're actually letting the pup lead the army."

"Hoi!" Sir Symon Loccart shouted, making James look up. "Look what I found me." Symon dismounted and pulled a sodden-looking squire off a mount. He gave the lad a push toward the three of them.

James tilted his head and examined Symon's prize as he chewed the tough beef. He swallowed and pointed his dirk at the pale-looking young Englishman. "What have we here?"

"Looks like a tiddler to me," Thomas said. "No more than a mouthful if we roast it over the fire."

"Too bony for that, and we have ample English cattle to slaughter. No need for roasting their squires." James stood up and sauntered to stand in front of the lad, who squared his shoulders, his jaw jutting with a mulish look.

"I'm not frightened of you." He narrowed his eyes to glare at James, but his face was pale as whey.

"Of course, you're not, lad. My lord earl was jesting. Now what name can I call you?"

"Thomas—Thomas de Rokesby."

James looked at Symon. "Where did you find him?"

"Scouting along the river. My men spotted him."

The lad kept sliding his eyes toward the dirk still in James's hand, so James sheathed it at his belt. "You're a long way from home. And riding near my army unasked is no safe thing."

Rokesby crossed his arms over his chest with a defiant look, but his thin hands were shaking. "The king promised a good reward to the squire who found you."

"Well, his finding me is taking long enough. It's what I'm here for."

Rokesby opened and closed his mouth a couple of times before he squeaked out, "It is?"

"Aye. So where is this king of yours that he can't find me?"

"Are you going to go attack him?"

James laughed and shook his head. "I'm happy enough here. Mayhap I'll let you go tell him where I am."

The lad's eyes widened. "Would you? He promised a knighthood and a land worth a hundred marks a year to whoever brought him word."

James grinned at Thomas Randolph. "What do you say, my friend? Should we send young Rokesby here back to receive his reward for finding us? He earned it."

Thomas's mouth was twitching with barely repressed laughter. "Why not? It will save us the trouble of finding them, and I'm growing right fond of this piece of England."

James gave the lad a hard look. "But I don't do favors for the English for nothing. I expect you to repay me. Now where is this pup of a king and his army?"

Rokesby squirmed a bit, twisting a foot in the mud. "At Haydon Bridge. I heard tell they thought you were retiring toward Scotland, and the king thought to cut you off. It's been—well, there hasn't been much food. The supply train was left behind. They brought out tents for the king and the lords." He gazed around the stark Scottish camp. "But—" he faltered. "I suppose you wouldn't know about those."

"Oh, I know the English fondness for them."

"We've been cold and wet. The Hainaulters and the archers are fighting—" He snapped his mouth shut as though realizing he had said too much.

James nodded as though the news meant nothing to him. "We'll let you carry the news to your king if Sir Symon has no objection."

Thomas strolled to stand beside James and looked the squire up and down. "You object to turning the tiddler loose?" he asked Symon who, after all, had claim to what little ransom the lad might be worth.

Symon shrugged. "You and Sir James are welcome to him."

"Then tell your king that we're as eager to fight him as he is to fight us," Thomas said to Rokesby, who had a look of astonished hope on his face.

"Be that as it may, we'll await his army on this spot." James smiled kindly. "Sir Symon, if your men will escort our guest half-way to the Haydon Bridge to make sure he is safe, I'd be most grateful."

Symon jerked his thumb toward Rokesby's horse and shouted for one of his men. James turned his back and said in a low voice, "I'll send my scouts toward the bridge. This should be – interesting."

* * *

For two days, James had sent out his scouts. His brother rode in with his two columns of men, beaming as he recounted that much of Dunbarshire was in flames and he brought more captured cattle. One of his men came complaining the graze was getting thin. Five men got into a brawl that left one with a broken arm. James thought about having them flogged. Donald of Mar sat in the entrance to his tent, scowling at the drizzle whilst Thomas supervised a squire polishing his mail and sharpening his sword. James whistled through his teeth and felt the edge of his dirk with a thumb.

In the morning, the sun broke through scudding gray clouds. "At last," Mar muttered.

James nodded as he rasped his dirk over a whetstone. The morning sun warmed his face, and he breathed in a deep lungful of air with no scent of rain. "The weather has broken. We may have fighting weather for a few days."

A scout galloped into camp calling out, "We found them!"

James sheathed his dirk that he'd honed to a razor's edge and stood. "What?"

The man threw himself from the saddle. "They're crossing Blanchland Moor."

Thomas ducked out of his tent. "How long to reach us?"

"Three or four hours, my lord." The man ran a hand through his sparse hair. "They're moving slowly, and the rain has the moor near impassible. When they reach the edge of the moor, they'll move faster."

"I need to see for myself." James looked about until he spotted Richert and shouted to him. "Form me a scouting party."

By then Thomas was shouting for his squire as Donald of Mar was ducking into his tent. "I'll form the men for battle," Thomas said as Richert led up James's horse.

"Where we discussed." James turned his horse's head and put his heels to its flanks. A score of men ran for their horses as Richert shouted for them to mount. Cantering to the hill-side near the camp past a towering gray spur that thrust skyward, James turned his horse in a tight circle to look over the field. It was muddy but mostly rocky ground, good for horses. Here, the ground fell away to the south bank of the River Wear. He turned the horse's head and trotted to the boulder-strewn edge of the racing river, raging from the heavy rains. Looking back over his shoulder up the slope, he nodded in satisfaction. His men would be out of bowshot from the north bank. If they fought this day, it would be here if the English could be brought to it.

His men raced into sight, so James headed for the best ford a mile downriver, and even it wouldn't be an easy cross-ing. The chill water boiled around his legs as his horse splashed, snorting, through the murky green swirling current. Richert rode to catch up and after riding beside him for a while asked, "What do you plan, my lord?"

"It depends on what they do. The real command will be with the earl of Lancaster and Jean de Hainault. They're canny enough. I want to see how badly we'll be outnumbered this time. Then we'll see."

They topped a small rise within sight of the moor. James raised his hand to call a halt and waited. In the far distance a horn winded, thin and lost in the winds of the moor. Marsh grass poked through pools of water that reflected the morning sun. The wet air was like a sodden blanket in the dazzling warmth. And beneath the morning sun, the might of the new king's army unfolded on the horizon like the opening of a leopard's paw, claws outstretched. James leaned forward in the saddle and caught his breath. *To have such an army...*

Even from a distance it was resplendent. In the center column, as big as a ship's sail, fluttered the leopard standard of the young Plantagenet king. Surrounding him, seven columns, all moved in good order. They would be exhausted though after days in the field chasing a foe they couldn't find, short on rations, wet through, tack rotting in the wet. But they'd be eager to punish the foe once they caught up.

"How many do you think?" Richert asked in an awed voice.

"Not so many as they had at Bannockburn. Fifteen thousand, mayhap." James turned his horse and spurred it to a gallop. He shouted, "Back to camp."

They raced across the river at a canter and up the sharp, rocky slope. Pebbles flew and skittered down the incline from under his horse's hooves.

His men had raised his starred standard next to the gray crag on the left flank. In front were ranks of men-at-arms with lances fixed, shields on their backs and swords sheathed. Behind, men formed a square of three rows, pikes gleaming like steel thorns in a hedge. In the rear, stringing their bows and their arrows thrust into the ground before them, the archers were arrayed into two long ranks.

The left flank was all chivalry and pikemen, three thousand all told that Thomas commanded, his men of the earldom of Moray. James saw the Randolph standard unfurled as the standard bearer shook the yellow banner. In the rear of his and Thomas's men, held in reserve, massed Donald of Mar's men-at-arms. He would hold and commit his forces where they were needed.

Sir Symon Loccart was pointing the Douglas men into position, riding through the ranks. "Sir James!" he shouted. "Will you review the positions?"

"You've done your job. No need for me to repeat your work. Join me here."

To attack their forces, the English would have to cross the swollen, roiling River Wear and storm up the rock slope. "Look," he said when Symon reached him. Past the foaming current, the enemy was before them, trooping over the ridge to spill in a shimmering flood into the riverland.

What I couldn't do with such an army, James couldn't help thinking. Triple the Scottish numbers at least, their leaders rode on barded horses, banners fluttering over their heads. Beside the massive leopard banner, James spotted the scarlet standard of Henry, earl of Lancaster, the four lions rampant of Jean de Hainault, the scarlet banner of Thomas de Brotherton, Earl Marshall of England, and hundreds of pennants of lesser lords. Rank upon rank of archers followed the chivalry, the longbows of the English, and the Hainaulters, who bristled with armor.

The English trumpets blew. *Harooo... Harooo...* James raised a hand and brought it down, the signal for his own trumpeter. They blared defiance. Would the English take the bait?

The trumpets died away and hissing filled the air and arrows pattered onto the rocks at the river's edge. Rocks flew as Thomas cantered up and reined his snorting mount beside James.

"Make sure they hold steady," James ordered Symon who wheeled his horse to trot back to the massed wall of lance and pike.

"Once I'd like to fight them on even terms," Thomas said. "Instead of being outnumbered."

"If they decide to fight," James replied. If they left it to the young king, they'd fight. Spies said he was eager to prove himself, but wily Jean de Hainault wouldn't be in a hurry to fight his way across a raging river and up a slope whilst his expensive mercenaries were ripped to bloody shreds. And James had never heard that the earl of Lancaster was any man's fool.

The rain of arrows had stopped. James shifted in his saddle and made himself more comfortable as he watched the English dismount. Archers dropped to the ground and sprawled to rest. Knights flung down their lances and shields.

Thomas pointed, "There's Edward." Edward of England rode down the slope through his host. Even from a distance the boy king was impressive on the back of a formidable black courser. His gilded armor shone like a second sun. The front of his surcoat was worked with gems into the shape of a lion reared and roaring. Another golden lion reared as a crest atop his helm. The king's banner was planted high on the crest of the slope, and he dismounted. Soon he was surrounded by his commanders.

"Yon is Jean de Hainault," James said, pointing at a burly man in plain gray armor. "Hainault spends his siller on his men, not shiny armor." Another man stomped up, resplendent in yellow and crimson—the earl of Lancaster. The other dozen men, James couldn't recognize.

"We might stand our men down," Thomas said in a doubtful tone.

James grunted. "They're well rested. A few hours in a schiltron will not hurt them." The English trumpets trilled a short blast and the men around King Edward parted. A herald shouted something that was lost on the wind and a handful of men scrambled toward the king and began to kneel in a line. James lifted his helm to rest it before him. "We'll have water brought to the men. It will be a long day."

Heralds ran messages, and there was scrambling amongst the English. Some carried buckets of drink and baskets of bread. James and Thomas sat watching the king go down a line of fifty or so squires, speaking words and drawing his sword to touch each on the shoulders. Thomas tensed suddenly and stood in his stirrups. "What's that?"

James leaned forward. "Those are archers—moving back."

"And men-at-arms. Look. A column of them following. What do you think?"

"I know what they think. That they'll flank us." James clicked his tongue on his teeth as he considered and then wheeled his horse. "Symon," he called. "Join us if you please."

"My lord?" The man cantered to join them.

"I don't want them to guess that they're spotted. I know where they'll cross. The two of you sit here and peaceably watch their little ceremonies whilst I meet our company."

He nudged his horse to a slow walk and called to Archibald, "Form your men past the boulders. And don't make a to-do." James continued his leisurely walk past the tall granite spur as he edged his horse away from sight of the river. He shifted in the saddle as he waited and scanned the valley beyond. Archibald trotted to ride beside James, the rattle and clop of five-hundred mounted men behind him.

"What's about?" Archibald asked eagerly. "Where are we going?"

"I'll show you soon enough." They descended into a valley rich with the scent of summer grass and damp earth. Pulling up, James pointed to dense oaks that began halfway up the hillside. "Half your men there." He pointed to the other side, strewn with boulders, where the trees were thin. "And half there."

Archibald frowned and scratched his cheek. "How do you know they'll come this way?"

"That's for me to see to." He smiled as he looked around and spotted Symon Loccart. He shook his head. "Give me your cloak, Symon."

The man raised his eyebrows as he unclasped the green cloak and handed it over. "Might I accompany you?"

"No, stay with here with him. You pretended to be one of Archie's men to accompany us, so here you'll stay." He twitched a smile. He'd trust Symon at his back, but this was a task he'd do on his own. "Command the left flank whilst Archibald takes the right. Hold until I give you the signal. Keep your men quiet but ready to move. I shouldn't be long if the English found the ford."

"I'd like my cloak back with no holes in it, pray you," Symon said and wheeled his horse, shouting, "Into the rocks!"

James flung the cloak around his shoulders and tucked it close. It didn't quite hide his entire surcoat and the three stars blazoned on his chest, so he pulled it tighter. With one last glance that his commands were being carried out, he kicked his horse to a trot. The English archers wouldn't move fast afoot, but he had to make sure he was in place before them. The slope led down to the ford he'd crossed only a few days before. He sat a bowshot above the river, just past the shade of a wide spreading oak. The azure and yellow of a pair of blue tits flashed high in its branches as they trilled. Below, the current burbled and splashed in the rocky bed. The wind was warm and sweet, blowing his cloak. He grabbed it and wrapped it close again. The birds stilled. In the quiet, he heard the rattle of armor and swords, the mutter of voices, a laugh, and the tread of a hundred horses. He had time to think that sometimes if one bait didn't work, another did, and shifted in the saddle.

And the enemy was there, beyond the gray-green froth of the river, advancing in ragged ranks, archers with their bows on their backs, screened by mounted shields and swords.

He gave his mount a gentle nudge of his knees and ambled into the open, turning so that his back was to the oncoming English. Another nudge and he slowly rode up the slope. Behind him, a horse whinnied and a voice shouted. Water splashed. Hooves clattered on rocks. James picked up the pace to a trot.

An arrow hissed by his ear. Another arrow clattered on

the stony ground. "Hold your fire, fool," someone shouted. "It's a knight. Take him alive, and we take the ransom."

He kicked the horse to a slow canter. *No need to let them capture him.* Hills rose on each side. Looking over his shoulder, he saw they were nearly where he needed them. One man-at-arm was near enough for James to see his scarred face. *Time to bring the fish to shore.* James spurred his horse to a gallop. It lengthened its stride, taking off with a surge. His cloak whipped behind him exposing his starred surcoat.

"It's the Douglas! The Douglas!" the man shouted. "A trap!"

Damn it to hell. "After them!" James bellowed. He reined his mount hard. It reared onto its haunches. His men boiled out of hiding. The noonday erupted with pounding hoof beats and shouting men. Cursing, James drew his sword, lifted his shield, and wheeled his mount. "After them!"

"Flee!"

"A trap! It's a trap!"

"A Douglas!" Archibald shouted as he gained James's side. James spurred his horse to a gallop. Around him the battle came to life, steel shrieking on steel, men shouting curses, the hammer of sword upon shield.

An arrow thunked into James shield and lodged. The man turned to run as James raced after him. James leaned to take him in the neck with his sword. The man swerved, dodging, his feet flew out from under him, and he went down, falling flat on his face, bow flying from his hand. James jerked his reins, his horse reared, iron-shod hooves coming down in a welter of blood. The man gave a hideous scream and James rode on. A knight looked over his shoulder as James gained on him. The valley ran with cries of "Douglas!" and the scream of dying men.

James thundered down on him, shield tilted. He smashed the edge into the knight's head, their horses slamming together. The knight flew forward and his horse galloped away. Once the man bounced before his foot jerked loose from the stirrup. He rolled onto his back groaning. James wheeled to look down at the man. "Yield."

The knight's leg that had been caught was twisted at an ugly angle. He pulled a sword from his belt and tossed on the ground.

James jerked his horse into a turn at the sound of hooves pounding behind him, but it was Archibald. "A prisoner. He'll be the only one. Some got away though."

James looked around at the field littered with corpses. His men came sweeping up to surround him. He pointed his sword at his prisoner. "Find a horse to throw him over. If we need a trade, he'll be of use."

* * *

James waved Sir Symon Loccart over. "Double the watch. I want them far enough out that we are well warned of an attack."

Symon cast his gaze over the English camp beyond the foamy ribbon of the Wear. "Aye. Do you think they'll try another sneak attack?"

Beneath a blaze of banners, pavilions had been raised for the English leaders in the midst of lines of fires that stretched out of sight along the river's bank. Smoke rose in thin fingers from thousands of campfires and hovered in a blanket over the army. Knights sat on the ground, honing their swords. Horses formed a hedge to the left in a long picket. They had settled in to rest, but James had no intention of trusting to that.

"Possibly. I'll not take a chance."

"What..." Symon exclaimed as three riders trotted toward the river and plunged into the water, a white banner snapping in the wind above their heads. Foam splashed around the men's feet, deep enough to reach the horse's bellies. One horse shied and reared, but its rider took it in hand, jerking until it joined its fellows in reaching the near bank and plunging up, slithering back on its haunches.

"Lord Thomas!" James shouted. "Company!" He strode through their men where they'd thrown down their pikes and taken off their helms. Squires scurried through the ranks of knights to lead away horses. The thud of an ax chopping firewood resounded. Men knelt rebuilding fires. Someone cursed.

Thomas wove his way through the tumult, bare headed but otherwise still fully armed. Donald of Mar followed, his helm tucked under his arm, his ferret face tense.

The three men climbed slowly from the saddle and approached. James raked a gaze over them—unarmed heralds in red and gold with a leopard sewn on their chests. The herald who stepped forward was a gaunt man barely past his youth. He raised his chin and strode, the other two trailing him. "My lords…"

Thomas nodded. "We'll hear your message."

"Lord Edward, our king, is as eager to do battle as you. He sent me to say that if you will cross the river to fight on level ground, he will draw back and give you space to deploy albeit tonight or tomorrow."

"A brave message," Thomas said.

"My lord earl." James jerked his head to indicate that he and Thomas should walk a few paces away to confer privily. "We should speak before we give an answer."

Thomas gave him a wide-eyed look.

Would the man never out-grow his foolish notions of what was fair in a war? Thomas Randolph as a good man for all of that, so James patted his shoulder and nudged him.

They walked together ten paces away, and Thomas said, "I

know they outnumber us. But we shall fight them, whatever their numbers."

James took a deep breath. "God be praised we have a noble captain with us to undertake so brave a fight. But, by St. Bride, if you trust me—" James gave him a look but Thomas darted his gaze away. "—we will do no such thing. There is no shame in the weaker side using what advantage it has. And it's foolishness to give up their advantage."

Thomas grimaced and turned to spread his gaze out over the English army below. "That is what my uncle would say."

James nodded. "I won't put it upon your honor. Let me speak for us." He gave Thomas's shoulder a friendly bump as he strode back toward the waiting heralds.

"Tell your king—" He looked into their faces one by one. "—we will do nothing whatsoever. It should be plain to him and his lords that we are in his lands. We have burned it and ravaged it. If this vexes him, he should cross the river and stop us. We are happy where we are. We shall stay here just as long as we please."

The herald's mouth worked like that of a landed fish. James thought he heard Thomas choke, but he kept his gaze fixed on the herald. He waved the gape-mouthed men away, so they clambered onto their horses. Once the clatter of their hooves on the stones turned to a splash as they re-crossed the river, James said, "I'll keep two hundred men in battle lines and alternate them through the night. They can keep themselves awake with battle cries. Let's see that our friends sleep as little as we can manage. Horn blowing in the dark should be a good thing. Young Lowrens has a bagpipe and we'll make use of it. We'll build the fires high and bright." He grinned. "This is exactly my kind of fight."

Thomas snorted. "James..." He shook his head. "After all these years, I should be accustomed to your idea of war."

"It's not that I mind a battle, my lord." James twitched a smile. "But I prefer to win."

* * *

The following day, James rubbed his chin and scowled at the glow of the sun as it westered toward the horizon, spreading its glow atop the far hills. The fact was they were near trapped. If the English dare not attack them, from this spot there was no easy road north to Scotland, except through English steel or through the great morass at their backs. One of his men gave a bagpipe a blow, its squall causing him to shiver. A trumpeter took up the challenge. "Wait until night-fall for your caterwauling," James called. He chewed his lip for a moment.

He motioned Archibald over. "Find Sir Thomas and Sir Donald for me, will you?" He sank down cross-legged and pulled his dirk. He tested the edge. It was sharp, but a dirk could never be too sharp, so he felt for his whetstone in his purse and whisked the blade over it as he waited.

Thomas strode up and crouched, breaking off half a bannock and handing it to James. "The men have eaten most of their oats. We'll soon be down to nothing but beef." He frowned as James bit into the flat bread. "How long can we hold out?"

"We have two hundred cattle. That will last us a bit." James stuffed the rest of the bannock in his mouth and chewed it. Donald of Mar walked up to listen as he chewed. "But we need to move our camp. There's a better place even harder to attack. It's no more than a half-hour ride. The ridge will act as a fence around it, has fresh graze for the cattle, trees for fires but open in the middle for our camp."

"Near to the river as we are now?" Mar asked.

"Aye, and a braeside they'll have to climb if they decide they want a fight."

Thomas took a bite of the half a bannock still in his hand. He nodded. "There might be deer we can kill too. That would help stretch our supplies."

"We'll build up the fires again and have the horns blown even louder than last night to cover our retiring." James tested the dirk on his thumb and then sucked off a drop of blood.

"I don't think they can blow louder than that." Thomas snorted. "I stuffed my ears with my fingers all night and didn't sleep for the yowling."

"Neither did the English." James twitched a smile. "Move the cattle first. We dare not lose them. The English have us trapped—for the moment."

* * *

The sun cast a gold sheen over distant hills through the drizzle. Dusk would soon be upon them, scudding clouds masking moon and stars, turning the night black as pitch. The English were scurrying like ants out of their ranks. Fires flickered and shouts floated on the wind. James watched, leaning a shoulder on a stone that made up part of the fence that formed a low wall around their camp. Two days camped here, and they were short on cattle with no salt, no oats. He'd have to find a way out of this corner soon, but for the nonce it would be wise to give the English something to think about.

He straightened and went in search of Thomas, past men hauling armloads of wood to pile high into bonfires to light up the night. "Good job, but make them even bigger than last night," James commanded. Two men led a bawling calf by a rope and another sharpened a knife for the slaughter.

Another stirred a bubbling pot made of hide giving up a scent of beef stewing.

James spotted Thomas crouched next to a pile of his armor beside his squire. He suspected it still smarted for Thomas to give up fighting the larger force. "I am taking men out tonight," he said as he stooped beside the earl. He stroked his moustache. "Keep the horns and pipes quiet until I return. I want the English to think they can rest."

Thomas eyed him unhappily. "On your own?"

James jerked a nod and rose. "Just a foray."

He spotted Richert and called to him to gather two hundred men and have them mounted to ride. "Half to carry lances and half swords," he ordered. Dropping a hand on his hilt, James narrowed his eyes as he calculated his intervals. By the time Richert had the men mounted, it would be full dark. The sky was clear and a quarter moon would give enough light. They would have to move slowly, quietly, and circle at least to the ford where he'd baited the archers.

Gawter led up two horses and gave James a hopeful look. James snorted but the lad was old enough. "All right. You may come." He wheeled his mount and nudged it to a walk, wending his way through the men. "Keep things quiet for now, lads," he said. "Save the noise for keeping me awake when I return."

"My lord, will you let me teach you the bagpipe tonight?" Lowrens called out and the men around him laughed.

"By the Rood, no!"

He waved farewell as he walked his horse away from the firelight. His men waited, black shadows in the night. James led his men along the heights above the river until the lights of their camp vanished behind him. Scattered fires flickered on the other side of the river through the trees. An owl screeched as he rode through the woods. A rabbit screamed when the hunter took it. Behind him, the sound of his men's horses trotting. Otherwise, the night was still.

They splashed across at the ford. James paused and said, "Afterwards, we meet here if anyone is separated," and he turned his horse to circle the stretch of the English camp. Away from the smells of camp, he breathed in the dusty scent of the dry summer air. Wind brushed his face and, a cloud scuttled across the white sickle of the moon. At last he turned again. The foe would not expect an attack from this direction, opposite that of the Scottish camp, but there should be a watch. The quiet made an itch between his shoulder blades, the ghost of a blade, and he twitched. Here and there the glow of dying campfires shined. A horse whinnied as they rode past, and there was a raucous laugh that was shouted down by sleepy voices. Far beyond, splashing the blackness, the Scottish bonfires spread against the horizon.

He heard the sound of horses and a voice grumbling about having the watch. And then, "I heard something. Quiet!"

James nudged his horse to a faster walk. "No ward, by St. George," he called in his best English accent.

"Good evening, sir," the sentry answered.

James grunted in response.

They rode on until the pavilions of the English lords sprouted like mushrooms against the light of the cook fires. "Now!" James shouted and spurred his horse to a gallop. "A Douglas!" He galloped into the midst of the sleeping men wrapped in cloaks. "Die, English thieves!" James saw a dozen men speared on the ground as they slept. One man scrambled to his knees. A swing of his sword took off the man's head in a geyser of blood.

The night was a furor of shouts and screams. "To arms!" someone shouted as Archibald buried a sword in his belly.

Others died, sharp steel ripping through their backs as they dashed for weapons. Richert's horse shattered a man's chest with a kick.

James slashed the ropes of a tent. It sagged and he slashed another as he rode by. It lurched sideways into a fire. The canvas flamed as someone inside screamed, "Help me!" James saw an Englishman snatch up an axe and run at Gawter, but the lad caught him full in the chest with his sword, hacking through muscle and bone.

He wheeled his horse. "A Douglas! A Douglas!" There was the boy king's tent. He spurred his horse toward the pavilion and jumped over an Englishman crawling, trailing a track of blood. A graybeard in a shift, scrawny white legs bare, scrambled toward the pavilion screaming, "To the king! To the king!"

"Die!" James shouted as he slashed into the bony chest. He hacked at a guy-rope at the corner of the king's pavilion.

Shouts behind him rose "To the king!" Horns blew, an urgent shrill that cried *Awake* and *To arms*. But he hacked a second rope and a side of the pavilion collapsed to the ground. A beefy man clad in a hauberk ducked out of the opening, sword raised, hauling the tousle-haired boy-king in a fine white shift behind him. A man with only a dagger in his hand, naked as a babe, flung himself in front of the king to shield him, knocking the boy to the ground. The lad gaped up from the ground as James thrust into his protector and jerked his sword free. The lad scrambled backwards, crab-like, but a guard with shield raised grabbed him and yanked him to his feet. Another guard flung himself in front of them.

The English horns blew again, brazen and desperate. A mob of Englishmen rushed toward the pavilion, screaming and bellowing, and behind James, Gawter screamed, "Help me!"

James wheeled his horse. He saw a tall Englishman who'd

managed to reach a horse swing at Gawter and the lad dodged, raising his shield. James charged.

His quarry met him with a slash at his head, but James slammed it aside. Tall and in a hauberk but with no helm, he bared his teeth in a snarl as he hacked at James. He bellowed, "Damn Scot!" and shoved in close, slamming a blow. James parried and buried his sword in the man's throat with a backslash.

"Retire!" James roared as he slapped Gawter's horse on the rump. The horse plunged to a gallop. "We're out of time. Retire! Retire!"

His men came sweeping past him at a gallop, flying by a flaming pavilion that threw sparks high into the air. All two hundred men surged past him, thundering silhouettes that rode down anyone who got in their way, jumping bodies that sprawled on the ground. He wheeled to be sure no one was left.

Suddenly, he felt a sickening crunch on his back. His vision wavered. He lurched in the saddle but managed blind a swipe with his sword.

Someone jumped back, dodging, and James raked his horse with his spurs. It took off at a gallop that nearly jerked his arms from their sockets. His stomach pitched. He clutched his horse's mane as he swayed half out of the saddle.

Behind him, he heard shouted commands and screams and moans as he galloped into the darkness. After a minute, he slowed to a trot. It wouldn't do to break his horse's leg by a gallop in the night. He flexed his back, twisting first one way and the other as he rode. No, nothing was broken, but his back throbbed at each thud of the horse's hooves. He'd be sore as the very devil for a few days.

At the ford, his men milled, and James heard voices raised in an argument. "We need to go back for him," Symon said.

"His orders were to wait—" Archibald's voice faltered. "But—"

"No need to go back," James called out. "I'm here. Back to camp."

When they reached their camp, Thomas was waiting, arms crossed over his chest, his face clamped in a frown. "What happened?" he asked as James climbed painfully from the saddle and grimaced.

"We drew blood."

"We should have gone together." Randolph paced in an angry little circle before he turned to face James. "We could have defeated them all. Now the chance is lost."

"It might have turned out well. Or we might instead have lost all. We risked enough. If we'd been there and defeated yonder, all would have been lost."

Thomas picked up a piece of wood and flung it into the bonfire. Sparks flew into the air and fluttered through the air. "If we can't defeat them with your tricks, then it's time to face them in battle. I shan't sit here and let them starve us into surrender, Douglas."

"A battle would be folly!" James shouted. He took a deep breath and gathered his patience, staring into the bonfire until he could look at Thomas without yelling. "We're outnumbered, and they're stronger every day. Merchants are bringing them food and supplies whilst we use ours up. You've seen the swarms of them. And we're in their country where no aid will reach us. We cannot count on rescue. We cannot forage. Supplies almost gone—" Now Thomas was nodding and listening, so James grinned. "So let us do to the English what I heard years ago that a fox did with a fisherman."

"A fisherman…?" Thomas said. He shook his head, rubbing the back of his neck. Then he gave a little laugh through his nose. "A fisherman."

James kicked a log closer to the bonfire. He motioned, and Thomas dragged one over and sank down, still shaking his head, his mouth twitching.

"So what did the fox do?"

"Once years ago, a fisherman lay by the banks of a river gathering in the catch from his nets. He had a hut there, a simple place with a fire and a door and a bed, nothing more. One night the fisherman was at his nets late, but when he returned home, by the light of the little fire burning bright, he saw a fox gnawing hard at his salmon. He ran to the door, so the fox couldn't escape, drew his sword, and yelled, "Thief, I have you now!" The fox looked about to find some bolt-hole, but the only way out was through the door, past the man and his sword."

James rubbed the side of his nose and winked. "Sound familiar?"

"So…" Thomas shook his head again.

"So the fox spotted the man's gray mantle lying on the bed. He grabbed it in his teeth and dragged it into the fire. The mantle caught fire, and the man gave a shout. He ran to grab his only mantle, jerking it out of the flames, and beating it out. The fox was away in a flash, through the door and to his lair. And the fisherman thought himself sorely used to since he lost his salmon, had his mantle scorched, and the wily fox got away."

Thomas shook his head. "No, I don't see where you're going with this children's tale."

"We're the fox and yon English, like the fisherman, think they have us trapped, but it won't be quite what they expect. I found a way out days ago." He chuckled at Thomas's growl. "We'll wet our feet, but we won't lose so much as a little page."

"Go on."

"After my surprise attack, our foes will think we're so stupid with pride that we'll give them open battle. Let them think so. On the morrow, we'll make merry, and at nightfall we'll build up our bonfires, blow our horns and keep them occupied whilst out of sight..."

* * *

It was the black of the night, a warm wind blowing scudding clouds across the tiny sliver of moon. James walked out from under the huge beeches into the clearing where a dozen bonfires roared, sending flames dancing higher than his head. He propped a foot on a woodpile and gazed around the camp. The bodies of half a dozen calves, throats slit, lay next to the fire. A lone cow bellowed and thrashed to escape, spooked by the scent of blood. It was the last to be slaughtered. A man cursed as he struggled to hold the ropes and another ran up with a knife. The camp stank of blood. He'd leave nothing, not even a single cow, alive for the English.

Richert came out of the shadows, leading his mount. His face reflecting the bright light of the fire. "We're loading the last of the split logs onto the horses, my lord." He handed James his reins.

James nodded. They had no time to lose, so he called to Lowrens, "Here. I have something for you."

The man swaggered over, grinning, his arm wrapped around his bagpipe and Dauid at his heels, a trumpet under his arm. "I'll not give you my bagpipe, my lord, no matter what you pay me."

"Just don't give it to the English. They might try my trick next time." James laughed as he took a handful of siller from his purse. "The two of you split this and hide it about you. You'll need it on your way home. I'll reward you well when you reach Lintalee."

Lowrens winked. "Don't fash yourself, my lord. We'll reach home."

James could only hope they would, but for their army to retire, he needed horns to blow through the night, so the risk had to be taken. "At daybreak, ride down to the camp." He grinned. "Ask them what they are waiting for since the Black Douglas is on his way home. We're leaving you sturdy mounts, so if the thieving English don't take them, you'll have an easy trip."

Lowrens nodded, his face becoming solemn. "Thank you for trusting us with your backs."

"We do." James turned to blink into the blackness, blind for a moment from looking at the light of the fires. Then he made out thousands of shapes under the huge trees, awaiting him, the long columns of his army ready to retire. He strode into the night. Behind him Lowrens's bagpipe skirled and the trumpet joined in.

"Let's go," Thomas said.

The two walked, leading their horses, at the head of four columns of men. As the ground under their feet squelched, water soaked into James's boots. He had scouted this bog thoroughly; he could lead them through it. When the water came to his calves, the sliver of the moon was reflected in the first dark pool. "Lay logs across," he said. "They'll reach." It would be a long night, but by daylight they would be miles to the north, foxes escaping to their lair.

CHAPTER 27

Norham Castle, England

The camp was buzzing with activity. Haunches of beef on spits sputtered as fat dripped into the flames, sending up mouth-watering scents. Squires dashed to and fro leading horses and raising pennants. A guard with a young pig under his arm bowed to James as rode by. "Riding in the tourney, my lord?" he asked as the pig squirmed and squealed.

"Indeed, I am," James replied with a grin.

Pennants outside the tents indicated their occupants: three pillows on yellow of Randolph, the stars on a blue field of Andrew de Moray, the white boar of Symon Loccart of Lee, the blue checky banner of James Stewart of Durisdeer, the blue of the knight of Liddesdale, James's mad cousin, the white and black banner of William Sinclair, the blue with a yellow bend of the earl of Mar.

On a hill overlooking the square red towers of Norham Castle, a long trestle table covered with a snowy white cloth was set up between two spreading pine trees. There beneath a fluttering banner with the royal lion of Scotland, King Robert de Bruce beamed genially as they broke their fast. James swung from the saddle and tossed his reins to a squire. Thomas Randolph, Donald of Mar, James Stewart and a handful of others had already taken places on the oak benches.

The cooks were setting the geese stuffed with onions and platters of immense salmons cooked in wine on the table.

"Your pardon, sire," he said taking a place. The scents made his stomach grumble and Symon Loccart elbowed him in the ribs as James filled his cup with ale.

The king nodded and said, "Thomas, I have decided that Norham Castle shall be yours, but I give the forests into the keeping of good Sir James."

"You always give him the forests, so he has better hunting," Randolph complained with a sly look at James.

"That's because I'm a better hunter." James watched William, a squire now, cut into the goose, and his mouth watered as a trencher of steaming meat was set before him. "I'm a better hunter than any of you, including his grace."

A gust of laughter went up around the table. Randolph smiled and shook his head. Neither of them expected to hold the lands they were taking in Northumberland, but the policy they'd both suggested of pretending to seize Northumberland, whilst holding tourneys and giving out grants of land had the king laughing as he hadn't since he'd first been ill. Even his cough seemed to be better these past few days.

The king was eating goose from his trencher and roaring as he jested. "It is a shame we have no English riding in the jousting. Where was the last you saw of Lord Percy? Mayhap I should send you to him."

"He was making a night march toward Newcastle when he realized my men were between his forces and Alnwick."

James took a bite of the goose and chewed it. "If I go hunting him, I'll miss the tourney myself, sire."

"I won't allow you to miss the jousting, Jamie. You'll ride against my nephew. I remember the tourney after my coronation. You hit him solid and knocked him flat onto his pride." The king was laughing so hard that tears ran down his face and James and Randolph laughed with him, remembering that spring day.

This was the strong king he had sworn to as a lad, James thought. His fears for the king's health were heedless worries. He would be well again, and the war would end. They would have peace to rebuild and to sail, even if his stomach roiled, in the king's birlinn to Moidart where they'd fled so many years ago. The young prince would have time to grow into a man to govern as well as his father. William would kneel to give him his oath. James could see it all.

"There are none of our ladies to admire our victories though. How can I enjoy defeating your nephew without a lady to applaud me?" His smile went deep.

Randolph snorted. "You always want there to be ladies. I think you still pine for not having captured Queen Isabella at York."

William bent to fill James's cut, his eyes bright with excitement, and whispered "Will you win the tourney, father?"

James laughed into his cup and drank before he said, "I always beat Randolph."

The laughter came freely and food tasted sweeter than any James had eaten in months. There was no need to pretend. When it was time for the tourney, James and Randolph mounted their coursers and rode with the Bruce down to the field together. The king took his place on a raised stand at the end of the field, his face flushed with laughing.

A horn winded long and low in the distance. James froze, his hands gripping the hilt of his sword. The guards surrounding the king's dais, turned their heads to the south, raising their pikes. Men stood still, listening. The horn came again.

The king stood. "Two. It is friends."

But James had ceased trusting years ago at the Battle of Methven. "To the king," he shouted to the pikemen who idled in the stands to watch the nobles ride at each other. "Now!" Men in studded leather jumped to their feet and pikes rattled as they were pulled from the stakes. Foot beats were like hail. A brisling hedge of steel three deep formed around the seated king.

Donald of Mar in his glittering armor sat gaping at the far end of the tourney field. Randolph nudged his horse and sat next to James as they watched. A horse stamped and whickered. The royal banner cracked in the wind above their heads.

James could see a banner flying as riders emerged from the green of the woods. Only one banner he thought as he leaned forward, straining to see. Dust kicked up under the hooves of the horses as they cantered in a long dusty column.

Randolph shaded his eyes. "Only one banner?"

James edged his courser a few steps ahead. "Not a banner," he said, his voice hoarse. "They fly a white flag."

The Englishmen spurred their horses, flag rippling over their heads as they came. In the lead was a lord, his armor enameled and burnished and with him two men in black gowns, fine wool under the dust, pleated and belted and sleeves with a touch of ermine at the wrists ad hats formed in elaborate folds. The leader rode a black stallion with a flowing mane and tail as dark as night. His yellow silk surcoat bore the blue lion rampant of the house of Percy and a yellow silk cloak was draped around his shoulders fastened with a sapphire broach.

So Percy had stopped running, James thought, as the man removed his helm. Beneath, his face was tight and grim. He had a few streaks of gray in his brown hair and an unlined face with eyes as dark as a moonless night.

"My lord Percy," Randolph said.

"I'm sent from the Queen Regent to Lord Robert." The man's horse made a restive step, and he took it in hand with a jerk. "On behalf of King Edward, I am to invite you to negotiate terms for a peace treaty. The Queen and Lord Mortimer would see the war between our kingdoms come to an end. If it should please his grace, Lord Robert, to receive us."

Percy's jaw was so tight, James thought his teeth might shatter, but it was the words that mattered. His heart thundered in his chest. *This will mean peace after a lifetime of war.* "I believe it will please his grace to hear your terms," James said mildly, careful to keep his face blank. Blood roared like a tide in his ears.

Peace.

"My companions are William of Dunham and William de la Zouche to aid in the negotiations. Terms must include a marriage between King Edward's sister and the young prince of Scotland."

James thought of his father the last day he had seen him before he was taken in chains to and English dungeon, of William Wallace screaming as he died, of young Andrew de Moray in his heroic pride, of Bishop Wishert going blind in a dungeon, of Simon Fraser and the gallant Christopher Seton following Wallace to his fate, of all who had suffered and died. Of his lifetime's struggle. Vindicated. *At last.*

CHAPTER 28

SEPTEMBER 1327

Cardross, Scotland

The king swayed in the saddle. James moved closer with a nudge of his knee and caught him to hold him erect in the saddle. Cardross was within sight and James said a prayer of thanks to St. Bride. The king had refused to stop to rest since a messenger had brought news as they rode that the queen had fallen and was giving birth, more than a month before the bairn should have come.

The king pushed his hands away. "I'm able to ride, James," he said but his words were hoarse.

Their army trailed a mile behind them in dusty columns. James exchanged a glance with Randolph who turned his horse's head and rode back along the lines of weary, silent men, giving orders for camp. In the distance, a bell was tolling. Robert de Bruce cursed and jerked erect. He put his spurs to his horse. It surged ahead. James kicked his horse to a trot and kept beside the king, ready to catch him if he fell as they clattered into the bailey yard.

The Bruce held onto his saddlebow as he climbed painfully from the horse's back. He dropped the reins and ran for the door as a guard threw it open. A knot of servants at the end of the hallway dropped bows and curtsies. For a moment, the king staggered and James reached for his arm. The Bruce caught himself with a hand on the wall and shot James a scowl as he hurried on. He blew out a relieved breath when Lady Christina stepped into the doorway of the queen's bower. Her face was calm though tear streaked her cheeks, her eyes red.

She held out her hands. "Robert—" she said.

The king shook his head. "Holy Jesu, no," he whispered. His sister rested her head against his chest for a moment, wrapping him in an embrace. His shoulders were shaking with silent sobs. "I should have been here."

"Whist..." Christina said. "You could have done nothing more than the midwives did. The birth... It was fast but the bleeding was terrible. It wouldn't stop. I'm sorry. I swear they tried everything. I *made sure* they tried everything." She pressed her hand to her mouth for a moment. "I never left her, Robert. Not for a moment. She didn't die alone, and she knew you were coming. But at last she closed her eyes, and they never opened."

The king kissed Lady Christina's forehead before he pushed past her. He looked back. "Leave us alone." He shut the door, closing everyone out.

James held himself up with a hand on the wall, empty with grief. "The babe?" he asked.

Lady Christina tears streamed down her face. "He's too small. So tiny."

James reached for her hand. She gripped it hard. "John... The priest christened him John, but I fear he won't live."

Randolph, Gilbert de la Haye and Archie walked silently into the hallway. James shook his head at them.

"We must prepare to leave for York," Randolph said. "The negotiations won't wait."

"I know, but—" He looked at the closed door. "We have a duty here as well."

Lady Christina nodded to them, the lines deep in her pale face. "I'll stay with my lord brother. Wash the dirt of the road away. Rest while you can. He'll need you by him when he's ready."

James kissed her hand before he turned for his own room. Duty would tear him away soon. Randolph was right, but he must be here for the king whilst he could. When he opened the door, Marioun turned from a fire on the hearth, her eyes red and swollen.

"James," she said. "Thank the Virgin you're here."

He nodded dully as he moved toward her and wiped her tear away with his thumb. He didn't even know what to say, so he curled his hand around the back of her head, fingers tangling into her soft hair, pulling her to him. The space between them vanished, taking weariness and grief at least for a time as they melded together, lips and hands rediscovering each other after too long apart.

The was a thrill of renewal and the comfort of long familiarity all at once; the softness of her breasts beneath his caressing fingers, the lush heat of her breath on his lips, a certain sigh as he trailed kisses down her neck, they were all things that he sought like a ship seeks safe harbor. Her hands skimmed a trail along his back, and he couldn't remember when he had needed her so much.

"There's wine," she whispered, but he shook his head.

"I need you more."

CHAPTER 29

JUNE 1329

The Royal Manor, Cardross, Scotland

Princess Joan was a chubby lass, barely seven, her cheeks round and dimpled, her hair a tumble of golden curls down her back. She curtseyed prettily to the king and bent to kiss his thin hand. A well-brought up princess, James pondered. Even when her mother had ridden away after the resplendent wedding feast in Berwick-upon-Tweed and left her behind with him and Randolph, she had not wept.

Her husband was already kneeling on the floor beside the king's chair next to a roaring fire, his arms around the rusty-colored deerhound. Sunlight from the tall windows of the solar flooded the room.

A trickle of sweat inched its way down the back of his neck.

"My lord father will give me a dog for my Saint's day," Prince David said proudly. "He has many of them."

Joan gave David a rather pitying look, not the first he'd received from her since James had escorted the children here after the wedding. But she was kind enough, even if she did treat her lord husband like a tedious child, and it made James smile.

The king had pretended to everyone, even James, that he had not attended nor taken part in the wedding because the King of England had chosen not to attend. He wanted no one to know that he was so weak he could no longer stand. James wondered whether it was only the sickness that was eating his body or part of it was the grief that had etched so deep into his face. Returning from England to find the queen dead and the wisp of a lad, John they had called him, dying from being born too early had seemed to leave him with no strength left to fight the dreadful sickness. The pilgrimage he had insisted on making to the shrine of St. Ninian had drained the last of the king's strength.

James squatted to be on a level with the children. "You may play for a while." He smiled at little David who was as noisy as a five-year old could be. "But quietly."

The king covered his mouth with a pink cloth and bent forward as he coughed and choked into it. He waved a hand toward James. "Let them be as raucous as they like. I would enjoy a bit of noise. You've all been so solemn." His voice was little more than a croak.

James twitched a stiff smile. "As it please your Grace." James cleared his throat of the rock that was constantly lodged there. *The king is dying. The king is dying.* The words tolled in his mind like a dirge. He rose to his feet. "I'll see that the preparations are complete for the Privy Council."

"In my chamber, not the council hall," the king whispered. "I have something important to say to all of you."

James's hands were trembling as he bowed and Randolph nodded that he would stay as James softly closed the door. Elayne, his own lady wife, and Lady Christina stood outside the door in the hallway with Christina's new husband. Over the years, Elayne had become skilled at ignoring that she was still James's wife.

Andrew de Moray raised his eyebrows at James. "How is he?" James shook his head. What a strange couple Lady Christina and Andrew de Moray made, the lady a good twenty years older than her flamboyant husband. But the king had been pleased his sister had finally agreed to wed. They were all happy to please him.

"The same. He will tax his strength no matter what Randolph or I say. Lady Christina, mayhap if you—"

"He has never listened to me." She laid a kind hand on his arm. "Besides, you know why he insists, Jamie. This is what he must do." Her mouth tightened into a tight line. "It's no easier for any of us, but pretending won't change it."

Marioun stepped into the hallway. Elayne nodded coolly to Marioun and smiled.

"Bishop Bernard is here. He is the last, and I showed him to his chamber."

James ran his hand over his beard and sucked in the stinging behind his eyes. After a deep breath he was sure he could sound as calm as he should, so he said, "A few more minutes with the children. I fear he won't be strong enough see them again."

Andrew de Moray nodded. "He doesn't want the prince to see him carried, so they should be taken into the garden."

It was as though James was stabbed. "He hates when anyone sees him helpless."

"Better that they go to the river and away from hearing—" Marioun swallowed. "I'll take them for a walk to feed the swans. Lady Joan likes that."

The door opened and Randolph stepped through. "Someone should take them," he whispered. James could hear the king's dry hacking. When Marioun held out her hands, the two children took them readily enough, but Lady Joan gave a look over her shoulder. She'd been through much in her short life, James thought. "My father died," she said pensively. "Perhaps Lord Robert is dying, too."

"He is not!" David replied, but Marioun hushed him. She smiled. She had been sad when she'd lost their bairn two years before, and it grieved her, he thought, that they had none of their own. But William was his heir, so more children didn't matter except to give her joy.

Marioun started for the door. "We'll have cakes, and then if you like, we'll see if the swans are hungry."

"They're always hungry," Prince David said as Marioun led them away.

Lady Christina nodded her understanding. She patted James's arm again before she turned and walked thoughtfully away. "See that everyone is ready for the meeting, will you, Sir Andrew?" Randolph said.

James waited until Andrew de Moray was out of sight before he took a deep breath. In this past month, this had become his especial task, the one that ripped at them both. He bent and as the king slipped a bony arm around his shoulder's, he lifted his liege's thin, emaciated body. He weighed no more than a babe. The king accepted being carried by him with no complaint, but no one could see. It was more than either of them could stand. They never spoke of it.

Randolph pulled the velvet bed draperies back as James placed the Bruce in the bed and drew the coverlet up over his chest. The king closed his eyes for a moment.

"My liege," James said, his voice thick with grief, "must you do this now? You should rest."

The Bruce took James's hand and squeezed feebly. "Would you have me continue like this, Jamie? My old friend." He managed a smile. "Once this is done, I can rest. Truly rest. Now call my council to me."

The Privy Council filed in: Thomas Randolph, Andrew de Moray, Robbie Boyd, Iain Campbell, Maol of Lennox, Angus Og McDonald, Bernard de Linton, now a bishop, Robert de Keith, Gilbert de la Haye. Propped up on pillows, Robert de Bruce turned his head and nodded at the men around him. "You've already sworn your fealty to my son. I trust your oaths, and I'll not ask you to repeat them. But there is yet a task I've left undone." The king looked at the grim and solemn faces. "You must not look so. You know the trials I've had. And you know the sin I committed to secure my crown. When I most wanted to pay for that sin, I couldn't." He coughed and paused while he wiped his mouth. "I vowed that I would go on a crusade, make war on the enemies of Christ and his church. But the Lord God denied me. So before my council, I put that duty upon one of you."

"I have no more gallant knight in my realm than you, Jamie. I beg you, my old friend, fulfill my oath for me."

James choked on the sob that was tearing its way out of his chest. He heard a groan ripped from Angus Og's throat. Maol of Lennox grimaced as he struggled against sobs.

"Listen to me." The king's voice was a little stronger. "When I am dead, have my heart taken out of my body and embalmed. Take such gold from my treasury as you need and such knights as you will. Let it be known as you travel that you bear the heart of King Robert of Scotland. Bear it into battle and when you can, take it to the Lord's Holy Sepulcher in Jerusalem."

Impatient with his weakness, James wiped his face dry with the heel of his hand. His throat felt raw and there was no breath in him. But the king was waiting. He knelt and gently took the king's hand. "My liege—I will do what you command. As I ever have." His throat closed up.

"You promise me? You swear it?" the king whispered.

"I swear it. I shall fulfill your oath as though it were my own."

"Thanks be to God." Robert de Bruce closed his eyes. "Now let me rest."

With a deep sigh, the king turned his head away. James was sure it would not be long. Master Ingram bent over the king and said something to him in a quiet tone as James closed the door. He went to find Randolph standing in the garden staring at the blue-gray mountains in the distance. His face was drawn with pain.

James had never noticed the white at Randolph's temples before. He suddenly seemed older. "You must—"

Randolph turned. "Must what?"

"You must—be careful." James bit his lip, a habit he thought he had lost years ago. "Who will have your back? When I'm not here?"

Randolph smiled a little. "The king trusts me, and you must as well."

"Holy St. Bride, I trust you. Of course I trust you. It's the English I don't trust."

"We're not at war now, Douglas."

"Not today. But when our king is dead?" He rubbed at his eyes, scratchy and tired from tears and grief. "You think they'll honor their treaty? As Longshanks honored his promises, that's how they'll honor it. With the king dead. With Walter Stewart dead. And Bishop Lamberton." James examined his feet, escaping Randolph's doubtful gaze. Peace was wonderful, but James feared it would not last. "You're a good captain, my friend. I've trusted you with my life more times than we could count. But you are only one man. Archibald is brave and loyal, and he's as thick as a plank of wood. My cousin of Liddesdale is a braw fighter, but murderous mad. Donald of Mar?" He snorted. "Robbie Boyd is a great knight but no leader. The same with Gilbert and

Maol, good men but no warlords. Iain Campbell is no more than a lad. The only one you can count on is Andrew de Moray. Keep him close to you."

He put a hand on Randolph's shoulder and squeezed. "Take care, my friend. Just take care and keep Andrew close. Until I return."

CHAPTER 30

AUGUST 1330

Near the Fortress of Teba, Spain

The sunbaked land seemed to go on forever. James drank deep from the watered wine in his bag. He had never been so thirsty as the weeks since he'd arrived in this ill-begotten land. King Alfonso's orange banner drooped like something dead over their heads in the still, hot air. He wondered if he had been wrong to accept King Alfonso's invitation to help him fight against the Saracen's, but the Bruce's wish had been to fight the church's enemies. The castle of Teba was stuck high on the cliff in the distance. The Castle of the Stars, they called it. James snorted. One of the trebuchets threw a stone at the fortress with a crash.

The young king's sour-faced commander rode up, dust puffing from the horse's hooves. "My lord Douglas, His Grace asks that you Scots take the left flank. We'll push Osmin back to be sure he does not make it over the river."

"As your king pleases. We're here to aid him."

A dozen Scots had already been with the Castilian king when James arrived with his following. With the dozen knights and score of squires in his company, they made a small but goodly band.

William de Keith scowled, his arm in a sling. "It is my luck to get hurt by a misfired trebuchet and miss the real fighting."

"There will be more fights. We have a long way to go and many battles before we reach the Holy Land." James nudged young Cailean Campbell. "Blow the assembly."

James looked over the ground where they would fight. It was flat, nothing but sand until the narrow strip of a river, then nothing but muddy shallows, bordered by reeds. He watched one of the Castilian knights ride down the line of the right flank, shouting and waving his arms. It was all chivalry on heavy destriers such as they rarely saw in Scotland. In the center, pikemen formed long bristling lines. The Castilian king, Alfonso, his resplendent armor reflecting the bright sun and surrounded by five hundred knights, took his place on a hill behind the pikemen. He had not been told, but James supposed King Alfonso would hold his men for the reserve.

The king's trumpets blew and blew and blew. Cailean raised his horn to his mouth. Symon Loccart grinned as he took his place to James's left. William Sinclair clanged his visor shut as he rode. William Logan and his brother Robert laughed as they took their places.

James led his men toward the river. The glaring sun rippled off the narrow strand of river.

He wheeled his mount and stood in his stirrups. "I know your courage, so I do not urge you to bravery. You are good and valiant knights," he shouted. "I do tell you that we fight a strong, fierce enemy, but we will show the Saracens how Scots fight. If we die here today, we die in God's service, and for King Robert whose heart I carry. Heaven's bliss will be our reward." He gripped the gold chain and the enameled coffer about his neck that contained the heart of his liege lord. "For the Bruce!"

King Alfonso's trumpets shrilled. James wiped the sweat from his face and clanged shut his visor. He put his spurs to his courser, and it took off at a canter. Suddenly, the enemy was before them, close ranks of Moorish cavalry a mile of them in flowing light-colored robes and turbans on high-stepping steeds. They stretched out of sight in both directions. Spears glistened in the light and curved scimitars flashed in their hands.

Trumpets shrilled and with a shout, James urged his horse faster. "A Bruce! A Bruce!" His men took up the shout behind him. *A Bruce! A Bruce! A Bruce!*

James splashed through the shallow water and thundered up the far bank. A tall Saracen was before him, a curved sword swinging as he came. James met him and they hacked at each other. The Saracen grunted some words James didn't understand, but James knocked his blade aside and lay his face open to the bone. He screamed as James buried his sword in his neck.

He wrenched his sword free and heard a ululating behind him. A Saracen came careening at him, a sword in his hand. He was spare and his face scarred, his turban tailing a long drape. James hacked at his face, but the man knocked it aside. The Saracen's horse was faster, and he circled James, raining blows on his shield. James hauled on his reins and his horse reared, steel shod hooves lashing in the Saracen's face. His head smashed and gore splattered.

He pulled up his horse and made a tight circle. The Saracens were behind them. He stood in his stirrups and stretched high, searching for the Castilians.

"Where is our right flank?" William Keith asked with a hint of panic in his voice. The Scots milled around James.

James looked down at his bloody sword and sucked on

his teeth for a brief moment. "They either didn't charge or they pulled back." The Saracens were reforming between James and the river, and the flanks moving in. *Trapped.*

Robert Logan cursed. "Alfonso let us walk into a trap. He's a cousin to the damned English king. I knew—"

James cut him off. "What matter now if it was a misunderstanding or if we were betrayed? We either cut our way through or we die."

The Saracens shouted, waving their swords and spears in the air. James was sure they had moments until their foes charged.

"Form a wedge. I led you into this. If God wills, I'll lead you out." He gripped the heart in its golden cask for just a moment as his men lined to each side in an arrowhead. "A Bruce!" He raked his spurs and his horse lunged so hard it ripped at his arms. "For St. Bride and the Bruce!" he shouted as he barreled into a Saracen, his sword swinging. They were almost through the thin line of their foe.

It slowed his mount but he knocked the enemy aside. Something sharp pierced his side with a sickening pain. He twisted and hacked at a spear. Blood poured down his side and he hacked again. He was falling, and he rolled. A sword slashed into his shoulder. He was on his knees, and he knocked a blow aside. Pain shuddered through him, and he was on the ground and trying to gasp for breath that would not come.

Then night rushed in on him.

When James rolled over, the battle had ceased. It was quiet except for a rustle of wind. He pushed his hand into soft heather that covered the ground and rose to his knees. He didn't recall how he got here. Dazed, he staggered to his feet and looked for his men. They wouldn't have left him lying alone. But his head cleared with the light of a soft Scotland morning. The weakness in his legs faded away.

A voice behind him called *Jamie, I'm waiting.*

At the top of a rise, silhouetted by the sunlight, Robert de Bruce motioned to him. *You've made me wait.*

James began to run toward the king. "Lead on, Braveheart!" James shouted. "And Douglas will follow as ever he was wont."

HISTORICAL NOTES

have tried as much as possible to weave my fiction into the known facts of this immensely complex period of history. Much information has been lost to time and the destruction of wars. Often even the dates of some events such as the details of James Douglas's last battle are unknown or in dispute.

The members of James Douglas's army to whom I refer to by name are fictional although I am careful to use names which records show were used during that time period in lowland Scotland. Nothing is known of the woman who James Douglas married; it was thought at one time that he hadn't married. However, in recent years evidence has come to light which indicates that he did marry, and his son, William, was his legitimate heir. He also had a bastard son born after his death who eventually became earl of Douglas. It is unknown who the mother of either son was.

None of the battles are fictional, and the techniques used in battle are as close as I can portray of what they used. The ladder I describe in *Countenance of War* and *Not for Glory* was invented by a Scot and used in sneak attacks including the one on Berwick Castle. When the English captured one after the unsuccessful attack on Berwick Castle, it was described with astonishment in the *Chronicle of Lanercost.*

My description of the Scottish policy of not attacking the English who didn't resist Scottish raids is not fiction; that was, in fact, the Scottish policy. Even the English *Chronicle of Lanercost* states that those who did not resist were left unharmed. It would have taken amazing control over an angry medieval army to achieve that.

This did not mean that the English of northern England didn't suffer under those raids. By the end of the period, much of the area was depopulated because of the loss of crops and herds. This combined with severe weather during the period meant a great deal of suffering whilst the King and nobles refused to make peace with the Scots and admit that it was an independent nation.

As for my historical references, the major ones are *The Brus* by John Barbour, *Chronicle of Lanercost* translated by Sir Herbert Maxwell, *Robert Bruce and the Community of the Realm of Scotland* by Geoffrey W. S. Barrow, *Robert the Bruce, King of Scots* by Ronald McNair Scott, *James the Good, The Black Douglas* by David R. Ross, and *The Scottish War of Independence* by Evan M. Barron, *The Chronicles of England, France and Spain* by Sir John Froissart, *The Scottichronicon* by Walter Bower, *The True Chronicles of Jean le Bel,* and *The Chronicle of Lanercost.*

LIST OF MAJOR HISTORICAL CHARACTERS

Sir James Douglas, Lord of Douglas – known as the Sir James the Good to the Scots and the Black Douglas to the English, Scottish soldier and knight, lieutenant and friend to King Robert de Bruce, Baron of Douglas, Lord Warden of the Marches of Scotland

William de Lamberton – Bishop of St Andrews who campaigned for cause of Scottish freedom under Andrew de Moray, William Wallace and Robert de Bruce

Robert de Bruce – King of the Scots

David de Moray – Bishop of Moray and supporter of Scottish freedom and of King Robert de Bruce

Sir Thomas Randolph – Earl of Moray, nephew of King Robert de Bruce

Maol Choluim II – Earl of Lennox and loyal follower of Robert de Bruce

Sir Niall Campbell – brother-in-law of King Robert de Bruce and husband of Mary de Bruce

Sir Robert Boyd – Scottish nobleman and loyal follower of King Robert de Bruce

Sir Robert de Keith – Lord Marischal of Scotland

Sir Gilbert de la Haye – supporter of King Robert de Bruce, Baron of Errol and Lord High Constable of Scotland

Angus Óg MacDonald, Lord of the Isles – Scottish nobleman and supporter of King Robert de Bruce

Walter Stewart – Hereditary High Stewart of Scotland

Bernard de Linton – Chancellor of Scotland

Edward II of England – King of England

Aymer de Valence – Earl of Pembroke, one of the commanders of the English forces during the invasion of Scotland

Robert de Clifford – Baron of Clifford, Lord of Skipton, English commander during the war with Scotland also first Lord Warden of the Marches of England.

AUTHOR'S NOTES / SCOTTISH AND ARCHAIC WORDS

In writing historical fiction, an author sometimes has to choose between making language understandable and making it authentic. While I use modern English in this novel, the people of 14th century Scotland, of course, spoke mainly Scots, and Gaelic and French. To give at least a feel of their language and because some concepts can only be expressed using terms we no longer use, there are Scottish and archaic English words in this work. Many are close to or even identical to current English although used in a medieval context. The following is a list of terms in which I explain some of the words and usages that might be unfamiliar. I hope you will find the list interesting and useful."

Aright, In a proper manner; correctly.

Aye, Yes.

Bailey, An enclosed courtyard within the walls of a castle.

Bairn, (*Scots*), Child.

Baldric, Leather belt worn over the right shoulder to the left hip for carrying a sword.

Banneret, A feudal knight ranking between a knight

bachelor and a baron, who was entitled to lead men into battle under his own standard.

Bannock, (*Scots*), A flat, unleavened bread made of ground oatmeal or barley flour, generally cooked on a flat metal sheet.

Barbican, A tower or other fortification on the approach to a castle or town, Especially one at a gate or drawbridge.

Battlement, A parapet in which rectangular gaps occur at intervals to allow for firing arrows.

Bedecked, To adorn or ornament in a showy fashion.

Bend, A band passing from the upper dexter corner of an escutcheon to the lower sinister corner.

Berlinn, Ship used in the medieval Highlands, Hebrides and Ireland having a single mast and from 18 to 40 oars.

Betime, On occasion.

Bracken, Weedy fern.

Brae, (*Scots*), Hill or slope.

Braeside, (*Scots*), Hillside.

Barmy, Daft.

Braw, (*Scots*), Fine or excellent.

Brigandines, Body armor of leather, lined with small steel plates riveted to the fabric.

Brogans, Ankle high work shoes.

Buffet, A blow or cuff with or as if with the hand.

Burgher, A citizen of a borough or town, especially one belonging to middle class.

Burn, (*Scots*), a name for watercourses from large streams to small rivers.

Caltrop, A metal device with four projecting spikes so arranged that when three of the spikes are on the ground, the fourth points upward.

Carillon, Music on chromatically tuned bells esp. in a bell tower.

Cateran, Member of a Scottish Highland band of fighters.

Ceilidh, A Scottish social gathering at which there is music, singing, dancing, and storytelling.

Chancel, The space around the altar at the liturgical east end.

Checky banner, In heraldry, having squares of alternating tinctures or furs.

Chief, The upper section of a shield.

Chivalry, As a military term, a group of mounted knights.

Chivvied, Harassed.

Cloying, To cause distaste or disgust by supplying with too much of something originally pleasant.

Cot, Small building.

Couched, To lower (a lance, for example) to a horizontal position.

Courser, A swift, strong horse, often used as a warhorse.

Crenel, An open space or notch between two merlons in the battlement of a castle or city wall.

Crook, Tool, such as a bishop's crosier or a shepherd's staff.

Curtain wall, The defensive outer wall of a medieval castle.

Curst, A past tense and a past participle of curse.

Dagged, A series of decorative scallops along the edge of a garment such as a hanging sleeve.

Defile, A narrow gorge or pass.

Destrier, the heaviest class of warhorse.

Din, A jumble of loud, usually discordant sounds.

Dirk, A long, straight-bladed dagger.

Dower, The part or interest of a deceased man's real estate allotted by law to his widow for her lifetime, often applied to property brought to the marriage by the bride.

Draughty, Drafty.

Empurple, To make or become purple.

Erstwhile, In the past, at a former time, formerly.

Ewer, A pitcher, especially a decorative one with a base, an oval body, and a flaring spout.

Faggot, A bundle of sticks or twigs, esp. when bound together and used as fuel.

Falchion, A short, broad sword with a convex cutting edge and a sharp point.

Farrier, One who shoes horses.

Fash, Worry.

Fetlock, A 'bump' and joint above and behind a horse's hoof.

Forbye, Besides.

Ford, A shallow crossing in a body of water, such as a river.

Gambeson, Quilted and padded or stuffed leather or cloth garment worn under chain mail.

Garron, A small, sturdy horse bred and used chiefly in Scotland and Ireland.

Gilded, Cover with a thin layer of gold.

Girth, Band around a horse's belly.

Glen, A small, secluded valley.

Gorse, A spiny yellow-flowered European shrub.

Groat, An English silver coin worth four pence.

Hallo, A variant of Hello.

Hart, A male deer.

Hauberk, A long armor tunic made of chain mail.

Haugh, (Scots) A low-lying meadow in a river valley.

Hen, A term of address (often affectionate), used to women and girls.

Hied, To go quickly; hasten.

Hock, The joint at the tarsus of a horse or similar animal, pointing backwards and corresponding to the human ankle.

Holy Rude, (*Scots*), The Holy Cross

Hoyden, High-spirited; boisterous.

Jape, Joke or quip.

Jesu, Vocative form of Jesus.

Ken, To know (a person or thing).

Kirk, A church.

Kirtle, A woman's dress typically worn over a chemise or smock.

Laying, To engage energetically in an action.

Loch, Lake.

Louring, Lowering.

Lowed, The characteristic sound uttered by cattle; a moo.

Malmsey, A sweet fortified Madeira wine

Malting, A building where malt is made.

Marischal, The hereditary custodian of the Royal Regalia of Scotland and protector of the king's person.

Maudlin, Effusively or tearfully sentimental.

Mawkish, Excessively and objectionably sentimental.

Mercies, Without any protection against; helpless before.

Merk, (*Scots*), a coin worth 160 pence.

Merlon, A solid portion between two crenels in a battlement or crenellated wall.

Midges, A gnat-like fly found worldwide and frequently occurring in swarms near ponds and lakes, prevalent across Scotland.

Mien, Bearing or manner, especially as it reveals an inner state of mind.

Mount, Mountain or hill.

Murk, An archaic variant of murky.

Nae, No, Not.

Nave, The central approach to a church's high altar, the main body of the church.

Nock, To fit an arrow to a bowstring.

Nook, Hidden or secluded spot.

Outwith, (Scots) Outside, beyond.

Palfrey, An ordinary saddle horse.

Pap, Material lacking real value or substance.

Parapet, A defensive wall, usually with a walk, above which the wall is chest to head high.

Pate, Head or brain.

Pell-mell, In a jumbled, confused manner, helter-skelter.

Perfidy, The act or an instance of treachery.

Pillion, Pad or cushion for an extra rider behind the saddle or riding on such a cushion.

Piebald, Spotted or patched.

Privily, Privately or secretly.

Quintain, Object mounted on a post, used as a target in tilting exercises

Retiral, The act of retiring or retreating.

Rood, Crucifix.

Runnels, A narrow channel.

Saddlebow, The arched upper front part of a saddle.

Saltire, An ordinary in the shape of a Saint Andrew's cross, when capitalized: the flag of Scotland. (a white saltire on a blue field)

Samite, A heavy silk fabric, often interwoven with gold or silver.

Sassenach, (Scots), An Englishman, derived from the Scots Gaelic Sasunnach meaning,originally, "Saxon."

Schiltron, A formation of soldiers wielding outward-pointing pikes.

Seneschal, A steward or major-domo

Siller, (Scots), Silver.

Sirrah, Mister; fellow. Used as a contemptuous form of address.

Sleekit, (Scots), Unctuous, deceitful, crafty.

Sumpter horse, Pack animal, such as a horse or mule.

Surcoat, An outer tunic often worn over armor.

Tail, A noble's following of guards.

Thralldom, One, such as a slave or serf, who is held in bondage.

Tiddler, A small fish such as a minnow

Tisane, An herbal infusion drunk as a beverage or for its mildly medicinal effect.

Tooing and froing, Coming and going.

Trailed, To drag (the body, for example) wearily or heavily.

Trebuchet, A medieval catapult-type siege engine for hurling heavy projectiles.

Trencher, A wooden plate or platter for food.

Trestle table, A table made up of two or three trestle supports over which a tabletop is placed.

Trews, Close-fitting trousers, usually of tartan.

Tun, Large cask for liquids, especially wine.

Villein, A medieval peasant or tenant farmer

Wain, Open farm wagon.

Wattles, A fleshy, wrinkled, often brightly colored fold of skin hanging from the neck.

Westering, To move westward.

Wheedling, To use flattery or cajolery to achieve one's ends.

Whey, The watery part of milk separated from the curd.

Whilst, While.

Whist, To be silent—often used as an interjection to urge silence.

Wroth, Angry.

NOVELS BY J. R. TOMLIN

Made in the USA
Monee, IL
09 February 2021